For Better or Worsted

For Better or Worsted

BETTY HECHTMAN

BERKLEY PRIME CRIME, NEW YORK

THE BERKLEY PUBLISHING GROUP
Published by the Penguin Group
Penguin Group (USA) LLC
375 Hudson Street, New York, New York 10014

USA • Canada • UK • Ireland • Australia • New Zealand • India • South Africa • China

penguin.com

A Penguin Random House Company

This book is an original publication of The Berkley Publishing Group.

Berkley Prime Crime Books are published by The Berkley Publishing Group.
BERKLEY® PRIME CRIME and the PRIME CRIME logo are trademarks of
Penguin Group (USA) LLC.

Library of Congress Cataloging-in-Publication Data

Hechtman, Betty, 1947–
For better or worsted / Betty Hechtman.—First edition.
pages   cm
ISBN 978-0-425-25294-9 (hardback)
1. Crocheting—Fiction.   2. Weddings—Fiction.
3. Reality television programs—Fiction   I. Title.
PS3608.E288F67   2013
813'.6—dc23   2013026936

FIRST EDITION: November 2013

PRINTED IN THE UNITED STATES OF AMERICA

10 9 8 7 6 5 4 3 2 1

Cover illustration by Cathy Gendron.
Cover design by Rita Frangie.
Interior text design by Kristin del Rosario.

Acknowledgments

This is one of my favorite pages to write. It is my chance to thank everyone for their help with the book. The first thank-you goes to my editor, Sandy Harding, who is wonderful to work with and does such a great job on my books. Natalee Rosenstein makes Berkley Prime Crime the best place to be. The Art Department keeps coming up with fabulous covers. I will never stop thanking my agent, Jessica Faust, because there would have been no crochet series without her.

You could say Molly introduced Linda Hopkins to me. She has become a friend and has graciously helped fine-tune the patterns.

Roberta Martia continues on as my chief cheerleader and crochet and knitting consultant.

A thank-you to Scott Tretsky for setting up the meeting with Hamlet in the park.

The Thursday group of Rene Biederman, Connie Cabon, Alice Chiredjian, Terry Cohen, Tricia Culkin, Clara Feeney, Sonia Flaum, Lily Gillis, Winnie Hineson, Linda Hopkins, Debbie Kratofil, Reva Mallon, Elayne Moschin, Margaret Prentice, Vicky Sostman and Paula Tesler offer yarn help, friendship and a place to show off what I've made.

Thanks to Delma Myers and Amy Shelton for continuing to

be my buddies at the Knit and Crochet Show. Suzann Thompson's wonderful polymer clay class provided me the perfect clue for this book.

Lee Lofland and the High Point Public Library put on another fabulous Writers' Police Academy in Greensboro, North Carolina. It was a great place to pick up small details like what a motor officer's boots really look like, to pick up big details like checking out a murder scene (fake, of course), and to meeting people like Sergeant Yahya of the Gilford County Sheriff's Department, who showed me his CSI van.

Finally, Max and Samantha, I hope you don't mind that I used your wedding as research. And Burl, what can I say, you are still the best.

For Better or Worsted

CHAPTER 1

YOU KNOW HOW THEY SAY WEDDINGS ALWAYS HAVE drama? Well, this one had an overdose. My name is Molly Pink, and the wedding in question was my friend Mason Field's daughter, Thursday's. Yes, that's really her name. I wasn't invited to the actual ceremony, which was for immediate family only, but I, along with two hundred or so others, had been invited to the reception that was being held in Mason's tented backyard. When I say *tent*, I'm not talking about some little open-on-the-sides thing. We're talking about a structure that took up the whole backyard. And it only looked like a tent from the outside—the interior was done up like an elegant ballroom. But I'm getting ahead of myself.

I would have already been inside the tent, but just before I was to go in, my friend Barry Greenberg, who is an LAPD homicide detective, happened to come by and I stopped to chat. The title of *friend* was a step down from his previous title as *boyfriend*. Don't get me started on that. *Boyfriend* for a man in his fifties? C'mon. And I don't think his arrival was an accident. It was a last-ditch effort to talk me out of doing something. The friendship between me and Mason was supposed to move up a notch after the wedding. He and I were to go up north for a get-to-really-know-each-other few days, if you know what I mean. Barry didn't know that before he had even arrived, I had already changed my mind and had decided to keep Mason's and my relationship at the friends-with-no-benefits level.

Barry had looked relieved, almost happy, until we both heard screams coming from the tent. Then we double-timed it inside. It was easier for Barry since he was dressed in comfortable jeans, a T-shirt and sneakers. But then he wasn't an invited guest and I was. The narrow bottom on my apricot ruffly dress didn't allow for a wide gait, and the heels—well, walking in them was a challenge, but running? Forget it.

When I got inside, it was as if the moment had frozen in time. Nobody seemed to be moving or talking. The only sound was the background music the DJ had put on.

I COULDN'T FIGURE OUT WHAT WAS WRONG, BUT then I looked across the wooden dance floor that had been laid over the grass and saw a long table toward the end of the tent. I didn't mean to gasp, but it was an automatic response when I saw Jaimee Fields, the mother of the bride, sprawled on the wedding cake, holding a bloody knife.

Barry had gotten up close to the table, and now he flashed his badge and told her to drop the knife. It hit the floor with a loud thud. You didn't have to be a detective to know that a bloody knife meant somebody had been stabbed. I was right behind Barry when he went around to the other side of the table. I almost didn't see the tuxedo-clad man sprawled on the floor. My eye went right to the white dress splattered with red as Thursday Fields tried to help her new husband up. Thursday Fields, or should I say, Thursday Fields Kingsley.

The DJ finally cut the music, and I heard a gasp go through the crowd. I turned, and I saw that Mason Fields had just come in from the house. He had a happy smile and was carrying a wedding gift, oblivious to what he was walking into. When he caught a glimpse of the crowd, he seemed surprised. "What's going on?" His question was met with the sound of two hundred-plus people sucking in their breath, and he seemed perplexed by the reaction. "I go into the house for a few minutes and the party dies?" Then he looked across the tent.

Mason was an attorney, and he mostly dealt with naughty celebrities who got themselves into sticky situations. But I doubt anything he'd ever seen equaled finding his ex-wife sitting in his daughter's wedding cake. And that was before he knew about the bloody knife.

Barry ordered everyone to stay put and leaned down to check the groom. Mason and a dark-haired man in a matching tuxedo ignored the command and came behind the cake table.

The dark-haired man pushed me out of the way and fell to his knees when he saw the figure on the ground. While Barry searched for a pulse, the man—who I now realized was Jackson Kingsley, father of the groom—cried out in grief and disbelief. Then his eyes fell on Jaimee, who was somehow still stuck in the cake.

"You stabbed my son," he bellowed in a deep voice.

Barry had already called it in, and it only took a few minutes before the place was swarming with blue uniforms and paramedics. The paramedics checked Jonah Kingsley, but I saw them shaking their heads; clearly, it was too late. They still got some business, though. A number of women grew faint as they were hustled to the tables that had been set up for dinner. As soon as the area was cleared, two cops stretched yellow tape across the whole end of the tent, and the area around the cake and Jonah Kingsley's body was being curtained off with tarps. Somebody had finally helped Jaimee out of the cake, and she was surrounded by uniforms. Jackson Kingsley was standing nearby on the dance floor with a much younger woman, who, judging by the ring on her finger, seemed to be his wife.

"What are you waiting for?" Kingsley said to the uniforms. "How much more proof do you need? Arrest her." He pointed accusingly at Jaimee Fields. I got the feeling Jackson Kingsley was used to being in charge and didn't like it when he wasn't listened to. And he had that kind of deep, melodious voice that got your attention.

Thursday was with another cadre of uniforms, and Mason was rushing back and forth between the two groups.

All I could think was that poor Thursday had only been married for a few hours, and she was already a widow.

I stiffened when I saw Detective Heather walking toward me. Her real name was Heather Gilmore, but with her Barbie Doll looks, I'd taken to calling her Detective Heather, of course, not to her face. There was a certain amount of animosity between us. Even though I'd helped her with cases a few times, she didn't like my sleuthing.

She had her pad out and was ready to question me, when

Barry interceded. "There's no reason to talk to Molly. She came in after the fact."

Detective Heather seemed disappointed, then almost annoyed when Barry explained that he and I had come in together. Apparently Heather still resented my relationship with Barry, even if he and I were just friends.

The whole tent had become a swirl of activity. Uniforms had spread out among the guests and help. The white-suited criminal-scene investigators had come in and were collecting fingerprints and DNA samples from the crowd. They had so much to deal with, it was mind-boggling.

After Detective Heather backed off, I watched the action, and for the first time, noted something odd. All the help had been gathered together, and they all looked the same. I mean, really the same. They all were wearing white shirts, black pants and white gloves, but it was more than that. For example, they all had their hair smoothed back, and if it was long, it was pulled into a small bun at the nape of the neck. And no one wore any makeup or jewelry. The androgynous, uniform look made it almost impossible to tell the men from the women or one person from another.

"Molly, it's okay, you can go on and leave," Barry said, coming up to me. As the police finished questioning the guests, each one was released and escorted out through the front entrance. Every time the door to the tent opened, I caught a glimpse of the newspeople already stationed out front. I dreaded going through the gauntlet of reporters.

Mason came by just as Barry was speaking. If it was possible, he got even more upset at Barry's comment.

"Oh," Mason said. I could hear the disappointment in his voice. "I was hoping you would stay, Molly. With your experience . . ." his voice trailed off, but I knew what he meant.

I was the event coordinator for Shedd & Royal Books and More. Let's just say many of my events had a dusting of disaster about them. I'd had authors who got carried away with cooking demos and set off the smoke alarm, bringing the fire department. There had also been a Mr. Fixit, who broke the plumbing and started a flood. The thing was that, even with the touch of disaster, the events were always a success, and one way or another, we always sold a lot of books. But did Mason really think I could save this reception?

His head shot toward the knot of uniforms around his ex-wife. "They wouldn't listen," he said in an annoyed tone. "They're taking Jaimee in."

Jaimee appeared shocked and frantic. Her hands weren't cuffed, but there was an officer on either side of her, holding her arms. Her cappuccino-colored dress still had hunks of cake stuck to it, punctuated with an occasional petal from the fresh flowers that had decorated the cake. I could hear her arguing with the officers as they started to move en masse toward the door.

"My ex is guilty of a lot of things, but not killing the groom," Mason said. He turned toward the cops surrounding his daughter, who seemed to be in a holding pattern as she stared dazedly at her beautiful white wedding.

Mason turned to Barry. "You're a father. You know how you want to protect your kids. If you need to question my daughter later, no problem. Just please don't detain her now." He and Mason weren't exactly friends, and asking him a favor wasn't easy. Jaimee and her cop escorts were going out the door. "I have to go," Mason said, quickly. "Jaimee's likely to say something stupid and get herself in more trouble." He looked back at his daughter in her elegant dress spattered with blood and let out a heavy sigh, asking Barry again not to detain her.

"Okay," Barry relented. "Your daughter can go. We've already got a statement from her, along with her fingerprints and a DNA sample."

Mason gestured to me. "Can you look after Thursday? Her sister isn't much help." He pointed to a similar-looking young woman in a champagne-colored maid of honor dress. She was leaning against a young man in a dark suit as a female officer stood over them writing something down. "Nobody here is much help for her. Everybody is too upset themselves." Mason walked backward toward the door. "I don't know when I will get back here," he said. "This is a hard thing to ask, but would you take Thursday home with you, Molly?"

Then Mason turned to Barry. "And could you help Molly get her out of here so she doesn't have to go through that?" he said, pointing to the tent opening where the frenzy of reporters waited with their cameras and blinding lights.

Barry made a sort of grumbling sound, but agreed. Mason took off and Barry went over and talked to the uniforms surrounding Mason's daughter. A moment later, Thursday was standing next to me holding on to my arm for support. She seemed to pay no notice to the blood spattered on her arms and dress. Barry glanced around the tent. "There must be another way out of here," he said.

Thursday finally spoke and said the best way was to go through the house. Barry escorted us as far as a tent entrance that connected to French doors leading into the house, and told the uniforms guarding it that it was okay for us to leave. Then he went back to help his associates.

It seemed strange to go from the tent directly into the den. I was used to the room having a view of the pool and the backyard, not the white sides of a tent. I heard Spike barking from somewhere. Mason's toy fox terrier sounded unhappy about being locked up. I followed Thursday out of the den and down the hall to the master bedroom. She suddenly noticed the blood on her and seemed horrified. She didn't resist when I pulled her into the bathroom and wiped off her arms and hands. There was nothing I could do about the dress.

I'd never seen Mason's bedroom. It was done all in earth tones and, as expected, was large and luxurious. But I only got a quick glance as Thursday led us through the room to another set of French doors. They opened out to a small private courtyard with a fountain and beautiful landscaping, surrounded by a stone wall. There was no time to spend admiring the secret garden, because Thursday took me out through a gate in the wall, and I saw we were once again in the backyard

I was disoriented, but Thursday pointed out a walkway that ran behind the tent. "This leads along the back of the yard, past the garage to the driveway," she said, lifting her skirt as we went down the stone path in the darkness. She stopped as we passed an open flap in the tent. "I guess we could have gone out that way." I looked in and saw that it was a service area, now deserted.

A dry wind was beginning to kick up and pushed against the sides of the tent. Somewhere in the darkness, I heard palm fronds rubbing together in an eerie cry. The wind was blowing in from the desert, and the air felt warm and unsettled. As we reached the garage, the stone path turned to sidewalk bordered by neatly trimmed bushes backed by the fence. Suddenly, one of my feet began to hurt big-time. It was no surprise since heels and my feet weren't friends. I slipped off both shoes, and my bare feet practically sighed with relief. When I bent down to pick them up, I realized I was standing beside something white and crumpled.

Instinctively, I reached for it and picked it up. It was wet and slippery. When I held it up, there was enough light reflecting from the streetlight to see it was a shirt, and it was splattered with something dark. I couldn't see colors in the darkness, but something told me the splatters were red.

CHAPTER 2

SOME PEOPLE THINK SOUTHERN CALIFORNIA HAS no seasons. We do, they're just different from the ones most of the country is used to. September brings hot, dry weather and the beginning of the Santa Ana winds, or as some people call them, the devil winds. They stir up the wrong kind of ions and would have made Thursday and me feel edgy even if we hadn't just slipped out of her wedding disaster. Still getting out into the dark street was a relief. All the newspeople and exiting guests were around the corner in front of her father's house.

We stopped along the row of deserted catering trucks parked on the side street, and I said something about wondering how I was going to get my car because I'd left it with a valet. A moment later, we were bathed in the headlights of the greenmobile, as I called my old teal green Mercedes.

It had come around the corner and pulled up next to us, and Barry got out, leaving the motor running.

"Thank you," I said with grateful relief. I reached out as if to hug him and leaned in close. "There's a white shirt in the yard. I think it has blood on it." I kept my voice to a whisper while Thursday went around to the passenger side.

He seemed a little disappointed when I didn't follow through with the hug. "I'll check it out," Barry said, going back to his detective persona. "I'm going to be lead detective on this case," he added, making a triumphant gesture.

"Oh," I said, suddenly understanding his manner. In the past, Barry had had to step down from a number of homicides because of a personal relationship with someone involved with the case, usually me. But that was when we were a couple. Maybe now that we were just friends, it didn't matter that I was a guest at the wedding.

"If it's okay, I'll call you later. I'm sure you'll want to know what happens," he said. I was stunned. In all the time Barry and I had been a couple, he'd never asked for permission to call me or come by my house. He'd always just shown up whenever and left the same way. I told him it was fine. Barry looked down at my bare feet and insisted I wear shoes to drive. I dropped the heels in the backseat and retrieved a pair of sneakers I had left on the floor.

"Nice outfit, huh?" I joked, doing a twirl in my ruffly dress and sport shoes.

He cracked a smile. "I'm sure it will be fine for the ride home." He started to leave it at that, but took a step closer. "I meant to mention before that you look really nice, even with the sneakers." He held the door until I got in and had my seat belt on, then he shut it, not stepping away until he'd made sure I'd locked it.

Thursday had crushed herself into the passenger seat and somehow managed to get her seat belt over the elaborate wedding dress. With its full skirt and train, it definitely wasn't meant for riding around in a car. As she adjusted herself in the seat, I heard the sound of fabric ripping and buttons popping off. Not that she seemed to care.

I put the car in gear and continued down the dark side street. For a moment I wondered what I'd gotten myself into. What if Thursday was like Mason's ex? Weren't daughters usually like their mothers? The thought of dealing with a junior Jaimee filled me with dread. Let's just say I could understand why Mason divorced her.

But Thursday didn't look like her mother. Even with her extravagant dress, professional makeup and flower petals twisted into her short hair, she was cute rather than pretty. I wasn't sure if it was the events of the evening or just the way she always sounded, but there was a little rasp to her voice that pulled at my heartstrings as she thanked me for helping her escape.

As I finally turned onto Ventura Boulevard and headed west for the short drive from Encino to Tarzana, I wondered how to make conversation. First I considered what I knew about her, which wasn't that much. All that Mason had told me was that she taught second grade at Wilbur Elementary, which was a few blocks from the bookstore where I worked. Mason had said little about the groom, other than he wondered if anyone would seem good enough for her. It seemed like a pretty common sentiment among parents, so I didn't take it to mean much.

I really wanted to ask Thursday about Jonah. If the cops

hadn't asked her yet who might have wanted to kill him, they would soon, and probably again and again. Even though I wondered what kind of person her late groom was, I didn't have the heart to ask her while everything was so raw and fresh. And I certainly didn't want to let on that she would probably be viewed as a suspect or a *person of interest*, the toned-down term common nowadays that really meant the same thing as *suspect*. Instead I asked her about her job.

"Jonah wanted me to quit," she said, sounding amazingly calm. "I'm glad I didn't. I just took off the time for our honeymoon." Her voice didn't falter, and for a moment I wondered if she understood what had happened or was simply in some la-la land of shock. There was nothing to do but let her talk and be ready to catch her when she finally fell. She turned to me. "My dad was very vague about your relationship."

When I hesitated, she kept talking and seemed relieved to be talking about something other than the wedding. "I know he tried to keep his social life separate from us. But who did he think he was kidding? Both my sister and I knew he was seeing somebody. And then when he kept talking about you . . ."

"What did he say?" I asked, curious.

"He said you worked at a bookstore and were in some kind of handicraft group, and that you were some kind of amateur investigator, and that he helped you out sometimes. It sounded like he had a lot of fun."

"And you don't mind if your father sees someone?" I said, still surprised by the line of conversation.

She chuckled just like her father, then caught herself. "I hope you don't think it's odd that I'm talking about my father's social life." She looked down at her dress. "I'm still processing everything."

I let out a breath of relief before she continued. At least it showed she had some recognition about what had happened and might be letting the pressure out a little at a time, like when you dropped a bottle of soda on the floor and all the fizz built up inside. If you opened the top quickly, it erupted like a volcano, but if you loosened the top slowly and let the pressure out in little bits, there's no Vesuvius of drink. I told her whatever she did was fine with me.

"Okay then, no, I don't mind if my father sees someone. In fact I want him to. I wish he'd get married again. Anything so he'd be happy." She looked at me. "So?"

What could I say to her? Should I tell her that her father and I were just friends, that he wanted it to be more than that, but I was trying to keep my life from being so complicated for a while? I had been married for just about all of my adult life when my husband, Charlie, died. I'd been a wife and a mother and never just me. This was my chance to try my wings and fly solo.

The truth was that Mason claimed to want just a casual relationship, but for now, I was glad to keep both Barry and Mason at arm's length. I really cared about both of them. Maybe even the *L* word, but I wanted some space. But that was too much to lay on her at the moment. Besides, I viewed our whole conversation as just nervous chatter, avoiding the pink elephant in the car with us.

Thursday had grown quiet as I pulled into my driveway, and I wondered if this was going to be the moment her emotions erupted. Instead she just got out and walked across my backyard, waiting while I unlocked the kitchen door.

"I hope you don't mind cats and dogs," I said, seeing that

my two dogs and two cats were waiting by the door. As soon as I opened it a crack, Cosmo, the small black mutt of indeterminate breed, ran outside. He screeched to a stop at Thursday's billowing white dress and began to sniff. Blondie was a terrier mix in name only and made a more hesitant move outside. She was one of a kind, a terrier with the aloof personality usually attributed to cats. She didn't even bark much.

I stopped the two cats before they walked outside. They'd come with my son Samuel when he moved back home. We only let Cat Woman and Holstein outside with supervision, and never at night.

Thursday seemed taken aback by the menagerie. She looked down at the black dog making his way around the base of her dress. "Can I pet him?" she asked.

I was surprised by her manner until she explained. "I've never had a dog," she said, still seeming hesitant about how to proceed.

"What about Spike?" I said, referring to her father's toy fox terrier, who was all terrier in the personality department.

"The first thing my father did after my parents separated was get Spike. My mother doesn't like dogs, or cats, or birds, or fish," she said with a shrug. She finally crouched down and offered her hand for Cosmo to sniff, and then he moved in and offered his head to pet.

I suggested we go inside, looking at her dress. "I'm sure you'd like to change." I said it half as a question, and she nodded.

I took her across the house, and I offered her a pair of cargo capris and a T-shirt, which was my summer uniform when I wasn't at work. Our builds were a little different, and the outfit hung on her like she was a hanger. But just getting out of the dress seemed to take a load off her mind. I changed into cargo capris and a T-shirt, too. They were a lot snugger on me, but definitely went with the sneakers better than the fluffy dress. Still, she hadn't said anything about what had happened.

"I know I haven't eaten, and I imagine you probably haven't, either." She followed me back into the kitchen.

Thursday started to shake her head and then looked down toward her stomach as it let out a rumble of protest. "Can I really be hungry after everything?" she said. I waited to see if she was going to say anything more about "everything," but she let it drop and said some food would be welcome.

I started to take out some cold cuts from the refrigerator until I noticed she looked uncomfortable. "Is there something wrong?"

"Do you have peanut butter?" she asked. When I nodded, she said she could make herself a sandwich.

"That's not much of a meal." I went to get the peanut butter for her, but something didn't feel right, and then I had a thought. "Are you a vegetarian?" I asked. She nodded, seeming relieved.

"I don't like to mention it. It's easier just to eat around stuff than answer people's questions or listen to their lectures about why they don't think it's healthy."

"How about eggs?" I asked, putting the peanut butter back in the refrigerator. When she nodded, I decided to make us both omelets with some salad on the side, along with toasted bagels. She wanted to help, but I urged her to sit at the built-in kitchen table. Exhaustion was beginning to show in her face.

I was back to having trouble starting a conversation

again. Everything I thought of saying sounded wrong. But silence made me feel tense, so I chatted about the animals and how they'd come to live with me. I whipped up the food and set it in front of her. She ate everything on her plate, and I could tell she was still hungry, though too polite to say anything. "How about some ice cream?" She agreed without even asking what kind.

I took out my stash of McConnell's Bordeaux strawberry. It was my personal favorite, and I'd been known to make a dinner of it. She scraped the bottom of the bowl, but when I offered seconds, she said she was full.

"Thank you," she said softly. "For everything." I heard the front door open and close. My son Samuel came into the kitchen a moment later.

"Do you know what happened?" he said before he was fully in the room. When he saw Thursday, he almost swallowed his tongue. My sandy-haired younger son was a barista by day and a musician by night. In all the excitement, I'd forgotten that he and his group were supposed to have been the after-dinner band at the wedding.

"Do you know Thursday?" I said, faltering when I got to her last name. I supposed it was Kingsley, even if Jonah was dead and she'd only been married for an hour or so. Obviously Samuel had recognized her, and before he could say the wrong thing, I got up and escorted him into the hall. He was already asking what she was doing there. "Mason asked me to get her out of there," I said.

Samuel said when they arrived at the reception, the cops had stopped them from bringing in their instruments and told them everything was canceled. He took a deep breath. "Is it true that her mother stabbed the groom?"

I gestured for him to keep his voice down and told him

about my entrance into the wedding and how I'd seen Jaimee Fields sitting in the cake holding the knife, but that didn't necessarily mean she'd stabbed him. Samuel started to laugh at the image, but I nudged him and he swallowed it.

"I'm just changing, and then I'm going out to meet some friends," he said. He shook his head as he headed down the hall to his room at the end. "When stuff like that happens, it makes you want to live every day." He stopped and looked back. "You don't think ending up at crime scenes is hereditary, do you?" he asked. I rolled my eyes, knowing he was referring to the title Crime Scene Groupie a channel 3 news reporter had given me. It wasn't my plan. It just seemed to happen. I told him not to worry.

Thursday helped me clean up, but I could see she still had some nervous energy. I didn't know what else to do with her, so I took her into the room I used for crocheting and keeping all my yarn. "This is where you made the hankie you gave me to carry in the wedding," she said with understanding, as she picked up an orb of white crochet thread. It turned out that along with never having a pet, Thursday had never learned any sort of handicrafts. When I offered to teach her, she quickly agreed.

It was embarrassing how quickly she picked it up, compared to how long it had taken me. I just had to show her once, and she was off and running. After making a swatch, she wanted to make something, so I showed her how to make a coaster. The one coaster became several, and I was surprised when I looked at the clock and realized it was after midnight. The phone rang, startling both of us.

"I know it's late, but I thought you'd want to know what was going on," Barry said after we exchanged hellos.

"Yes, I do," I answered, stepping into the living room to be out of Thursday's earshot.

"The first thing is we released Jaimee Fields," Barry said. "The consensus was, there wasn't enough cause to arrest her. Not that any of us were sorry to see her go. What a ruckus that woman made. She used her one phone call to call the producer of some ridiculous reality show, *Housewives of Mulholland Drive* or something. They sent a camera crew down to the station." Barry made an incredulous grumbling noise. "I was actually glad to see Mason show up and take over."

There was a knock at the kitchen door, and I took the phone with me as I went to answer it. Through the glass door I saw Mason standing outside. Barry heard the sound of the door opening and asked what was going on. When he heard it was Mason, he asked if Mason had called first.

"Why do you ask?" I said. Barry reminded me that I'd been upset by his just showing up when we'd been a couple and wondered why it was okay for Mason to just show up.

I let out a groan. "I wouldn't call this a regular night for him," I said, which was the understatement of the century.

I let Mason in and pointed toward my crochet room and then took the phone outside. I thought it would be easier now that Barry and I were just friends, but he went on making a point of how he'd called instead of just knocking at the door unannounced. I got a funny feeling when he said that.

"Where exactly are you?" I asked.

There was a moment of silence before Barry muttered that he was at the front door. I went back inside and heard Mason and Thursday talking as I went to the front door and let Barry in. He glanced toward the sound of their voices, but I had him follow me outside into the backyard.

"Did the bride say anything?" he said, gesturing toward the house. I was in mid-shrug as an answer when Barry continued. "She probably knows more than she told us."

"You've decided that she's a suspect?" I said, thinking of the person I'd sat crocheting with. I didn't buy it and thought of trying to talk him out of it. But I knew he would say that just because you liked somebody didn't mean they hadn't killed somebody.

He hesitated and then said, "Maybe." I reminded him of the shirt I'd found.

"Thanks for that. The lab people have it. We're pretty sure there is blood on it, but there's other stuff, too. Maybe wine and food and some dirt, which will make finding evidence somewhere between hard and impossible. The scenario we came up with was someone could have come in dressed as one of the servers, stabbed Jonah Kingsley and went out through the yard before anyone realized what had happened. And Heather thinks the stabbing makes it seem like revenge as a motive." He made eye contact. "You know, stabbed in the back."

I was surprised—Barry didn't usually share this much about cases with me.

The door clicked open and Mason joined us. There was always tension between Barry and Mason. It was partly due to the fact that Barry was a homicide detective, and Mason was a criminal attorney. And it was partly due to me. They were still competing for my attention, even though my relationship with both of them was described as just friends. And as much as they claimed to accept that designation, I wondered if they really did.

*   *   *

MASON SHOWED THE WEAR OF THE EVENING. HE didn't have on the jacket to his tuxedo, and his bow tie was untied and hanging around the open collar. I think there were even some cake stains on his shirt. This from a guy who usually wore designer suits with a perfect drape and dress shirts with an impossibly high thread count. The only thing that seemed usual was the lock of dark hair with flecks of gray that always fell across his forehead, somehow giving him an earnest look. As our eyes met, I saw that he looked exhausted.

"I suppose Barry already told you they released Jaimee. It was ridiculous to have detained her in the first place." Barry started to protest, and Mason put up his hand to stop it. "I know, she was holding the murder weapon, and Jackson Kingsley was insisting she killed his son." Mason looked at the outdoor chairs as if he was thinking of sinking into one of them. "But Jaimee was just going to check on the cake," Mason began, before Barry stopped him.

"I already told Molly what happened." Did I note something smug about Barry's tone? "You look beat. I'm sure you just want to collect your daughter and go," Barry said to him before turning to me. "How about I make us a couple of cups of tea?"

Mason sighed. "There's a problem with that." He turned to me. "Thursday doesn't want to leave."

CHAPTER 3

"MOLLY, ARE YOU ALL RIGHT?" THE VOICE ON THE phone asked while I was still in the process of saying hello, groggy from being awakened. Without waiting for an answer, she continued, no doubt figuring that since I'd answered the phone, I must be okay. "So, tell me everything." The voice belonged to Dinah Lyons, my best friend and an instructor at Beasley Community College. Dinah was known for being able to whip unruly freshman English students into shape, and maybe everybody else, too. I had resisted calling her after Barry and Mason finally left. The fall term had just started and I knew Dinah had an early class. I looked at my watch and saw that it was barely seven. She had already heard about Jonah Kingsley's murder. It was all over the local morning news and even the national news on *Good Day USA*.

I wasn't surprised, because the story had all the elements

to whip newspeople into a frenzy. Who could blame them, really? How many times does a groom get stabbed with the knife meant to cut his wedding cake? And how many times does someone go from wife to widow before the reception is even over?

In their hurry to get the story up, the newspeople had called Jaimee "the alleged murderer-in-law" as they showed her being escorted away from the reception by a number of uniforms. The reporters were quick to point out that there was cake still sticking to Jaimee's dress while she was ushered into the backseat of a cruiser.

Dinah said that the news reports had only mentioned she'd been taken in, but not what had happened afterward. She was surprised when I said they'd released Jaimee without arresting her.

"How did Mason manage that?" Dinah asked, repeating what the news had said about Jaimee being found almost standing over the dead groom with the bloody knife in her hand.

"When I tell you, you're going to laugh," I said. I explained that Mason, Barry and I had ended up having tea together, and I'd heard the whole story. "Mason didn't really have to do anything but let Jaimee tell the story herself. And do a demonstration." I'd heard some crazy alibis, but Jaimee's was a prizewinner. "You know how women of a certain age have something called batwings?" I began, referring to the loose flesh both Dinah and I had on our upper arms. It made wearing sleeveless garments an act of courage.

"You might not have noticed it, but Jaimee's dress had a spaghetti strap top, and in order to hide the jiggle of her arms, she'd bought this shapewear. It looked like a lacy shrug worn over the dress, but it was made of strong, stretchy stuff, and it was meant to make her upper arms appear trim. She tried to tell the cops that it limited her range of motion so much that she couldn't have raised her arms high enough to stab somebody."

"That must have been embarrassing," Dinah interjected.

"Wait, it gets worse, and I think she was telling all this to Detective Heather," I said, thinking that Detective Heather was too young to be worrying about fleshy arms yet. "Mason said that the cops didn't buy the excuse, and she had to let them try to lift her arms up. It took a lot of pulling to raise her arms, and when they let go, her arms snapped back to her side. The cops were still skeptical, like maybe she was faking it. I think she was almost willing to go to jail rather than tell the rest of it. Mason told me he had to do it for her. He said she'd bought the shapewear online, and in a moment of vanity had ordered an extra small, when a medium was really her size." I heard Dinah laughing. "Wait, there's more. She started arguing with him that the shapewear ran small because there was no way she really needed a medium."

When Dinah got finished chuckling, I backtracked and told her how Mason had asked me to take Thursday home with me. "So, then they finally all left last night?" Dinah said.

"Not exactly. Thursday wanted to stay on," I said.

"And you let her?" Dinah said, and I could imagine her shaking her head at me. "You don't even know her."

"What could I say? It's only for a night or so. The poor girl is numb with shock."

"You mean like not talking and staring at the wall?" Dinah said.

"Not exactly. She talked a little." I was still sitting in my bedroom and really wanted to go across the house to make some coffee, but I didn't want Thursday to hear our conversation, even if it was only my side of it. It was times like this that I wished I had a coffeepot in my room.

"What about the groom? Did she talk about him? Like what kind of guy he was and who would want to kill him?"

"She didn't say much about him, other than repeat 'poor Jonah' a few times with heavy sighs. It was too soon to start interrogating her about him. She mostly acted as if nothing had happened. I'm sure she's just holding it all in, and it will come busting out eventually. But for now, she wants a place to hide out. Who can blame her? I bet there's a news crew set up on the street in front of Mason's house right now. And her mother's house. Between her mother being sort of a suspect and starring on that reality show, I bet the camera crews are tripping over each other. Mason said the reality-show crew couldn't get enough shots of Jaimee leaving the police station. And Jaimee loved every minute of it. Her other choice was to go stay at the condo that was supposed to be the home she and Jonah were to settle in after their honeymoon. Can you blame her for not wanting to go there, either?"

"Hmm," Dinah said. "Have you considered that it might not be shock at all that's making her act the way she is? Wasn't she crouched next to her dead husband?"

I hated to admit it, but the thought had crossed my mind, though it seemed even the news media was talking about her being the tragic bride who'd been widowed on her wedding day. "I don't even want to go there," I said to Dinah. "I like Thursday. She can't be a murderer."

"I hope you're right, but doesn't Barry always say you can't tell a killer by looking at them?"

Just then, Dinah noticed the time and gasped. She reminded me she wouldn't be making it to our crochet group's meeting that morning. And then she hung up.

Free from the phone, I walked across the house to make some much-needed coffee, passing the door to the room where Thursday was sleeping. I had hastily fixed up the smallest of the bedrooms for her last night. I used it as an office and guest room, but Thursday hadn't cared that it was tiny and plain. She'd taken the chamomile tea I'd offered her, shut the door, and, I assume, gone to sleep. The door was still shut when I left for work.

For me, at least, life went on, and I had to get to Shedd & Royal Books and More. It was a short drive from my house to downtown Tarzana. I was about to turn into the parking lot when I saw a cop car pulled to the curb with its doors open, along with a throng of people on the sidewalk. Everyone was looking up and pointing.

Someone had gotten the idea that all the San Fernando communities along Ventura Boulevard ought to have some kind of decoration to set them apart. Tarzana, due to the Tarzan connection, had gotten the Safari Walk. What it amounted to were some metal cutouts of jungle animals hanging from the light posts, an occasional topiary of a giraffe or elephant, and something they had the audacity to call mini parks. There were no trees or grass or even space, just a block of sidewalk replaced with red brick and one or two boulders.

The heavyset cop and the others were staring at a light post. I didn't get it at first, but then I saw the metal cutout of a monkey hanging above the street sign and something else about it. It was now attired in some kind of striped jacket.

I parked the car and came around to the street to join the crowd.

"What's going on?" I said. Someone in the group said there'd been a yarn bombing.

"Yarn bombing?" I said. The woman pointed to the little jacket, which hardly looked dangerous.

"It's like guerrilla crochet," another woman in the crowd explained.

"Gorilla?" a man asked, pointing at the metal form hanging from the light post. "It looks like a monkey to me." The woman who'd done the explaining, rolled her eyes at the man and spelled out *guerrilla* for him. "What's that supposed to mean?" he said.

"It's supposed to be a surprise splash of color and something soft and handmade," the woman said. "I've seen street signs covered, mailboxes, even a car. But that was all somewhere else. This is the first time I've seen it around here."

"It looks harmless enough to me," I said.

"It's like yarn graffiti," a man in the group said.

"I like to think they're random acts of whimsy," a white-haired woman in a red dress said.

"However you want to describe it," the cop said in a grumpy tone. "It's illegal." He asked if any of them had access to a ladder. The white-haired woman leaned in close.

"One thing is strange. Most of what I've heard of has been knit, but that looks like crochet."

Something went off in my mind like a bomb. I knew somebody who was always trying to champion crochet. But how far would she go? By now the cop had gotten a ladder from one of the stores and leaned it against the light pole. It didn't look that stable, and the cop didn't look like he really wanted to be climbing it. Finally, he reached the monkey and stripped it of its jacket and threw it into the crowd. I caught it. Yup, it was crochet all right. I stuffed it in my pocket and went toward the bookstore.

The Santa Ana wind had died down to a breeze, but the air still felt silky and dry. It was too hot to think about sweaters, even for a metal monkey. Who would figure that September would be one of the hottest months of the year? But the Santa Anas were like a hot breath blowing in from the desert, and it was the one time when the city side of the Santa Monica mountains lost their sea breeze, leaving it to roast along with us.

Though the temperature still felt like summer, the bookstore window was all done up for Halloween and fall. There were piles of paper leaves and a display of spooky books. The entrance had been decked out for harvesttime and Halloween. A pile of pumpkins and gourds topped a small stack of bales of hay. The front tables held Halloween paper goods and fancy candy in the shape of bats and witches. More and more, the bookstore was turning into an everything store, set up with little boutique stations like the serenity table with its books on Zen, candles of all sorts, aromatherapy oils, lavender-scented eye pillows and yoga videos.

My boss, Mrs. Shedd, was looking over a small selection of Halloween costumes we had this year. She thought it was okay because they were unusual characters like Albert Einstein and Edgar Allan Poe. I knew she had probably already heard about the murder at the wedding, but I was hoping she hadn't connected it with me. She kept mentioning that dead bodies seemed to show up wherever I went, and I kept trying to make it sound like it wasn't so. I wouldn't have much of a case if she brought up the events of the night before. I felt the monkey jacket in my pocket, reminding me of the yarn bombing.

"Have you seen Adele?" I said, referring to my coworker. Mrs. Shedd looked at me quizzically, and I realized that because it was Adele, my question could be taken two ways. I could have been asking for Adele's location, or it could have been a rhetorical question about Adele's latest outrageous outfit. I quickly made it clear it was Adele's location I was after.

"She must be here somewhere, I saw her things in the back room." Mrs. Shedd glanced around the large interior of the bookstore. "I'm glad you're here," she said, changing the subject. "It's good you set things up for today's group in advance." She directed my attention to the alcove in the window that we used as our event area. "They got here early."

Originally, my job as event coordinator and community relations person had mostly been putting on author events, but lately Mrs. Shedd and Mr. Royal, the two owners, were looking to bring more customers into the bookstore. So we kept broadening the kind of events we put on. We were just starting to host a young adult writers' group. Mr. Royal had found someone to act as the leader for the group, but I did all the organizing and setup.

Adele Abrams had been more than a little put out that she wasn't in charge of the kids' group. The kids' department was hers, and she was always concerned about being overlooked. It wasn't likely if you had eyes. She was known for her colorful clothes and the costumes she donned for reading time.

THE WRITING GROUP WAS AIMED AT TEN AND above, and somehow the kids' area, carpet decorated with

cows jumping over moons and low tables, seemed too childish for the group.

There were two boys and a girl waiting at the table I'd
set up. We had arranged the first meeting of the group for
this Monday morning because the kids had no school. But
after today, it would meet after school. I noticed a woman
standing off to the side and nodded a greeting, figuring she
belonged with the kids. I welcomed the kids and told them
I expected a few more.

"Your group leader, Mr. Sherman, should be here any
minute," I said. Actually, I hadn't met him yet. All I knew
was that he had a master's degree in writing and had some
credits. Mr. Royal had done the hiring before he'd taken off
on a trip. For years, he'd traveled around acting as Mrs.
Shedd's silent partner, but now that he'd been back for a
while, he'd gotten itchy feet and was gone again for some
kind of extended retreat.

"Hi," I said to the woman. She came forward and introduced herself. "Emerson Lake," she said. "Lyla is mine." She
pointed at the girl, before explaining that the two boys belonged to neighbors. "I brought them, too. We decided to
kidpool." Emerson laughed and said it was kind of a play on
carpooling. With her shoulder-length dark hair and arty appearance, she looked vaguely familiar, but then, everybody
did. This was the only bookstore in Tarzana, so everybody came in here to shop.

"I hope it's not a problem, but I thought I'd hang around
for this first session." She left it at that, but I understood. I
would have wanted to see what the group was like firsthand,
too, before I just left my kids on their own.

Lyla got up and joined her mother. "Can I show you
something I want for my birthday?" the girl said. Seeing

her, I realized we'd made a good decision not to hold the writers' group in Adele's domain. Between Lyla's trendy outfit and her manner, she was quite grown up, and the set of books she showed her mother were aimed at tweens. I knew because I'd read *Joy on Her Own,* which was about a high school girl juggling her social life and trying to keep secret that she was bringing up her siblings on her own. And the Savannah books—they were about a geeky girl who built a time machine and had a ghost sidekick. It was a trilogy that came with a crystal bracelet matching one the heroine wore. I admit, I had one.

Her mother seemed a little surprised and said the books might be too old for her.

"Mother," she said as she rolled her eyes skyward. "I'm going to be eleven." There was some discussion about her upcoming party. When Emerson said she'd booked the pizza place that had all the games, Lyla looked stricken. "You didn't, Mother. That's for children."

I was familiar with the place and had to agree with Lyla, though I wasn't going to say anything. I think Emerson must have seen her daughter's point, too, because as I excused myself to get some young adult books on writing, I heard the mother say something about rethinking it.

By the time I'd come back with the books, Mr. Sherman was there. I did a double take. I don't know why, but I was expecting someone with a white beard and wire-rimmed glasses. Mr. Sherman, or Ben, as he told the kids to call him, was young, with a mop of unruly black curly hair and an overly serious attitude. Several more kids had joined the group. Their parents hung around for a few minutes, and then I saw them, along with Emerson, make their way to the bookstore café.

Somehow I felt responsible for the success of this new program at the bookstore, so I used setting up a display of writing books as an excuse to hang around and see how it went. Ben won them over in a flash, particularly when they heard his credits.

"I suppose you want to know what I've written. Some of the stuff you'd probably find pretty boring, but how many of you watched *The New Adventures of Janet and the Beanstalk*?" Lyla and the two other girls raised their hands. The boys didn't look that impressed. "Who says girls can't be heroes?" Ben said. He looked at the boys and mentioned writing some episodes for *Zeon, Spaceship Mechanic*. He glanced in my direction and described some literary stories in several academic anthologies. He told the kids and me that it was good not to lose touch with the real world when you were a writer. He managed that by dabbling in the food industry. I got it. Food industry was his way of saying he was a waiter.

I didn't want to hover too much, so as soon as he gave them their first writing exercise, I walked away.

The event area was on the side of the bookstore that faced Ventura Boulevard. The back corner of the bookstore had recently been turned into a yarn department, which I was in charge of, too. It was also the spot where the crochet group, the Tarzana Hookers, met. Once we'd put up a permanent worktable in the middle of the colorful department, some of the Hookers were almost always hanging around, even when it wasn't a real meeting time.

Though this morning was a regular get-together. As I approached the table, I was surprised to see how full it was and that there seemed to be some new members. CeeCee Collins had her position at the head of the table. We all thought of her as the leader of the group. Along with being a superb crocheter, she was also our resident celebrity, not that that had anything to do with her leading the group.

Everybody recognized her from some part or another of her career. Long ago, she'd had her own sitcom, *The CeeCee Collins Show*, but now most people recognized her from her reality show, *Making Amends,* or her supporting lead in the film *Caught by a Kiss*, which featured Anthony, the vampire who crocheted. There was even a rumor that she might get an Oscar nomination.

She was always the best dressed of us, concerned that the paparazzi could pop out from behind one of the bookcases and snap her picture at any time.

"Molly, dear, are you joining us?" She held up the multicolored piece she was working on and explained it was a pet mat she was going to donate to the pound. "So those poor dears don't have to sleep on the cold cement floor." She made a broad gesture around the table. "It's not a group project," she said sounding disappointed. "Everybody seems to be doing their own thing."

For the moment, all seemed peaceful and I pulled out a chair. But before I'd sat all the way down, all heads turned my way. "We heard about the wedding," Rhoda Klein said. She was a no-nonsense person with a thick New York accent, even though she'd lived in Southern California for twenty years. Her brown hair was short and neatly cut. Her clothes were always comfortable looking, which was a nice way of saying dull.

"Molly, were you there when it happened?" Sheila Altman said in a hushed voice. Her face looked tense as she turned to the rest of the group. "I knew the victim. Sort of, anyway." The words came out in a nervous squeak. She pointed down the street to Luxe, the lifestyle store where she worked, but she didn't say more.

Sheila was the youngest in the group, still in her twenties. She was pretty much alone in the world, and we all looked after her.

"I heard they arrested the mother-in-law," Elise Belmont said. She had a birdlike voice and wispy brown hair to go with it. In fact, all of her seemed wispy, like a good wind would carry her away. She sighed and looked down at her project. None of us said anything to her anymore. We just accepted that everything she made was going to be vampire style, as she called it. It all had to do with her almost worship of the character Anthony, the vampire who crocheted. It meant she exclusively used the half double crochet stitch because she thought it resembled fangs, and almost everything she made was black and white with a splash of red somewhere.

"But they let her go, didn't they?" We all jumped at Eduardo's deep voice. We should have been used to it by now. He'd been a part of the group almost from the beginning, but we still reacted anyway. At least we didn't all stare at him anymore. He was striking-looking, with long black hair he wore in a ponytail. But then he had been a cover model in his younger days. When he'd gotten to the age where he started being cast as the pirate's father instead of the pirate, he figured it was time to branch out. He'd bought the Crown Apothecary, which was a fancy name for a drug and sundries store.

"I guess Adele isn't coming," I said. "But we have new people." I looked to the two women who were sitting at the far end of the table. Both were dressed in somber colors, and I was surprised to see that one of them was knitting.

CeeCee dropped her voice and gestured with her head. She was trying not to smile. "Dear, maybe you should look again."

More than look again, I walked down to the end of the table. The knitter was definitely someone new, and I started to introduce myself when the woman next to her looked up.

"Adele?" I said, far louder than I intended to. You have to understand. Adele never blended in anywhere. She naturally chose wild colors and unusual outfits that seemed more like costumes than clothes. The woman who sat before me was wearing navy blue pants and a white polo shirt with a little lip gloss, and the only hint of crochet was a tiny pink yarn flower on her collar. I did another double take when I looked at her project.

Adele tended toward big projects in bold colors. So what was she doing working on a dainty necklace? I was a little surprised to note that she was crocheting with soft wire and adding tiny pink seed pearls. But that paled in comparison to something else: Adele had no reaction to the fact that the woman next to her had long needles clicking together.

We all thought crochet was the superior yarn art, but none of us made a fuss about it. Adele, on the other hand, viewed knitters as her natural-born nemesis. It all had to do with a not-so-nice stepmother who was a knitter, and even after all these years, it was a sensitive spot with Adele. When I say sensitive, I mean over-the-top sensitive. Yet here she was sitting next to this knitter without batting an eyelash.

Something was definitely up.

CHAPTER 4

"QUIT STARING AT ME, PINK," ADELE SAID. SHE was the only one who called me by my last name. She'd started out doing it because it annoyed me. She thought she should have been promoted to event coordinator and was more than a little miffed when Mrs. Shedd hired me from outside. It didn't matter that I had some PR experience when I worked with my late husband. Calling me Pink was her way of having a little revenge.

But by now it had become a habit, and I wondered if Adele even remembered why she'd started doing it in the first place.

"Why don't you tell us more about the wedding?" she said with an uncomfortable glance toward the woman next to her.

Something was definitely up. Adele never wanted to give up the spotlight.

"Molly Pink," I said by way of introduction, as I held out my hand to the mystery woman.

She set down her knitting and threw Adele a disparaging glance. "I guess we're casual here and introduce ourselves. I'm Leonora," she said. I noticed that she didn't offer her hand and guessed that she didn't think handshaking was a woman's domain. I rested my hand on the table as if that had been my plan all along.

Before I could pull out a chair, the bookstore cafe's barista and cookie baker, Bob, showed up bearing a plate of brownie morsels.

"There are two kinds." He pointed to the plate and said one side had nuts and the other didn't. "I need your vote." He began to go around the table, letting everyone pick out a brownie bit from each side.

"I shouldn't," CeeCee said. "The camera puts on ten pounds." But CeeCee took two pieces from each side, despite her comment. Not a surprise—her sweet tooth was as well known as she was.

The rest of the table followed suit. When he got to Adele, he held out the plate to her. Adele started to reach toward it, but caught sight of Leonora shaking her head.

I think we were all shocked when Adele retracted her hand with a no, thank you. When Bob offered it to Leonora, she actually pushed the plate back at him.

"I never eat sugar," she said. "Except for the five grapes I have for dessert at lunch." There was something very proper about the woman's posture. It was almost as if she had a rod up her back making her sit so straight. She had a long face framed by nicely styled, highlighted brown hair. She began packing up her knitting before she turned to Adele. "You see it isn't hard practicing willpower. That drink powder will help you." After that, she got up and said it was nice to have met us, and then she rather abruptly left.

"I might as well give this to you now," Elise said, sliding a green shopping bag across the table to Adele. I noted a sticker that said, "Want to lose weight? I can help."

"It's a gift from her." Elise pointed to the front door that was just swinging shut after Leonora's departure.

Rhoda waylaid the bag before Adele got it. As Rhoda started to examine the contents, her eyes opened wider and she turned to Elise. "You're selling supplements now?"

Elise put down the vampire-style pot holder she was making. "Yes, and if any of you want to order anything, let me know."

Eduardo examined the contents of the bag. "I wanted to sell this weight-loss tonic at the Crown Apothecary, but the company only sells it through distributors like Elise."

"My title is supplement adviser." She waved at Adele to get her attention. "I just want you to know that I'm here to help you on your weight-loss plan."

The bag finally made its way to Adele, and she took out one of the packets. Elise urged her to mix it with a glass of water immediately because it would help her ignore the brownies.

Dinah asked to see it first. "I'd like to see the ingredients. You should know what you're taking."

Elise took offense and insisted the powder was fine. She got up and returned with a glass of water and mixed the powder in. It got kind of thick-looking and turned light brown. We all watched while Adele reluctantly drank it. She made a face, no doubt expecting it to taste foul, and swallowed. Elise told us it tasted like red berry. Was that really a flavor?

Adele set the empty glass down and said it tasted better than it looked. Still, she didn't seem sold on it. I can't say I blamed her.

"Okay, what's going on, and who is Leonora, and why didn't you care that she was knitting?" I said.

"So, Pink, are you going to investigate the marriage murder?" Adele said.

What? Adele usually tried to downplay my investigative skills. Did she really think any of us would fall for that?

"Let's cut to the chase," Rhoda said. "Adele, we all know something weird is going on."

Adele held her ground and continued to deny anything was strange, but her lip had begun to quiver.

"Dear, we're like family. You can tell us what it is," CeeCee said. I certainly hoped Adele appreciated how caring everyone was being. If the shoe was on the other foot, I honestly wonder if she would have been the same.

Adele took a deep breath, then let it out, before she tried again. "I know you all think I'm my own person, and I never bend to what other people think, but it's different with Leonora. She's my boyfriend Eric's mother." Then the story came out. Leonora was visiting from San Diego, and Eric had asked Adele if she could tone things down while his mother was here. He'd intimated that any future they had together required a vote of approval from his mother. There was more. Leonora had told Eric that she'd always dreamed his bride would wear her wedding dress.

Oops. Leonora was half a head shorter than Adele and a whole lot of pounds lighter. Now I got the diet supplement.

"I don't know what I'll do if she gives me a thumbs-down," Adele said in almost a wail. "You have to understand. Eric is the one. The yin to my yang. My soul mate, life partner."

I tried to get Adele to lower her voice when I saw that Emerson had wandered into the yarn area. I remembered how I had hung around, waiting while my boys took swimming or art classes when they were Lyla's age. I got up from my chair as Emerson looked through the cubbies.

"Do you knit or crochet?" I asked before offering my help.

She shook her head. "My thing is flower arranging. But I love the way you have the yarn colors arranged like a rainbow." She glanced at her watch and sighed as she looked back at the event area. She smiled when she saw Lyla and the two boys walk out. The boys headed to check out the graphic novels, which was a fancy name for comic books. Lyla came toward us.

She joined her mother for a moment, then went over to the table and walked around it, looking at everybody's work. "Is that knitting?" Lyla asked, pointing at CeeCee's project.

Rhoda put a hand on Adele's shoulder to keep her in place, expecting her to overreact to Lyla's question. I was surprised to see Adele stay put and glare at us.

"What?" she said. "I'm a changed person. I can deal with knitters now."

CeeCee didn't look convinced and explained to Lyla that she was crocheting. She even demonstrated a couple of single crochets. Lyla wanted to know what CeeCee was making.

"I'm using up scraps of yarn and making a pet mat. We donate them to the pound so the dogs and cats will have something soft to lie on." Lyla's eyes got big as she listened to CeeCee, and she asked if it was hard to learn.

"I love animals, and I'd like to make something for them," the girl said.

Emerson was watching her daughter and then turned to

me. "Do you have a kids' crochet group?" When I told her we didn't, she waved to her daughter and said it was time to go.

As they started to walk away, a bunch of things came together in my mind. Mrs. Shedd was continually telling us the bookstore was on shaky ground, and we needed more revenue streams. Then I remembered hearing about Lyla's upcoming birthday and the fact that she wasn't happy with the idea of a pizza party at a place with a bunch of games. A party needed an activity. Lyla wanted to learn how to crochet. Maybe her friends did, too. And suddenly an idea was born.

I rushed after them. "We don't have a kids' group, but we do crochet parties."

CHAPTER 5

"A CROCHET BIRTHDAY PARTY. I LIKE IT," DINAH said. After work, I'd stopped at my friend's house. She lived down the street from the bookstore, so it wasn't even out of my way. She'd hated to miss the Hookers get-together and was anxious to hear all the news. Particularly about Adele. Dinah still couldn't wrap her mind around Adele wearing plain clothes and not having a hissy fit when someone next to her was knitting.

"I wasn't sure how Mrs. Shedd would react to the idea, particularly since I'd gone ahead and offered it to Emerson and her daughter without asking my boss. But not only did Mrs. Shedd like it, she thinks we should make a business out of it. I suggested calling them Parties with a Purpose."

"Great idea," Dinah said. "You could do more than just birthday parties."

"Adele is going to be helping me." Dinah started to roll

her eyes, but I explained we'd sort of worked it out. I would do all the planning and handle the party; Adele would be in charge of teaching the kids how to crochet. "There is one small issue, though," I said. "We need the first party to be flawless, or it might just end up being the only Party with a Purpose."

Dinah squeezed my shoulder. "I'm sure all the Hookers will want to help. I know I certainly will. Now, what's going on with the wedding murder?"

In the excitement over the party idea, I had put the whole wedding episode out of my mind.

"You remember how Barry used to always tell me to stay out of investigations when we were a couple?" Dinah nodded, and I continued. "Well, this time I couldn't even if I wanted to. Did I tell you that Barry is working this case?"

"Several times," Dinah said.

"And did I tell you that he doesn't seem to be keeping me out of the loop like he used to? I suppose it's a benefit of not being his girlfriend anymore and the fact that Thursday is staying at my house."

Dinah responded with a little laugh. "Maybe, or maybe he likes having a reason to talk to you."

As I got up to go, Dinah followed me to the door. "If you start investigating on your own, I'd love to be your Watson."

"I wouldn't have it any other way," I said before I left.

By now, I probably should have been used to not knowing what I was going to find when I came home, but I was still surprised by the scene when I walked into my living room. Thursday was sitting on the couch, and Barry was in a chair with his notebook out. Clearly it was an official visit. His tie was pulled tight, and instead of his Tahoe being parked in the driveway, his Crown Vic was in front of the house. I had noticed some other cars, too.

Mason was standing up, hovering between them, and Jaimee was pacing in front of my fireplace, muttering to herself. Then I noticed another man I didn't recognize standing near Thursday. Who was he?

It all came to a stop when I walked in. That is, except for the banging coming from the door in the den that led to my bedroom area.

"I tried to stop them," Barry said, giving Mason and Jaimee a dark look.

"Stop them from what?" I asked, wondering how it was that I had so totally lost control of my own house. Mason came up to me.

"I'm sorry, Sunshine, but when Jaimee saw the cats and dogs she got hysterical. She said she felt faint." Mason rolled his eyes and grinned. For a moment, he became the Mason I was used to as he took my arm and led me to the kitchen. He glanced back toward Barry. "No more questions until I get back."

Once we were in the kitchen, Mason leaned against the counter and let out a tired sigh. "I'm sorry for all this. Thursday called and said that Barry had come over supposedly to give her an update on the investigation. So, I came over to make sure that was all he did. I had no idea Jaimee was following me. She seemed to think we were trying to keep Thursday's whereabouts a secret, and she thinks Thursday should come home with her. That woman is too much. She could have just asked." Mason let out another sigh.

"What about the other guy?" I said. "Is he a detective associate of Barry's?"

"Not even close. He was following Jaimee while she was

following me. He's Jackson Kingsley's lawyer. Apparently now that Jackson's son is dead, he doesn't want Thursday to be a Kingsley." When I didn't understand, he explained more. "The only thing I can figure is that he's afraid that as his son's widow, she might make some claims on the family business." Mason threw up his hands in hopelessness. "He's trying to get Thursday to sign something saying the marriage was a fraud so they can get it annulled. I understand he's grief-stricken, but it's a terrible way to treat my daughter."

There was a sudden uproar in the next room, and Mason was there in a flash with me close behind. The Kingsleys' lawyer had taken the opportunity to wave a check in front of Thursday, along with the papers he wanted signed.

"She's not going to sign anything," Mason said, intercepting both items and pushing them back at the man.

"It's been a long day, and if you are all finished," I said, making a not-too-subtle sweeping gesture toward the door. Before I could remind them that it was my house, and my animals were supposed to have the run of it, a bunch of conversations erupted. The attorney had been instructed that once he found Thursday, he was not to leave without the papers being signed.

"Thursday isn't signing anything, and unless you want him to arrest you for trespassing," Mason said, pointing his shoulder in Barry's direction, "you should leave." The attorney shoved the papers in his leather briefcase and angrily went to the door.

With the lawyer gone, Barry started to talk to Thursday. "For now, we're following up on the idea that someone slipped in dressed as a server, did what they came for, and then left before anyone realized what had happened." I noticed that he didn't mention that my finding the bloody shirt probably had a lot to do with them coming up with that scenario. "We think the motive is some kind of revenge—"

Mason interrupted, "And Kingsley is trying to say the revenge motive is aimed at me. He thinks it's because of some client I got off." Mason shook his head in disbelief. Most of Mason's law practice was involved with keeping celebrity types out of jail. Their crimes were usually relatively minor, so it was hard to think of someone being worked up enough to want revenge.

Barry retook the floor. "Fields, don't be so quick to dismiss it. Someone could be blaming you for getting someone off who they think ruined their life."

Mason looked at his daughter. "You should know cops don't really like lawyers."

Barry shook his head. "Nobody likes lawyers, Fields."

Jaimee got up, insisting that her daughter should be staying with her rather than her father's girlfriend. Barry flinched at the girlfriend remark and said he just wanted to ask Thursday a few more questions. Mason jumped into the middle of it, wanting to know what the questions were. Was I really powerless in my own living room?

"Get your things, Thursday," Jaimee said. Mason's ex was fidgeting and tapping her foot, both signs of her impatience.

"I just wanted to show you some pictures," Barry said, sliding several sheets out of an envelope and passing them to Thursday. He turned to Mason and Jaimee. "You can look at them, too. They are copies of the photos from the reception your photographer got to me. We're looking for someone who doesn't belong."

Thursday looked over the pictures and shrugged. "All the serving people looked like robots." She glanced at her mother, making it clear it had been her idea.

Jaimee started to defend herself, saying it was the caterer's idea. "She said it was the trendy thing now to have the men and women look alike. All with slicked-back hair and no makeup or jewelry to set anyone apart. The white gloves were to give it that English butler touch." Jaimee looked at all of us. "I didn't know there was going to be a murder, or I would never have made it so easy for someone to slip in." Her voice had an escalating edge to it. "And I certainly didn't expect to be detained or called a murderer-in-law," she said. She took the pictures from her daughter and started going through them. She shrieked when she saw that the photographer had gotten a shot of her sitting in the cake holding the bloody knife, and she pushed them on Mason.

His eyes were glazed over by the time he'd gone through them all. "With all the people at the reception, and the cookie-cutter help wearing white gloves, I don't know how you'll be able to sort out what's evidence."

Barry took the comment as a challenge. "This isn't one of those TV shows where they pick out a fiber that solves the crime, and it all takes place in a few minutes. But we have our ways," he said. "Personally, I mostly depend on finding suspects through tips. Somebody remembers something." He looked at Thursday. "Like you remember that one of the servers looked different or acted a little strange. Then before you know it, we have a good idea who did it. It might take a while to get enough evidence to bring charges, but we know who the guilty party is."

He gathered up the proof sheets and slipped them back in the envelope. Jaimee turned to her daughter, who was still sitting on the couch, and gestured for her to get ready to leave.

Jaimee realized that Thursday wasn't getting up and repeated another time what she'd said about her daughter getting her things. Thursday shook her head and didn't move off the couch.

All the color drained from Jaimee's face, and I thought she was getting faint again. "But I'm your mother. I'm supposed to be the one you stay with at a time like this." She looked to Mason. "Do something."

Mason looked at me and shrugged. "And you were upset when I kept you out of my family?"

It was then I noticed that Thursday had the crochet hook and yarn I'd given her in her lap. She picked up the hook and began to work on another coaster as her parents discussed options of where she could stay. Okay, she'd gotten to me. She was the first person I had taught to crochet.

Thursday looked at her mother. "If I stay with you, I'll end up in the middle of the *Housewives of Mulholland Drive*." She turned to her father. "And your house is too much of a reminder of what happened. And the condo Jonah and I were supposed to live in—it would feel too strange. And besides, it belongs to Kingsley Enterprises, so I probably wouldn't be welcome there anyway." Her gaze finally rested on me. "I'll be going back to work in a little over a week, and I'm going to find my own place. But in the meantime, could I stay here? I'd be glad to help with the animals and anything else you need."

Jaimee looked horrified, Mason appeared hopeful, and Barry did a slight negative shake to his head. I didn't hesitate. I leaned down to hug Thursday and to tell her the room was hers for as long as she needed it.

Barry's cell phone went off, and he stepped away to answer it. I could tell by his expression it was business and wasn't surprised when he said he had to go. It seemed natural to walk him to the door. When we got to the entrance hall, we stood facing each other for a moment.

"Do you really think it's a wise idea to let Thursday hide out at your place?" Barry said in a voice barely above a whisper. He gestured toward the living room and the rising and falling of conversations that sounded like an argument. "I thought you were so interested in being alone."

I had to stand close to hear him and shrugged before giving a tired laugh. "I think that ship has sailed. It seems there's always someone or some animal showing up at my door." To punctuate the comment, the banging on my bedroom door increased in volume. Something had been on my mind, and I decided to ask for his professional opinion. "Do you think it's strange that Thursday is acting so, well, so as if her world hadn't been turned upside down? She seems so calm."

Barry let down his bland detective demeanor and became Barry my friend. "Yes and no," he said, clearly liking that I was asking for his input. "It could mean that she doesn't care that her groom got stabbed, or worse—that she was involved."

I started to react with a vehement head shake, but Barry continued. "Or it could be her coping mechanism. She may have shoved everything under her mental rug for a while. Eventually, it will come out, and then the you-know-what will really hit the fan."

I started to ask Barry why he hadn't mentioned the bloodstained shirt I'd stepped on, but he touched my arm and totally changed the subject. "I was wondering if you

would like to have dinner with me and go to Jeffrey's play?"
He mentioned a day and time.

My eyes narrowed as I imagined having dessert alone and
sitting next to an empty seat at his son's play because something had come up at work and he'd had to go. His eyes
flared and I knew he knew what I was thinking. "It won't
be like that. Look, I'm giving you advance warning and I
have the night off. I'll even turn my phone off."

"So, you're asking me on a date?" I said, blanching at the
juvenile term for people our age.

"Take it any way you want. In case you haven't noticed,
I'm a changed man. No more pushing for things my way. If
you don't want to get married, no problem. You want to be
just friends, fine with me." He looked at me expectantly.
"Well?"

CHAPTER 6

"So, what did you say?" Mason asked as we sat together on my couch. Jaimee had accepted that Thursday wasn't leaving with her and left. The animals had been released from the bedroom, and the two dogs and two cats did some major sniffing to find out who had been there. Thursday had hugged her dad, taken her crocheting and retreated to her room. Once we were alone, I'd told Mason about Barry's invitation. He seemed less than pleased and even more agitated when I said I'd accepted.

"I wouldn't want to miss Jeffrey's play," I said. "Barry says he's a changed man. He has no problem with us being just friends." Mason leaned back deeper into the leather cushions. The concept of Barry being different seemed very upsetting to him.

"There's no reason to go overboard on the platonic thing

with him. I thought this was going to be a time for us," he said in a disappointed tone.

I looked around at the living room that just a few minutes before had been full of commotion, and then toward the fourth bedroom where his daughter was holed up. "You're kidding, right? Things are complicated enough."

Mason tried, but he couldn't come up with an argument for that. "Maybe when everything settles," he said hopefully, and I nodded in agreement, thinking I would worry about it then. I got up and checked Thursday's room. The door was shut. When I came back to the living room, I led Mason into the den. I wanted as much distance between us and Thursday as possible before I said anything.

"I was just wondering," I began, "is it normal for Thursday to be acting the way she is? You know her better than I do. I would think under the circumstances she'd be more distraught."

"I kind of expected something different, too," Mason said. "But Thursday has always been very independent and kept things to herself." Mason hesitated. "It does worry me, though."

I asked him about Jonah, since I really didn't know much about the groom. "He seemed nice enough," Mason began. Then he chuckled. "As if anyone is ever good enough for your daughter. I didn't really know him. Like I said, Thursday is very independent. I didn't even meet him until they were getting engaged." Mason went on to say he and Jaimee had gotten together with Jackson Kingsley and his second wife. Jonah's mother had died years ago.

"Kingsley seemed happy that his son was getting married. And happy with Thursday. If you want to know the truth, I thought Jonah was on the bland side." Mason stopped and cocked his ear toward the other side of the house, obviously concerned Thursday might be up and about. "There was someone else before Jonah. I never met him, but I gather that Thursday was really in love with him. He broke it off with her."

"And you think that she met Jonah on the rebound?" I said. Mason nodded. Then he sighed deeply.

"It's terrible to say this, but if the motive was revenge, I'm just glad the victim wasn't Thursday." He looked in the direction of Thursday's room, and I knew he wanted to go and hug her, grateful that she was there. Instead, he gave me the hug and reluctantly said that he'd better go.

Not that he stayed gone long. During the next few days, Mason stopped by on each of them to check on Thursday and bring clothes he'd gotten from the condo. He wanted to be there when Barry made his daily stop to talk to Thursday. Barry claimed he was stopping in to give her updates, but I wasn't so sure that was his motive, because he always seemed to say pretty much the same thing. The detectives were going through all the statements they'd taken at the reception and going back to talk to some of the people, but so far no one seemed to have seen what happened to Jonah.

Thursday stuck close to the house. I don't think she went outside for three days, other than to go into the backyard.

On the fourth day, she came into the kitchen as I was making coffee. Staying locked away like that didn't seem healthy, so I suggested she come with me to the bookstore and spend some time with the Hookers.

I was expecting to have to talk her into it, but she surprised me and readily accepted—she just needed a few minutes to get dressed.

Cosmo and the cats followed us to the front door. In the

short time Thursday had been staying with me, they'd already accepted her as part of the family. Blondie seemed to like her, too, but it was hard to tell with the terrier mix because she kept to herself so much. Just before we went out, Thursday turned to give them all a good-bye pat. She slid into the passenger side of the greenmobile, and it felt very natural to have her company.

Don't get attached. Don't get attached, I warned myself as I pulled onto the street. But it was so easy. She had taken up crochet when I taught her. She liked my animals, my house. She wanted to stay with me.

The winds had stopped for now, but all the junk they'd blown around was still in the street. Though the palm trees bent and swayed with the wind, the fan-shaped fronds didn't do so well. I had to steer around a number of the long woody stems with sharp, pointy leaves. The sky was a bright blue without the hint of a cloud.

"What's going on?" Thursday said when we got to Ventura Boulevard and Vanalden. A police motorcycle and a cruiser were parked at the curb. The cops and several people were standing in the open gate to the Tarzana Cultural Center. Even from a distance, I couldn't miss the big crocheted hearts in different shades of pink hanging from the white gazebo.

I'm not sure if it was curiosity or just nosiness, but I pulled over and we got out. When I got closer, I recognized the barrel-chested motor officer as Adele's boyfriend, Eric Humphries. He was standing with the two uniforms from the cruiser talking to several women. Thursday was right behind me as we approached.

Eric recognized me and nodded a greeting. "Do you know anything about this?" he said pointing to what he called crocheted graffiti. Before I could even tell him I knew nothing, he was explaining to the women that my name was Molly Pink, and I was one of the Tarzana Hookers and knew all about crochet. The women sparked on the name and crochet comment and suddenly looked at me suspiciously.

"We don't mind the hearts," one of them said, pointing at the decorations dangling from the gazebo, "but *whoever* did that came onto the cultural center property when it was closed."

"It's trespassing, plain and simple," one of the uniforms said.

"And it's illegal, just like all that tagging with spray paint," Eric said. I didn't want to bring up that it was hardly as permanent as spray paint. A few snips of some scissors, and they could be rid of the yarn bombing if it bothered them. I suppose it was trespassing, but with the idea of adding a little color and fun. Eric pulled me aside.

"Is there anything you want to tell me about who is doing this?" he said. I knew what he was really asking. He knew what a fanatic Adele was about crochet and wondered if she was involved. There was something so proper about the tall motor officer. Not a scuff on his knee-high boots or the slightest wrinkle in his shirt. He was an absolute rule follower, which made him an odd pairing with Adele. I told him the absolute truth. I had no idea.

I explained the concept of yarn bombing to Thursday as we drove the rest of the way to the bookstore. Once I'd parked the car, she followed me around to the front, admiring the display in the window before we walked in.

We went directly back to the yarn department. Most of the group was already there, and I put my arm around her shoulder as I prepared to introduce her.

"Everyone, this is Thursday," I said. I was about to add a last name, but floundered. Should I say Kingsley or Fields? It wasn't as if they needed her last name to know who she was. Thursday wasn't exactly Mary in the first-name department. As they realized who she was, a wave of sucked-in air passed through the group, then they were tripping over themselves to pull out a chair for her.

A ripple of surprised ahs went through the group as she took out the cotton yarn and hook, along with a partially done washcloth. She'd moved up from coasters to washcloths as a way of trying out other stitches.

"She knows how to crochet," Rhoda said to the others. I said I'd taught her, though then she had taken over learning on her own. I was just a touch jealous at how fast she'd progressed by herself.

"Dear, if you need any help, just ask me," CeeCee said. Thursday nodded a thank-you, and then it registered with her who CeeCee was. Our resident actor and leader of the group lived for that moment when people recognized her. She instinctively patted her hair and struck a pose similar to the one in her publicity shot.

Rhoda interrupted by introducing the rest of the table. I added that Dinah was my best friend when Rhoda got to her. Adele's lip quivered from across the table, but she didn't say a word since Leonora was next to her. Rhoda described Leonora as a guest from San Diego, leaving out who she was visiting. The lip quiver was because Adele had said more than once that I was the best friend she had, and she was upset that the relationship wasn't mutual.

Eduardo complimented Thursday on her skill, and Elise suggested she might want to make a vampire-style washcloth. Before Sheila could say hello, Thursday was admiring the mohair shawl she was making in blue, green and lavender mixed together.

I was about to let out a sigh of relief. I'd been worried about how they would react or what they would say to Thursday, and I'd wanted to talk to the group first, but it appeared to have been unnecessary. I say *appeared*, because in the next breath, Rhoda asked Thursday for the real details of what happened at the wedding.

"I'm just trying to get the facts," Rhoda said, after getting nudged and gasped at by the rest of the table. "And who would know better?"

There were rumblings of Rhoda being insensitive, but Thursday stopped them. "All I can tell you is what I know. I saw my mother fidgeting around the cake, and I went to see what was going on." Thursday stopped, and for the first time I saw emotion welling in her face and her eyes filled with water. "I tripped over something, and when I looked down I saw Jonah was on the ground. I was trying to help him sit up, but——" she stopped, clearly unable to go on.

Was this the moment when the you-know-what hit the fan that Barry had warned me about? I looked around the bookstore, glad that it was relatively peaceful if she was going to have a meltdown. Only Mrs. Shedd and Ben Sherman, the kids' writing instructor, were around. When I looked back at Thursday, she had swallowed back her tears and regained her self-control. To make sure things stayed calm, I changed the subject to the crochet birthday party.

Dinah got what I was doing and gave me an affirmative nod from across the table. For Thursday's benefit, I explained the whole situation. "It all started with a little girl bored with pizza parties," I said before going into the girl's encounter with the crochet group. When I explained the Parties with a Purpose idea, Thursday brightened.

"What a wonderful idea. I'm a teacher, you know," she said to the group. "The kids all spend so much time with electronic things these days, they will love actually doing something with their hands."

I told her I appreciated her enthusiasm and then got to the challenging part of the party planning. "When I offered to do the party, I was thinking we'd just offer the place and the crochet lesson, but the mother is expecting me to take care of everything. All they want to do is show up." I heard Adele clearing her throat in a pointed manner from down the table.

"Molly really isn't doing this party business on her own. I'm functioning as the crochet instructor," Adele said. I was a little stunned by the restraint in her manner and the fact that she had called me Molly instead of by my last name, Pink, as she usually did. I was beginning to hope that Eric's mother never left.

"In any case, the whole thing falls on us. We can't just teach the kids to crochet, we need to give them a project that, if they can't finish completely at the party, they can get a lot done and know how to finish it."

"What a wonderful idea," Eduardo said. "It would be a whole new business for the bookstore, making optimum use of the same space." His whole focus on things had changed since he bought the Crown Apothecary and started reading books on business management. I think it was important to him that we realized he was more than just a pretty face.

"There's another issue. We only have one chance to make

this right, otherwise it will be our only party." I gave Adele a pointed look, and she threw it right back at me.

"My children's programs always come off perfectly. It's your author events that end up being a problem." Adele was still watching her words and how she said them. She was being so careful, she was beginning to sound like English wasn't her native language. I didn't bother to add that it was her costumes and behavior that had had a part in some of the fiascos. Who could forget Adele dancing on the table in purple sequins as the cops rushed in?

The group promised to help come up with a project that would work for the kids. Thursday even volunteered to help with the kids.

"At least we won't have to decorate," I said, gesturing to the colorful backdrop of yarn. For a while the group fell into silence as they all worked on their individual projects. When it came time for the group to break up, Adele headed back to the children's department, saying she was working on an important author event. It seemed as if her comment was mostly directed toward Leonora, who didn't seem terribly impressed. I was so used to Adele and her flamboyant clothes, I did a double take when I saw her outfit. Then I realized she'd copied what I usually wore—khaki pants and a shirt. I wasn't sure if I should take that as a compliment or a comment on how dull my clothes were.

Dinah stayed behind with me as I cleaned up after the group. We both watched Thursday as she wandered through the bookstore displays. Now that she was alone, I noticed her demeanor had changed. The smile had become a straight line and her shoulders seemed to slump. I felt good and bad. I was sorry to see her looking so down, but at the same time relieved as it seemed a more natural response.

Thursday stopped in front of a display of pens, journals and books about writing. I went back to what I was doing, but Dinah nudged me a moment later.

"Who's he?" she said. I followed her gaze and saw that Thursday was talking to someone. His head was down, and it took a moment for me to register who the tumbling black curls belonged to.

"That's Ben Sherman, our kids' writing teacher, ah, I mean facilitator." I still had a hard time with that term. It sounded pretentious, but then I guess the idea was that he was to help it all happen instead of teaching anybody how to do it. I stopped brushing off the snippets of leftover yarn while both Dinah and I watched them for a moment.

"Maybe it's from being your Watson, but I'm deducing that they haven't just met," Dinah said, noting that he had touched Thursday's arm.

"But they don't want anybody to know it," I said, pointing out that instead of facing each other they were both facing the display as if that was their focus.

"Ooh, aren't we the detectives," Dinah said, giving me a high five.

"There you are, Sunshine," Mason said, coming into the yarn department. "Do you ever check your phone messages?" I was relieved to see him back to his usual self. The happy grin, the flop of hair over his forehead and the twinkle of fun in his eye. "I told Thursday I'd meet her for lunch so we could talk over her next steps. I left a message inviting you."

"I can't get away now. But Thursday is over there." I pointed toward the display and noted with surprise that Thursday was now alone.

CHAPTER 7

"Food!" I said out loud to myself as I manned the customer service desk. The woman I'd been helping figure out when the next Anthony book was coming out looked up in surprise at my abrupt comment. I'd had a nagging feeling that there was something about the party I hadn't thought of, and then out of nowhere the answer came. Dinah had left for an English department meeting. Thursday and Mason had gone off for lunch and I had gone back to work.

"Sorry for startling you," I said with a sheepish smile. "We're starting a new venture of putting on parties at the bookstore. We call them Parties with a Purpose. The first one is a girl's birthday, and we're going to teach them to crochet."

I was on a roll now and probably giving her far more information than she wanted, but in the back of my mind I was also trying to get the word out about the parties. I explained I had just realized I hadn't thought about the food.

"You know cupcakes are quite the thing these days," she said. Then she said she'd be interested in hearing how the party went. "It sounds like a fun idea, and it might work for something I'm planning."

I thanked her and gave her one of the store's business cards after writing "Parties with a Purpose" on the back. More things I hadn't thought about. If this was going to be a business, we would need to make up a brochure and add the information to our website. But first I needed to pull off Lyla's party.

Cupcakes were a perfect idea. I considered talking to our barista and cookie baker Bob about doing them in-house. But for this first party, I didn't want to take any chances and decided Caitlyn's Cupcakes was the way to go.

As soon as I could take a break, I walked down the street and crossed Ventura. Caitlyn's was on the corner. The building had housed several different businesses in the past, but had been redone to accommodate the cupcake bakery. The front had been made into a retail area with cases of different kinds of cupcakes. A number of tables shaped liked giant cupcakes were sprinkled around on the black-and-white tiled floor, and a bar with stools faced the window. The back two-thirds of the building was where they did the baking.

I had hoped it would be quiet when I went in so I could discuss all the possibilities with Caitlyn, but the place was crowded. A line of people were waiting to be served and all the tables were filled. It smelled delicious and reminded me that I'd missed lunch. The only thing I could do was join the line and wait.

It was a neighborhood place and the atmosphere was

friendly, which meant that everyone was talking to everyone else while they waited. I shouldn't have been surprised that the topic of conversation was Thursday's wedding. It had all the makings of a conversation piece. It was local, it was weird and murder was involved.

"The TV newspeople are calling it 'nuptial nightmare.' Did you see the photo of the mother of the bride sitting in the wedding cake, holding the bloody knife?" a woman said.

"I heard her referred to as the murderer-in-law," another woman said. "The newspeople love catchy phrases."

Someone else brought up the shapewear defense, and someone else said the same thing had happened to her. "I couldn't even lift my arms enough to dance with my son at his wedding."

I was glad I didn't have Thursday with me. It would have been her worst nightmare.

The line moved up slowly, and then even when they'd gotten their cupcakes, people stood off to the side continuing the conversation. The place had become so popular that Caitlyn had hired more baking help and several part-time people to man the counter. Since I was a regular customer, I knew all the counter help. I saw that Kirsty Frazier was assisting Caitlyn today. It was nothing personal, but I hoped when my turn came I'd get Caitlyn, since she was truly a cupcake expert.

"I was at the reception," the woman behind me said. Everyone turned to face her and began to shoot questions at her. I scrutinized her as well to see if I recognized her. She was blond with some help, somewhere in her forties with an overeagerness about her. It was obvious she liked being in the center of the discussion as she gave details about the event in the tent. Someone mentioned that she'd heard the cops thought it was someone who slipped in and pretended to be a server.

"It wouldn't have been that hard. The servers looked like something out of that old video. The one with Robert Palmer and all the women musicians who looked the same. Someone came by with a tray of baby quiches, and I couldn't tell if it was a man or a woman."

"Were the quiches good?" the woman next to her asked. The question caught everyone off guard and there was a titter of laughter as I finally stepped up to the counter. Just my luck Caitlyn was helping another customer and I got Kirsty.

"I'm not sure you can help me," I said. Kirsty did a double take. She had dark brown hair pulled back with a headband that showed off her dangle earrings.

"You don't need the boss to put some cupcakes in a pink box," she said, making a tsk sound and rolling her eyes. She waved her hand over the counter. "Tell me how many you want total so I know the size box and then you pick what kind you want."

"That's just it. I'm not here to buy cupcakes, well, maybe one, but what I really want is advice," I said.

Kirsty gave me an odd look. "What? You think cupcakes have taken the place of cocktails, and us counter people are like bartenders who you tell your problems to?" Then she apologized for being short. "Too many jobs, too little sleep," she said with a yawn. "I guess I might as well get used to it. Med students are notoriously sleep deprived."

All ears were on me now and eyes, too, though everyone was trying to act like it wasn't so.

I began the story about the Parties with a Purpose, explaining that the first one was for an eleven-year-old's birthday, and I was trying to line up the food and thought cupcakes might be the way to go.

"Absolutely," Kirsty said. She pulled out a menu of party options and slid it across the counter. "Our newest are the filled cupcakes. They look nice, but they are a little pricey."

"I'm not sure what Emerson wants to spend," I said.

"Emerson Lake?" Kirsty asked, and I nodded. She looked toward the crowd. "She did the flowers for the wedding you're all talking about."

The woman behind me spoke up. "That's right. She's the hot flower person for events now. She's known for her personalized service. Her trademark is decorating the cake with fresh flowers. She always does it on-site."

"Even so, she had to dress like the rest of the servers," Kirsty said. Caitlyn looked up from her customer and gave Kirsty a sharp look. Kirsty flinched and got back to business. "So, do any of those cupcakes work for you?"

All the choices were a little overwhelming, so I asked if I could take the menu and discuss it with Emerson and Lyla. I asked about how much time they needed and other details, and then bought a cornbread cupcake that almost passed as lunch.

One of the seats became available, and I sat down to eat my cupcake before going back to work. I was surprised when Kirsty abandoned the line and came out from behind the counter and over to me.

"Could you do me a favor?" she said, waving to the line that she'd be back there in a moment. She held out an earring. "Could you tell Adele I want another one like this?" She tried to hand it to me, but I was concerned that I might lose it. Instead, I offered to pass on the information to Adele.

"Fine," she said in an annoyed tone. "I'll keep it in my cubby if she needs to see it." She rushed back behind the counter, telling the fussing mob not to get their shorts in a knot. The blond woman who'd been behind me came up to me while she was waiting for her order. This time when we looked at each other, we recognized each other, at least sort of. She knew I worked at the bookstore, and I remembered her as the cookbook collector, but until now there had been no names involved. I gave her mine, and she introduced herself as Isa Susberg.

"Isa?" I said. "That's an unusual name."

"It's really Isabella. I went by Bella for years, but then it became too common, thanks to some vampire books. I sure hope nobody names a character Isa," she said with a smile. "I couldn't help but overhear what you said about the parties you're putting on. I'm hosting a baby shower and I was looking for something different. I think everyone is tired of the silly games. The idea of learning how to do something and actually making something sounds great. Could you handle a baby shower, or are you strictly kids' parties?"

"We can do any kind of event," I said. Unfortunately, she asked what kind of parties we'd done, and I had to tell her that Lyla's party was actually the first one we were doing.

"Oh," she said, sounding dubious. I sensed her backing away, and in an effort to keep the conversation going, I told her I'd been at the wedding, too. I asked if she was on the bride's or groom's side of the guest list.

"Actually, both. My husband does business with the Kingsleys' company, and I know Jaimee Fields from our women's club." She confided that she'd been questioned by the police and asked to give a DNA sample. She wanted to know if I'd been asked for one.

"I came in after the event, so I guess they didn't need one from me," I said. What I didn't tell her was that I'd been so close to so many crime scenes by now, I was pretty sure they kept my prints and DNA on file. Isa seemed uncomfortable with giving the sample.

"What if the cops make some kind of mistake?" she said in a concerned voice.

I assured her they were very careful about who they blamed and, besides, it would take forever to get any results for DNA stuff. By then they would probably have a suspect in custody.

"You didn't happen to see anything strange?" I asked. It had become second nature to me now to ask those kinds of questions.

She gave me an odd look. "You must be the one I heard about. Tarzana's answer to Nancy Drew. What's this, the Case of the Wronged Wedding?"

I gave her an uncomfortable smile and said I'd been involved with some investigations, but that I never gave them names.

"I'll tell you what I told the cops. I was there for a wedding. Everybody was standing around having drinks and appetizers. I wasn't expecting anything like that to happen, so I wasn't looking for anything weird. It just seemed like a regular wedding reception until the screaming started."

I thought she was going to leave it at that, but she leaned in close. "I'm not a detective, amateur or otherwise, but I think there was something going on between the bride and groom. I couldn't hear what they were saying, but he was holding her arm so tight that when he let go, it left a mark where his hand had been."

CHAPTER 8

THURSDAY WAS WAITING OUTSIDE THE BOOKSTORE when I finished for the day. She was more dressed up than I was used to seeing her. It seemed like she was going for a business look with the black jeans and rust-colored cotton jacket. She wore makeup down to lipstick, and her short brown hair looked styled. "Thank you for doing this," she said as we walked to the parking lot and her car. "I need to handle this myself." She glanced at me. "But maybe with some moral support."

She'd come back to the bookstore after lunch with her father, and asked for my help. Part of the reason for their lunch together was to bring Thursday her lime green Volkswagen and to discuss her future. "I'm all for moving ahead and making a new start, but I can't leave these loose ends hanging. I just want to talk to Jonah's father and clear the air."

I asked her again if she was sure she didn't want to talk

to her parents about it or have them accompany her, but she was insistent she wanted to do it this way.

"You're an impartial bystander. My father would want to handle the whole thing, and my mother—she's still so upset that Jackson Kingsley insisted the police detain her. You get the picture?"

I could see her point. Though I wasn't totally impartial, either. I was curious to see what I could find out. She drove along Wells Drive past the turnoff for my house. I was glad she knew the way because as she turned from one twisty street to another, I lost track of where we were.

Finally she pulled into a steep driveway and cut the engine. I followed her up to a house that sat on a finger of land above Corbin Canyon.

The Kingsleys were expecting her and seemed surprised and not altogether pleased that she wasn't alone. I checked out the house as they led us into the living room. It seemed to be all windows with a fabulous view of the valley. The furnishings were elegant without being gaudy, but it was a little too perfect for my taste. It didn't look lived in.

Jackson Kingsley was a little too perfect for my taste, too. He somehow managed to make a pair of jeans look stiff and formal. Maybe it was the tucked-in dress shirt or the belt. His wife, who introduced herself to me as Margo, was friendlier, but then Jonah wasn't her son, so there was less baggage.

"Why don't you entertain Molly," Jackson said to his wife, gesturing toward the living room. "Thursday and I can go into my office." It was hard to read his voice, other than to notice how nice the deep quality was. He seemed cordial, but not kind. I looked to Thursday to see if she wanted me to stick with her.

"It's a good idea for us to talk alone," she said as she followed Jackson across the house. I had to admire the way she handled herself. She seemed to be ready to face him head-on.

Margo and I sat down in the living room. She poured herself a glass of red wine and offered me one. I declined, but noticed that she dropped several ice cubes in it. She saw me staring.

"It's a habit I picked up from Jackson. He absolutely insists on ice in his wine." She sat back down and glanced in the direction Thursday and her husband had gone. "He's doing a good job of keeping it together, but he's still broken up. Jonah was his only child," she said.

"What about you? You're Jonah's stepmother?" I said, and she made a face.

"Stepmother sounds so awful. I never really thought of myself that way. I never thought of being any kind of mother to him. And Jonah wasn't looking for a replacement. In case you didn't know, his mother died when he was small. Jackson and I have only been married for five years. Jonah never lived with us." She moved closer to me. "Jonah and I never really hit it off. He tried to bust things up with his father and me." She suddenly realized what she'd said. "I didn't mean that. Please forget I said it. What I really meant to say was that Jonah and I had a polite relationship. He was a wonderful young man."

It was hard not to laugh when she called him a young man since I was pretty sure she was only ten years or so older than he was.

She drank some of her wine and quickly changed the subject to the bad job the police were doing. "Jackson is pretty upset with the police work. He's pretty upset with everything. He's being okay to Thursday right now, but I have to tell you, he blames her and her family for what happened to Jonah."

"You mean he thinks that Thursday and her mother were involved in his son's death?" I asked, and Margo nodded.

I asked her what she remembered from that night. She started to recite it as though she'd repeated the same thing many times. Someone had just replaced Jackson's boutonniere. He had a glass of merlot and asked one of the servers for some ice cubes. The clumsy server put the ice in his glass, and then as Jackson was about to drink it, knocked it out of his hand, spilling the red wine all over their shirt and gloves.

"Then what happened?" I asked.

"Jackson got another glass of merlot and a few minutes later all the screaming started."

I asked if she knew who had put the fresh flowers in the lapel of Jackson's jacket and she shrugged. "I wasn't really paying attention," she said, "and all those people looked the same anyway." She thought a moment. "It was probably the same person who put the first boutonniere in his lapel before the ceremony." I looked at her expectantly. "It was whoever did all the flowers."

I wanted to ask her about Jonah's job, but before I figured out how to segue into it, Thursday and Jackson returned. Neither of their expressions revealed how things had gone. Thursday just thanked him, and he gave her a wooden hug.

"What happened?" I said when we got into her car.

"I went there to tell him how sorry I was about everything. And to talk to him about returning the wedding gifts. I don't know what the proper etiquette is in a situation like this, but it feels wrong to keep them. I let him know that I didn't expect anything from Jonah's estate."

"That must have smoothed things over."

Thursday drove on toward the bookstore. "I don't think it really helped. He didn't come right out and say it, but I think he believes that my mother and I plotted to kill Jonah and that my walking away from Jonah's estate is just a ploy to throw everyone off the track." She let out a heavy breath. "And we talked about Jonah's funeral. Well, he talked about it. I have no say in it," she said.

She drove me back to my car and followed me home. We both pulled into the driveway and parked so we wouldn't block each other. "At least he said he'd have someone from his office handle returning the wedding gifts. I just don't think I could deal with that right now."

When we went inside, she took over the care of the animals, and I looked in the refrigerator for something to make for dinner.

"Let me help," she said as she came to stand next to me. She was about my height and her demeanor had changed completely from when she'd picked me up. Then she had seemed hopeful somehow, but now she looked discouraged.

"I think we need comfort food," I said. Her eyes brightened as she nodded in agreement. We finally made tomato soup and grilled cheese sandwiches.

"Please don't tell my dad about tonight," she said. "He told me not to talk to Jackson Kingsley. He was afraid I might make things worse with him, and I'm afraid I have."

CHAPTER 9

When I came home the next night, my living room was buzzing with activity. Mason, Thursday, Barry and another guy were gathered around something on the coffee table.

"What's up," I said, relieved to see that my animals were loose.

When I got closer, I saw that the new guy had on rubber gloves and was swabbing an envelope sitting on the table.

"I told you it wasn't sealed," Thursday said. There was some kind of greeting card sitting next to it. I sucked in my breath when I got close enough to see the artwork.

"Lots of people gave me envelopes at the reception," Thursday explained. "I didn't open any of them. I just stuffed them all in my bag." Her voice cracked. "I started looking through things, so I could begin returning the gifts." Thursday glanced at me, and when no one was looking, she put her finger to her lips in a gesture that clearly meant for me to be quiet about her trip to the Kingsleys'.

The card was handmade with a layer of patterned paper glued to the card stock. The skeleton bride and groom were a collage created out of layers of glued-together magazine photos. The wedding cake had been drawn in and colored in black and decorated with bloodred roses. The overall impression was jarring. And when I saw the inside, it was worse. The message had been created out of cutouts of words and letters. It read simply: "Time to pay for what you did."

"Was it just guests who handed you the envelopes?" I asked. Thursday took a moment to think back.

"I don't know," she said. "There was so much going on. It just didn't register who was handing me things."

The man who I now realized was a CSI technician took pictures of the card. Barry cleared his throat. "It obviously was meant as a message, and the fact that they gave it to Thursday makes it look like your family was the target of revenge." He looked at Mason.

Thursday's face clouded over. "That's ridiculous. Nobody wants revenge against my father. Who? Most of his cases are things like celebrities hitting stop signs and driving away. Maybe it was just given to me because other people were handing me cards."

The technician was packing up his equipment. "It's doubtful there's any evidence on it. You have to assume that if it was intended as a calling card, the person who made it wore gloves. The fact the envelope wasn't sealed means they probably knew about leaving DNA and trace evidence."

"Would you have even called me about the card if I hadn't stopped over?" Barry said to Mason and Thursday before turning back to me. "I brought some more photographs for Thursday to go through."

Mason and his daughter looked at each other, and some silent communication passed between them before they both denied what Barry had said.

"I hope you're spending as much time talking to the Kingsleys. If there is revenge involved, it seems more likely it would be aimed at Jonah, no matter what Jackson Kingsley says," Mason said in a terse tone.

It got more awkward after that. Barry insisted that they were checking everything and everyone. I got an uncomfortable feeling when it seemed like he was looking at Thursday as he said it.

Each man appeared to be waiting for the other to leave. Samuel came home with a bunch of friends, and they headed for the kitchen. I'd been through all this before, so I handled it in my own way. I left.

"Come in," Dinah said when I landed at her doorstep. She laughed when she heard about the chaos at my house. "You could just tell all of them to leave. Including Thursday. She isn't your responsibility." Dinah knew how to handle an awkward situation better than I did. But then she'd had years of experience with difficult students.

"But she seems so vulnerable, and when I taught her how to crochet, she kind of got to me. You saw how nice she was at the group. She even offered to help with the party. And it's only temporary. She'll be going back to work soon and she's going to find her own place."

"So you've adopted her," Dinah said. "The daughter you never had."

"Maybe a little," I said.

Dinah's face grew serious. "Just be sure that she isn't playing you. The crocheting and her offer of help are all very nice, but it could just be part of a plan to win you over." She mentioned students she'd had who were oh-so-friendly, brought her cups of coffee, and complimented her on the long scarves she always wore. "And expected an A, despite the fact that their class work stunk."

I didn't even want to think about it. "Let's talk about something else." I told her about my trip to Caitlyn's and the possibility of another party. But then the conversation came right back to the wedding reception when I told her about Emerson doing the flowers for the event and being there.

"I wonder if she saw anything," Dinah said.

"I'm going to ask her about it." I was going to tell Dinah about the creepy card, but there was a knock at her door.

"It's Sheila," Dinah said as she got up to answer. Sheila was juggling fewer jobs these days, but she was still renting a room in a house. A house that had a whole family of kids and no peace. "She's seeking asylum, too," Dinah added on her way to the door.

Sheila was still going to school to study costume design, but most of her time was spent at Luxe, the lifestyle store on Ventura Boulevard near the bookstore. The owner had turned over more and more of the responsibility to her. It had also become a place for her to sell the scarves, shawls and blankets she made that resembled Impressionist paintings with their mixtures of blues, greens and lavenders.

"We can have our own little Hooker gathering," Dinah said after letting Sheila in.

"Okay by me," Sheila said, sitting on Dinah's chartreuse sofa. We all pulled out some yarn, hooks and works in progress, and started to crochet. The silence lasted about thirty seconds, and I remembered that I hadn't told Dinah about the card.

Both Dinah and Sheila shuddered when they heard what it looked like. "Mason is upset because the Kingsleys keep insisting the revenge motive is aimed at him."

"They're probably crazy with grief," Dinah said. "What could be worse than having your son killed?"

"It's not really *they*," I said, before explaining about the current Mrs. Kingsley. "Maybe they are, but they're being horrible to Thursday," I said. Dinah turned to Sheila.

"Molly has adopted a daughter," she said with a grin.

"I have not," I said. "Well, not exactly, anyway." Then I told them about accompanying Thursday to the Kingsleys'. "I don't know if I should refer to them as her in-laws or what. She's grieving, too. It was her husband who was murdered. Just because she's keeping it all inside doesn't mean she isn't hurting."

"You'd think they would want to be close to her after what happened to Jonah," Sheila said. She'd been brought up by her grandmother who'd died recently, leaving her alone in the world, so she was particularly sensitive.

"Close? No way. If anything, it seems like the opposite. I think Jackson Kingsley wants to cut the tie. He sent a lawyer to talk to her. She's the one that made the move to go to the Kingsleys and discuss things face-to-face," I said.

"It sounds to me like he's blaming Thursday for what happened to his son," Sheila said.

"But you have to remember that Jaimee Fields was holding the bloody knife, and Thursday was next to the body," Dinah added. Her point was well taken. Their fingerprints were probably all over the knife, and the killer's probably weren't, if they'd worn the white gloves. Would Jackson Kingsley buy Jaimee's shapewear alibi? Probably not.

"Someone could think they worked as a murder team," Sheila said.

"Okay, I can see how they might think that. The shape-wear story did seem rather far-fetched, even though the cops supposedly tested trying to lift one of her arms and as soon as they let go, it snapped back against her side." I paused after that. I didn't want to say anything about Thursday, but the truth was she had been next to the body with blood on her hands and dress.

Dinah picked up on my silence. "And why is it that you're not considering the possibility that Thursday had anything to do with it?"

"She just couldn't," I said a little too quickly. My real reason was that I liked her too much. After living in a house full of men and then being around Barry and Mason—well, the most I got was an occasional "you look nice" with no details. Thursday had noticed that I'd added a summer-weight cowl to my usual bookstore outfit of khakis and a shirt. She'd noticed that instead of the usual white, I'd worn a turquoise shirt. And she'd said it looked nice with my hair color. A murderer wouldn't say that, would they?

Sheila looked up from her work quickly. "I forgot. I know something strange about the groom."

"Spill," I said, quickly, realizing I still knew very little about him. In one of Barry's more candid moments, he'd admitted that who a person was had a lot to do with who had killed them. It was all related to the idea that most victims knew their killer.

Sheila wasn't used to being the one in the know, and she was a little stunned by my command. And it immediately turned into an attack of nerves. She pulled out the string and hook she used as a portable tranquilizer and began to make a long line of chain stitches and went back over them with single crochets. She didn't even look at the stitches or seem to care that they were all over the place. This was just about the rhythmic activity rather than the end product.

Dinah countered my abrupt order by asking Sheila in a soothing manner to tell us about it. Sheila's chin-length brown hair had fallen forward to block her round face, and she pushed it behind her ears and took a few deep breaths.

"Okay, here it is," she said. "Jonah Kingsley bought his groomsmen's gifts at Luxe and something special for his best man. Only," Sheila stopped and took a deep breath. "About a week ago, he came in and wanted to change the engraving on the best man's gift."

I asked what he was like.

"He was clean-cut and very nice-looking. And polite. He apologized for the last-minute request." It seemed like she was finished, but then she remembered something else. "Oh, he also bought an antique armoire."

"He bought it without consulting Thursday?" Dinah said. I looked at Dinah and got her point. It was kind of overbearing. Then I remembered that Thursday had said the condo really belonged to the Kingsleys' business, and I told Dinah and Sheila.

"It doesn't sound like it was their place as much as it was his place," Dinah said. "I don't think I would like that."

"I wasn't trying to tell you that he bought a piece of furniture. It was about the best man's gift."

"I think we got it," I said. "He wanted to change what he wrote on it."

"I didn't explain it right," Sheila said, getting into a tizzy.

"He wanted to change the name on it. So that means at the last minute he changed who his best man was." Once that was out, Sheila went off into how she'd had to tell him it was too late to stop the order. "He ended up getting something else entirely with no engraving."

"I bet that means he had a falling out with the original best man," Dinah said, then she giggled. "I just love playing Sherlock Holmes and deducing things."

"And maybe the former best man wasn't so happy about being dumped or was angry from the falling out. He would have known about the wedding plans and could have just slipped in as one of the servers, stabbed his former buddy and left." It sounded perfectly plausible to me.

"Are you investigating this murder?" Sheila said. I glanced at Dinah and shrugged.

"I guess I am. It's kind of hard to stay uninvolved when Thursday is staying at my house," I said. "So, tell me who the dumped best man is."

Sheila's eyes went back and forth as she searched her memory, and then she seemed disappointed. "Sorry, all I can remember is that it was a weird name."

"Well, that's that," Dinah said. "You should mention it to Barry."

I shook my head. "No way, not unless I have more to give him. I think Jackson Kingsley just stonewalls whenever Barry asks him any questions that make it sound like the motive had anything to do with his family."

"Can they do that?" Dinah said.

"Yes, nobody can make them talk," I said. Dinah said something about that wasn't the way it worked on TV shows.

"They only have an hour to solve the crime," I said.

Sheila was listening to our conversation and then brightened. "I just remembered. The name might have been written on the outside of the box the tray was in." When we didn't understand, she explained that the gift was one of those trays for a dresser top. "It's for your coins and the stuff from your pocket. It came in a velour box with a white sleeve around it to protect it," she said.

Dinah and I were waiting for her to get to the point. She explained that the best man's name had been written on it, and she'd taken it off before the box had been gift-wrapped. "I think I wound some yarn around it." She went on describing a hank of yarn she'd been trying to wind into a ball and the cardboard had worked as a center.

"Where is it?" I said, interrupting her involved explanation.

"Oh, it's still at Luxe. I keep a project to work on when things get slow," Sheila answered.

"You have keys to the store, right?" Dinah said, getting up.

"I do, but I don't know if I should use them. I'm just supposed to use them to open and close the store. It might look strange if we went into the store when it's supposed to be closed." Sheila had gone back to her nerve-relieving crochet. "I mean, what if a police car went by and knew the store was supposed to be closed, but the lights were on?"

I didn't want to tell her that it was doubtful the police were that knowledgeable about store hours. "What if you left something there and went back to get it?" I said, standing and joining Dinah.

"Couldn't you just wait until tomorrow?" Sheila said.

"We could, but if we get it now, by tomorrow we'll know who this guy is and hopefully where to find him."

Sheila put down her hook and string and reluctantly got up. "If we went in the back way, nobody would notice," she said.

A few minutes later, we'd walked the short distance from Dinah's house to the parking lot that ran along the back of the stores. The leaves were beginning to rustle as the desert winds started to pick up again. It felt unsettling, like rubbing a cat's fur the wrong way.

Dinah's long scarf caught in the breeze and wound around her neck. She seemed a little panicked by how tight it had gotten, and she pulled it off, stowing it in her pocket. My shirt caught a gust of wind and floated up behind me. Only Sheila's short skirt and gauzy peasant top seemed windproof.

With the stores closed, the parking lot was almost completely empty. The few cars that were there were parked along the back wall and seemed a little creepy. "Let's get this over with," I said, leading the way to the back door of Luxe. I glanced at the window next to the door and it appeared dark.

Sheila took out the key and put it in the lock. "There's an alarm," she warned. "Let me shut it off first." She walked inside and then came back. "That's funny. It isn't on. I'm sure I set it before I left."

Dinah and I told her she must have forgotten, but not to get upset about it as it didn't seem like anything bad had happened in the meantime.

The three of us went inside and closed the door behind us. A hallway led to a door that opened into the actual retail area. There were several doors leading off the hallway. I knew that one led to a restroom and the other to the office of Luxe's owner, Nicholas. But once he'd admitted to writ-

ing the crocheting vampire books that our fellow Hooker
Elise was so enamored with, he rarely came into the store
anymore, and I heard he'd gotten a fabulous hillside home
with an office that looked out over the whole valley.

"What's in there now?" I said as we went by the closed
door.

"Storage, I guess. Nicholas didn't give me the key." Sheila
moved quickly down the hall. She had this phobia about
turning on the lights, sure that it would look suspicious, so
the three of us felt our way to the door that led to the front
of the store and went inside. The street lamps illuminated
the interior enough so that I could make out the racks of
interesting clothes and shelves of shoes, scarves and house-
hold items, and the occasional piece of furniture.

Sheila went behind the glass counter and started feeling
her way for the ball of yarn. I knew it didn't make any sense,
because we were only there to get something that belonged
to Sheila, but somehow being in the darkened store made
my heart begin to thud, and I felt like a criminal.

"What was that?" Dinah said. In the semidarkness, she
cocked her ear in the direction we'd entered. I heard a definite creak.

"You locked the door when we came in, didn't you?" I
said to Sheila.

"Maybe I didn't," she began to wail. "If I forgot to set the
alarm, I could forget to do anything. Suppose there were real
burglars in one of those cars and they followed us," she said.
There was another creak, and I could've sworn I heard a
footstep. The adrenaline was shooting through my body,
and even my whispered command telling the two of them
to hide sounded high-pitched. Carefully, I walked toward
the door leading to the back. I'd grabbed an Italian leather

boot to use as a weapon. What was I going to do, poke whoever in the eye with the pointy toe?

I had my hand on the door handle, counted three and threw it open, making some kind of karate noises, and threw the shoe into the dark hallway just as a hand grabbed my wrist.

"Nicholas!" Sheila squealed when the lights came on and she saw who the hand grasping me belonged to. "What are you doing here?"

"I could ask you the same thing." He glanced over at the three of us. Poor Sheila looked like she was going to faint. Not only was Nicholas her boss, but she also had the hots for him. This wasn't going to help her case.

To save Sheila, I took the rap and said we'd talked her into coming in to get something. His face broke into a good-natured smile and he shook his head. "I just bet it has something to do with Tarzana's best-known crime fighter." He went into the hall and picked up the Italian boot, which had made a little dent in the back wall—maybe I wasn't so off base choosing it as a weapon after all.

"I should have told you," he said to Sheila. "The office with the view is too distracting. I've been coming here at night for a while to work." He gestured toward the closed office door. "Well, now you know, in case you come back here again." By now, Sheila had the ball of yarn. She showed it to Nicholas to make it clear she'd only come for something that belonged to her. He let us walk ahead of him toward the back door before he stopped at the one to his office.

I hung back, wishing I could get a glimpse inside. I'd seen the inside once, and there'd been that coffin, a Hollywood version of a vampire's coffin, and that bottle of red liquid in the refrigerator that I'd heard was Bloody Mary mix, but who knew for sure? And why didn't the light show through the window?

Nicholas opened the door, and I grabbed a quick look. The window was covered with blackout curtains, and the coffin was still there. He offered me a friendly nod as he stepped back inside. I rushed on to join Dinah and Sheila outside. I told them about the coffin and the curtains that kept out any light. "It makes you wonder," I said.

Dinah rolled her eyes at me. "You're beginning to sound like Elise. Vampires only exist in fiction."

When the three of us had collapsed onto seats in Dinah's living room, Sheila took out the ball of burgundy-colored yarn and began to unravel it. When she got to the cardboard core, she unrolled it and the three of us looked at the name: Paxton Cline.

"Well, you were right. It is a weird name. Paxton. I wonder what they called him when he was little. Paxie?"

Dinah had already gone to her computer and was typing in the name. A few moments later, she let out a triumphant sound. "Found him."

The three of us gathered around the screen. It was filled with a news story about Paxton Cline and his family's business, Cline's Yarns.

I recognized the name of the company, but had never realized it was local. I'd bought from them for the bookstore, but through a trade show.

"I think I know where we're going tomorrow," I said.

CHAPTER 10

MUCH AS I WOULD HAVE LIKED TO HAVE GONE right to Cline's Yarns, there were other things to take care of first. Like my job. "How are the party plans coming?" Mrs. Shedd asked when I came in the next morning. Yes, she'd put me in charge of the parties, but ultimately she was in charge of everything that went on at the bookstore. She tried to keep her voice light, but there was an edge of nervousness.

"I have the food covered. Caitlyn's Cupcakes has a special birthday package. A platter of cupcakes put together like a cake with decorations and 'Happy Birthday' written across the middle."

Mrs. Shedd's expression faded a little. "I was hoping we could keep the food in-house." She left it at that, but I knew the bottom line was the bottom line. She was looking for ways to make the parties more profitable. We discussed it back and forth, and I convinced her to do it this way for the first party. Then we could see if there was a way our barista and cookie baker could come up with something for the parties. I mentioned the possible baby shower and Mrs. Shedd perked up immediately.

"That's what I want to hear," she said, asking for details. When she heard Isa Susberg was waiting to commit until after the birthday party, Mrs. Shedd gave me a pointed look. "I don't care what you have to do, but you have to pull off that first party."

"No worries," I said brightly. She wanted to know what other details I'd locked in for the birthday party and was concerned when I said I was still working on most of them. But what she really wanted to know was if I had a deposit from Emerson.

"It's too easy for her to just change her mind," Mrs. Shedd said when I told her no. I could see her point, and I put my plans to go to Cline's Yarns, Inc., off until later.

At least Mrs. Shedd had no objection when I left shortly after getting to work, because it was for the new enterprise. Rather than calling Emerson, asking her for the deposit and then trying to arrange a time to get it, I just went to her place of business. Once I knew she'd done the flowers for Thursday's wedding, all I had to do was call Mason to get the location.

The small storefront was tucked into a strip mall on the border of Tarzana and Woodland Hills. The display window featured a metal floral arrangement and a sign that said "Event Florist."

A bell on the door tinkled as I walked inside. The first thing I noticed was the smell, or should I say fragrance, of flowers mixed with the freshness of something green. There was a counter with a book of designs on it and a small cooler with some arrangements in it.

An open doorway led to a back room where several women were working with flowers and talking. Emerson looked up from a worktable on the other side of the tiny back room. When she saw it was me, she smiled and set down the stalk of white gladiolas she was about to add to a spectacular arrangement of assorted white flowers.

She took off a pair of almost-flesh-colored cotton gloves as she walked into the outer room.

"We don't do walk-in business," she said, assuming I was there for flowers. "This isn't the way I dress for customers," she said gesturing at her well-worn jeans and pale yellow polo shirt. She pointed to the cooler behind her and then to the book on the counter. "Those are just samples. We do strictly special events." She started to say something about making an exception and letting me have one of the samples, but I stopped her and told her I wasn't there about floral arrangements.

"I wanted to talk to you about Lyla's party."

Emerson seemed concerned. "I don't want to make this into a big production. The pizza parties were easy to plan. All I had to do was make a reservation, order the pizzas and hand out a bunch of tokens for the amusement things at Bucky's Pizza Palace."

I assured her that all she would have to do was show up once we went over a few things. Included in that was the deposit, but I thought I'd work my way up to it. As soon as I mentioned getting cupcakes from Caitlyn's, she looked happier.

"That's much better than a traditional birthday cake," she said when I showed her a picture of a tray of cupcakes with "Happy Birthday" written across them. "I'm sure Lyla will love it."

One of the women came in from the back room and said there was a problem with the hydrangeas dropping blossoms and mentioned the wedding they were for. It reminded me that she'd done the flowers for Thursday's wedding.

"I hope this one is more peaceful than the Fields–Kingsley reception," I said. Then I explained that I'd been an invited guest.

Emerson seemed to flinch as I mentioned that I'd heard she'd done the flowers for it.

"I have tried to put it out of my mind," she said. I asked her if she'd been questioned by the cops at the reception.

"Actually, when I left, everything was okay. My specialty is decorating the wedding cake with fresh flowers. I do it on-site, literally just before the start of the reception, so there's no chance of wilted flowers," Emerson said. I smiled benignly, wondering if she'd seen what happened to her work after Jaimee fell into the cake.

"I did a final check on it as the reception was getting under way, and then I left," she said.

"And you gave out fresh boutonnieres," I said. She seemed surprised when I mentioned that I'd heard it from Margo Kingsley.

I couldn't help myself and started to ask if she'd seen anything suspicious, like someone who didn't belong. "How could you tell? Everybody who was working at the reception in any capacity, including me, had to have that stupid robot look. I had to use a jar of goop to slick my hair back and then put it in a bun."

"And the white gloves," I added.

"They weren't the right kind to wear when you're

working with flowers. I had brought my own. I'm just glad most of the weddings I do don't make an issue about what I wear." As a way of turning the topic back to the birthday party, she picked up the photo I'd brought of the cupcakes. She asked about the crochet project and what kind of supplies the kids would have to work with. She caught me off guard, and I had to admit that those details were still being arranged. I did my best to assure her that teaching them to crochet would be easy, and we would have a project they would like. Then I brought up the deposit.

Emerson seemed to hesitate as she got out her checkbook. "I am sure you will do fine, but I would feel a little better if you taught Lyla to crochet first. Then it won't be all new to her at the party."

I got it. She wanted us to audition. As soon as I agreed, she wrote the check and handed it to me. We set up a time and I assured her that we'd give Lyla more than one lesson if needed. Adele would no doubt fuss that I'd agreed to the pre-party crocheting, but I had no choice.

I rushed back to the bookstore just in time to tell Mrs. Shedd I was going to lunch. "Mission accomplished," I said, handing her the deposit check.

Dinah was waiting outside. She had a break before she had to be back to Beasley Community College for her afternoon class, and we'd agreed to use the time to check out Paxton Cline, the deposed best man.

"I love playing detective with you," she said as we walked to my car. Cline's Yarns International, Inc., was located in a business park in Chatsworth. It was an easy drive up Corbin to get there, and we tried to come up with a strategy as we went.

"This should be easy," I said to Dinah as we turned off

onto Plummer. I'd even come up with a reason why I was coming in to see them. "The only thing is we have to make sure we talk to Paxton."

"Uh-oh," Dinah said, pointing to the police car in the parking lot as I pulled in.

"I wonder what's going on?" I said as we got out of my car. Nobody could accuse us of being afraid to walk into trouble—we practically ran to the white double-door entry. We slowed when we reached a reception area and saw two uniforms talking to a woman wearing glasses.

I edged close enough to overhear. "You recognize this knitted thing?" a heavyset, olive-complected officer said, waving something made of colorful yarn. "We're trying to track down the person who made it." I recognized him from the first yarn bombing. He'd been the one to climb the ladder and strip off the monkey's jacket.

The woman took it from his hand and looked up with an amused smile. "This isn't knitted. It's crocheted." The officer shrugged off her comment.

"Knitted, crocheted, what's the difference? All I know is, it's trouble."

She started to explain the difference, then seemed to realize it was probably a lost cause. "It is our yarn," she said. She had laid the rectangle on the counter and pointed out some variegated yarn that was their trademark. "But we can't trace it to a single user. The best I could do is give you a list of yarn shops in the area that carry our line." She looked at it again. "Where did you say you found it?"

"Wrapped around a light pole on Ventura Boulevard," one of the uniforms said. "This yarn bomber seems to be stepping up the attacks."

Attacks? Was he kidding? How was adding a little color

to a drab light pole an attack? Calling it vandalism seemed a little extreme, too. All they had to do was cut it down.

The woman with the glasses went to get them a list of stores in the area that sold their yarn. Great, the bookstore would probably be on the list.

While we waited our turn, I looked around the lobby area. Wow. They had items made up from their yarn on mannequins and hanging on the walls. There were a couple of desks behind the counter. Behind them I saw a doorway leading to what appeared to be a warehouse full of yarn. I was wondering how I was going to zero in on Paxton when the front door opened and a man in his late twenties came in carrying what appeared to be a food order. On a chance, I called out, "Paxton," and the bland-looking young man with close-cropped brown hair turned at the sound.

"Molly Pink," I said, holding out my hand. "And this is my associate Dinah Lyons." Dinah gave him a little wave, and poor Paxton looked confused.

"We had an appointment," I said. Okay, I was totally winging it, making it up as I went along. The cops got their list and left, and the woman with glasses looked over the counter at us.

"Can I help you?" she said.

"No, no. It's Paxton here I was supposed to meet," I said. I remembered that the article Dinah had found online had said that he was working in all aspects of the business, which no doubt included sales.

"Can we go somewhere and talk?" I said, looking at the box he was balancing.

"Uh, sure," he said, handing his load to the woman with the glasses.

Dinah was looking at me and I could read her thoughts. She was wondering what I was going to say. So was I.

I explained that I handled the yarn department at Shedd & Royal. "We're going to be doing parties at the bookstore." I explained the whole Party with a Purpose concept and how we'd be teaching groups of people to crochet, and they'd be making a project. "I'm looking to buy kits," I said. "They'd have yarn, the tools needed and some kind of tote bag."

Before I asked him if they could do it, I segued into the first party and brought up Emerson. From there, I brought up what she did and how she'd done the flowers for a wedding reception where there was a murder. I just kept on blathering about how terrible it was about Jonah Kingsley. Then I just stopped and looked at Paxton. I watched as a cloud passed through his amber eyes. This was it. He was going to start to spill his guts. Or maybe not.

"I did hear something about that," he said. I waited for him to say more, and when he didn't, I tried to coax it out of him.

"He was right around your age," I offered. "I don't suppose you knew him."

"Only in the vaguest sense," he said finally. He gestured toward the front door. "Kingsley Enterprises, Inc., is across the street." He seemed thoughtful for a moment. "I was at a baseball game the day of the wedding."

Dinah and I nodded with interest and I waited for him to elaborate. He didn't, even when I gave him plenty of dead air.

"Really?" I said, finally. "He worked across the street and you weren't invited to his wedding?"

Paxton chewed on the inside of his cheek. "I didn't know

him. Like I said, I didn't go." He looked at me intently. "What are you? Some kind of private detective?" I shrugged as an answer and let the air go dead again. This time it seemed to make him nervous. "I have nothing else to say. Like I said I was at a baseball game." He quickly turned the conversation back to the kits. "What did you have in mind?"

When he heard I only wanted eight, and they needed to be very reasonable, in other words, cheap, he looked dubious.

"If it was up to me, I'd try to do something for you, but my grandmother calls the shots. She's the one who started the business and keeps saying she's going to start taking time off, but she doesn't."

He'd barely finished talking when he ushered us toward the door.

"He was certainly lying," Dinah said when we drove away.

"It could be that he's just scared and thinks that if he denies knowing Jonah he can stay out of the whole thing. Maybe he realized that being fired as the best man gives him a motive, or maybe he's the one who stabbed Jonah."

CHAPTER 11

By the end of the day, my head was spinning, whirling between thinking about Paxton, all the unsettled details of the party, and my regular work. I still had to manage the yarn department and think about upcoming bookstore events.

I was really concerned about the project for the party. Whenever I went into the yarn department to help someone or straighten up, I took the opportunity to thumb through the crochet books, hoping something would pop out at me. It had to be simple enough for new kid crocheters to do, it had to be something fun, and it needed to be relatively quick.

"Hey, Sunshine." Mason caught up with me as I walked out of the bookstore. I startled, even though his appearance shouldn't have been a surprise. He'd called earlier and suggested dinner. He thought it would be nice for the two of us to go somewhere.

I'd barely said hello to Mason when Barry came from the other direction and joined us. "Greenberg," Mason said with a note of surprise, and not the good kind, either. Mason tried to be dismissive by saying "See you later" to Barry and putting his arm through mine. But Barry made no move to leave and ignored Mason's comment altogether. Instead, he brought up some sports game. Mason commented on it, and the next thing I knew they had a conversation going about balls and playoffs.

The ever-observant homicide detective commented that it looked like we were on our way to dinner and then stunned me by suggesting that he join us. "We *are* all just friends," he said. "And we can talk about the murder case."

Barry's eyes flitted toward me with a little smile. He knew he'd hit Mason's tender spot. And the next thing I knew, the three of us were walking into the family-owned Italian restaurant down the street. The air smelled of garlic and tomatoes, and I was already salivating at the thought of their homemade Caesar dressing.

We took a table by the window, and as soon as we'd ordered, Mason turned to Barry. "So?"

"We'd hoped to have a suspect by now, but things aren't progressing as quickly as we'd like. Having all the workers dressed the same didn't help. It's almost like somebody deliberately planned it."

Mason put up his hands. "It wasn't my idea. Talk to my ex."

Barry gave a weary nod and I knew what he was thinking. He had already talked to Jaimee and didn't want to talk to her again. "We're talking to all the servers again, trying to see if they noticed any of their own that didn't quite fit in. So far, all I have is that someone thought one of the staff people was wearing different gloves."

I flinched, knowing he was probably referring to Emerson. I wondered if I should mention that I knew her and explain why her gloves hadn't been the regulation kind, but I decided it was better to stay out of it. I also wondered if Barry knew whether Jonah had any enemies? But then Barry would want to know why I was asking, and I didn't want to bring up Paxton Cline—at least not yet. I'd investigate on my own, and if there was something worthy, I'd pass it on.

"Basically, what you're saying is that you aren't any closer to a suspect," Mason said with a touch of annoyance.

Barry dealt with the comment by totally changing the subject to the yarn bombings. "It's not my area," he said, focusing on me, "but since it involves yarn. Do you know anything?"

The food arrived and Mason waited until the waiter left. "You don't have a suspect in the murder at my daughter's wedding, and you're wasting time trying to hunt down some kind of yarn tagger."

"I wouldn't call them a tagger," I said. "Taggers go around spray painting their logos on stuff. The yarn pieces hardly seemed to have a signature or an identifying quality to them. Even calling them graffiti seems over-the-top."

Barry said they were afraid the yarn pieces were just a gateway to something more.

"You're kidding, right?" I said, checking his expression as it lightened a smidgen.

"Maybe I agree with you, but some other cops are more concerned." He pushed his salad away to make room for the plate of lasagna. "Your coworker Adele's boyfriend for one."

"I get it. Is this your subtle way of saying he thinks it's Adele, and I should get her to cease and desist with the yarn attacks?"

"If you want to take it that way," Barry said, "I'm not going to talk you out of it."

Mason seemed unhappy with the line of conversation, maybe because it was going on between me and Barry. "Are you really making a fuss over some kind of yarn snuggie on a mailbox?" Mason said.

"You saw a crocheted cover on a mailbox?" I said. Mason nodded, and said there was one on Ventura near the Walgreens.

"Instead of it being USPS dark blue, it was wearing a wild piece that was all different colors. Personally, I thought it was an improvement. It was certainly cheerful," Mason said.

Barry's eyes lit up. "Aha, so then it is escalating. First it's an innocent little jacket on a metal monkey, then hearts on a gazebo, a sock on a street sign, and now it's a cover for a mailbox."

Mason groaned and steered the conversation back to the murder investigation. "Really, you're still interviewing and re-interviewing the same people?"

Barry got defensive. "There were over 250 people there, if you count the help. None of them was expecting to be a witness to a murder. Getting information out of them isn't easy. We're still sorting out who was there. We're still trying to get a list from the caterer. They pay cash and don't keep the best records. It's not exactly a profession, and all their people have other jobs, sometimes several. Lots of actors and writers, and waiters." Barry looked up at the young man refilling his water. "I'm just curious. Have you ever worked for Laurie Jean's Party People? The caterer?"

The waiter seemed surprised by the comment, and then nodded. "I'm really an actor. You might have seen me in the crowd scene on last week's *L.A. 911.* But yeah, I have."

With that opening, Barry asked him about the wedding. The waiter's eyes narrowed. "Nope, not that one. It makes me glad I had a shift here. What a crazy world. A few minutes after you're married, you're dead." He held the water pitcher with both hands and got ready to leave. "Personally, I'm going with the murderer-in-law theory."

When the waiter had gone, Barry turned to Mason. "How involved was your daughter with the planning?" I saw Mason's expression grow tired.

"Greenberg, I know where you're going. You're thinking that whoever planned the wedding could have decided on the robot look, so that somebody could slip in and kill Jonah. It was all my ex's idea." Mason finished with his entree. "This dinner was supposed to be a chance for Molly and me to get away from it all for a while." Mason put his hand over mine in a possessive manner.

Barry stared at Mason's hand. "Is hand-holding permissible? This whole idea of friends is new to me, and I'm not familiar with the rules."

I rolled my eyes to myself. The whole idea of keeping both men as friends was supposed to make things less complicated. Now I had to worry there were rules?

CHAPTER 12

"A hug in greeting is okay." "A light kiss as a parting gesture." "No baggage, and no expectations." "No cuddling and definitely no sleepovers." After I gave a replay of the evening and explained how Barry had asked about the rules, the comments kept coming from around the worktable.

"What are we talking about?" CeeCee said as she fluttered up to the table.

"Molly had dinner with her two men friends. Only it sounds like *she* views them as friends, but typical men, they don't get that kind of relationship. For them, it's some kind of competition and Molly is the prize."

CeeCee let out a burst of her musical laugh. "It's just like the two neighbors Troy and Rock on *The CeeCee Collins Show*. My character kept saying they were just friends, but Troy and Rock kept trying to sabotage anything I had with the other. It was a while ago, so everything was very innocent. In those days, even married couples were only allowed a peck on the cheek."

"If Eduardo was here, you could ask him," Dinah said. "I think he gets the idea of women as friends. I haven't noticed him putting the moves on any of us."

Adele was dressed all in brown and blended in so much with the table, I didn't even see her until she spoke. "Speak for yourselves. He definitely had a thing for me, but I had to set him straight and make it clear we would never be more than fellow Hookers." As the last words tumbled out of Adele's mouth, she froze. "Did I really say that?" She looked around frantically. Some yarn and knitting needles were on the table next to her, but the chair was pulled out.

"Leonora went to the restroom," Elise said. Adele began to gasp and started biting her lip. "Thank heavens, she didn't hear me. She must realize I have a past, but there's no reason for her to know that Eduardo was one of the men in my life."

I never thought I would be happy to see Adele act outrageous, but she'd been so proper lately, trying to hide under a bushel basket of plain clothes and dull comments to please Eric's mother. It only lasted for a minute, and as soon as Leonora even got near the table, Adele went back to her fake demure self.

"Yes, Molly, I would be happy to teach little Lyla how to crochet," Adele said in crisp diction as Leonora returned to her seat. Acting surprised, Adele turned to her. "Oh, Mother Humphries, I didn't see you come back. We were just talking about the first party we're hosting at the bookstore." Adele seemed ready to say more, but she began to bite her lip to stop herself. Could it be that she was finally recognizing how outrageous most of what she said was? I don't think Leonora liked her moniker. I heard her grunt when Adele said it.

In the meantime, everybody showed off what they were working on. CeeCee went first and showed off another pet mat she was making. "I'm using up all my colorful scraps. No reason for the poor dears not to have something bright and cheery in the shelter."

ADELE BROKE IN WHILE WE WERE STILL ADMIRING the pet mat, showing off some earrings she was making by crocheting wire and attaching beads. When I saw them, it reminded me of what the girl in the cupcake shop had said, and I told Adele the girl needed a mate to an earring. Adele muttered something about having made the beads and having to make a whole new pair.

Dinah was next. "Did I tell you my ex's kids with his newest ex are coming for Halloween?" She held up a partially done orange bag and explained she was making bags for them to take trick-or-treating. Leonora seemed confused and started to ask questions about Dinah's relationship to these children. Adele's eyes went skyward and she swooped in to point out what Elise was working on. That is, until she saw Elise was putting a red tassel on the black-and-white, worsted-weight, striped beanie. Sheila was easy. She was quietly working on a ruana in her trademark heathery colors, no doubt to be sold at Luxe.

Rhoda held up the lapghan she was making. She had a pile of small balls of different colors of yarn on the table. "We give them to cancer patients when they're getting chemo."

Leonora seemed impressed. "Finally a project I can identify with. Personally, I knit chemo caps." I saw it register on Adele's face, and she stopped biting her lip long enough to explain that making a chemo cap was her next project.

I was about to show off the ruffly scarf I was making, when Bob interrupted. Maybe *interrupted* is the wrong word. How could someone showing up with a tray of yummy cookie bars be interrupting? He focused directly on me.

"I understand you were in Caitlyn's talking about cupcakes for a party at the bookstore." There was a little edge in his voice, as if he thought I was some kind of traitor. "Cupcakes are already passé," he said. "If you want to be ahead of the curve, cookie bars are it." He began to circle the table, and he didn't have to ask anyone twice, until he got to Leonora.

She waved them away. "I never eat sweets, except for the five grapes I have with my lunch." Bob stopped by Adele next. Adele gazed at the cookie bars with wide eyes, and I bet she was already salivating. It didn't help that the rest of us were eating them and saying how delicious they were.

"I really should taste one. As the party coordinator, I should be involved with the food decisions." Adele started to reach for one, but I heard Leonora suck in her breath, and Adele pulled her hand back like a naughty child.

Bob finished where he'd begun, with me. "Well?" he said putting his hand on his hip and looking at me expectantly.

I explained the importance of the success of the first party and that I'd thought cupcakes would be the best choice for a bunch of kids.

"I can do a giant cookie bar birthday cake," he said. "It would be much less messy. No little paper cups all over and cake crumbs ground into the carpet. Or, instead of one giant bar I could make the bars bite-size."

Geez, Bob wasn't making this easy. Finally, I said I would present the option to Emerson and Lyla and see which one they liked, reminding him that the customer ruled.

My cell went off and I answered. I'd taken to leaving it on while I was at work, since that was the number I was giving out regarding the parties. Good thing I did. It was Emerson asking if we could come to her rather than her bringing Lyla to the group for her lesson.

"The customer rules," I mumbled to myself as I clicked off. Adele was fine with going, but I needed to check with Mrs. Shedd. I found her across the bookstore near the event area, talking to Ben Sherman. His mop of black curls was cute in an unruly way, but despite the rumpled hair, he was a little too serious for my taste. He was on the slight side, barely taller than Mrs. Shedd, and wore as always, a slightly rumpled dress shirt over slacks. I heard a snippet of their conversation. He was pitching her the idea of starting a writing group for adults.

"I like it," Mrs. Shedd said. "Writing groups, parties, all these new start-ups with the fall." My boss saw me and pulled me into the conversation, explaining I was the event coordinator for the bookstore.

He repeated his pitch to me. It would be a short story workshop, and we could print them up at the end and sell them at the bookstore. Before I could say it was a good idea, Mrs. Shedd was already talking about all the coffee drinks we'd sell to the participants and how they'd browse in the bookstore. She began to describe displays we'd set up of books with famous short stories, because wasn't it true that they should read what they wanted to write? We'd have a table of writing books and supplies for them, just like we did for the kids. "It sounds like a good idea," I said. Everything went well until we got to discussing the time to have it. We agreed on once a month, but when it came to settling on an evening, we hit a snag. Mrs. Shedd and I thought a weekday evening would be good, but he was more interested in Sunday morning.

"I have another job," he said. "Well, jobs, and I can't predict when I'm going to be working. I could guarantee Sunday morning."

"Writing jobs?" I said.

He seemed a little defensive. "I've got some spec scripts out, but with all these reality shows now, it's tough." He seemed to want to leave it at that, but I was curious about what else he did, and I used the dead-air trick I'd picked up from *The Average Joe's Guide to Criminal Investigation*. I just didn't say anything and let the silence hang in the air. It always worked, except this time.

A short time later, Adele and I headed toward my car. "I could really go alone," Adele said, "since I am the one giving the crochet lesson. I am in charge of the children's department, and I handle story time all by myself." She made references to a story time she had coming up, which was top secret and going to be so stupendous, Mrs. Shedd would want to make her an assistant manager. Now that she was away from the bookstore and Leonora, she was reverting to her old self.

Even if I'd been willing to go along with it, Mrs. Shedd wouldn't. But she was fine with us leaving to give Lyla a private crochet lesson, as long as we both went, and it was less than half an hour. Clearly, she worried that you just never knew what Adele would do alone.

I have discovered the best way to deal with Adele is simply to tell her how it is. So I flatly told her we were both going.

"Okay, waste your time if you want to," she said as she slid into the passenger seat of the greenmobile. Emerson lived in a condo on the other side of the 101 on the dividing line between Tarzana and Encino. On the way there, I brought up the yarn bombing.

"Did Barry say that Eric thinks I'm the yarn bomber?" She sounded incredulous.

"Not exactly, but he implied it and said I should get you to stop."

"But it isn't me," she squealed. "If it was me, the pieces would be a lot better. I'd do it with embellishments, like maybe tie a bunch of crochet flowers to a stop sign." She stopped to think. "Imagine if I made a really giant flower and hung it from a bridge over the freeway." Then she stopped herself and turned to me.

"Pink, we have to find out who's doing it and stop them. I know I'm winning Eric's mother over, but if he thinks I'm the yarn bomber, it won't make any difference. He plays by the rules, and no way would he accept having a yarn graffiti artist as a fiancée."

"Fiancée?" I said with surprise.

"He hasn't said anything for sure yet, but you heard the comment his mother made about always wanting Eric's bride to wear her wedding dress."

I nodded noncommittally, but I was thinking that all the diet powders in the world weren't going to shrink Adele enough to fit into the dress of a woman who ate five grapes as her treat for lunch.

I parked the car, Adele grabbed her bag of tools and yarn, and we walked up the street to Emerson's town house.

I guess because she was in the flower business, I was expecting to see floral arrangements and floral patterns all over her house, but when Emerson ushered us inside, I instantly saw that I was wrong. I admit to being nosy and immediately began to check out the living room. There was lots of color, and it was obvious she was very creative, whether she made the things herself or just appreciated handmade items. Throw pillows with bright strips of primary colors decorated a blue suede couch. Instead of the usual carpeting, there was a wood tile floor with throw rugs that added more color and softness to the room. The small round wood dining table at the end of the room marked a dining area and beyond a half wall was the kitchen.

The fireplace was an unexpected bonus, and it made the room seem even more inviting.

Emerson had her hair tucked back off her face and was wearing a peasant blouse over some washed-to-a-pale-blue jeans with a scarf thrown on for color. I wish I could manage that nonchalance.

"I'm afraid we can't stay very long," I said, explaining we had to get back to the bookstore.

"No problem," Emerson said. "I appreciate you coming here. I just thought it would be easier for Lyla if she learned here."

Adele was all business and asked where she should set up. Emerson pointed to the table. As if on cue, Lyla came in the room. She looked like a miniature of her mother, down to the clothes she wore.

I was pretending to admire the fireplace, but I kept

glancing at Adele. I had no idea how she would be teaching a child. There were photographs on the mantelpiece, which I focused on. I certainly didn't want Emerson to know how concerned I was about Adele, so to cover it up, I picked a photograph at random and examined it. The man was wearing a white coat, and I asked if it was her husband.

Emerson said it wasn't and explained that she and her husband had an unusual situation. "He works up north in Silicon Valley and is here only on the weekends, which is when I'm usually working." She laughed and said at least they never got tired of each other.

"That's my grandpa, but he's dead. That was his pen," Lyla called out in reference to the photo. I glanced down and saw a fountain pen with a metallic amber body. "I wanted to take it to school, but my mom won't let me use it."

Emerson's face clouded over and she shushed her daughter, telling her she should concentrate on crocheting. But when she turned to me, she threw up her hands and said, "Kids," in typical mother exasperation.

"I didn't realize two of you would come," Emerson said, quickly changing the subject. I couldn't tell her the real reason I was there, so instead, I said I wanted to talk over the food options and mentioned Bob's cookie bars. She was firm on the cupcakes, but seemed a little confused. "What do you usually do for a birthday?"

I must have seemed a little befuddled because Emerson appeared concerned. "How many of these parties have you put on?" When I'd first suggested the party idea to her, I had alluded to the many bookstore events I'd put on, but now that she was asking directly I told her the truth.

"So, we're your guinea pigs," she said.

"I'd rather refer to you as our premiere clients." I was

relieved when Emerson smiled. Lyla had left Adele at the table and joined us.

"What exactly will we be making at my party?" Lyla asked. I was a little taken aback by her mature tone. I was still getting used to how grown-up kids were these days.

"We're still designing it," I said. *Designing* sounded better than *trying to come up with*.

"I'd like it to be something wonderful and maybe something for animals," Lyla said.

"I'll make note of that," I said. Adele didn't want to be the only one at the table, so she joined us, too.

"I'm doing a special animal story time that day," Adele said. "Maybe we could move your party up so they coincide."

Both Emerson and Lyla looked horrified at Adele's suggestion. "The party isn't going to be in the part of the bookstore with the cows jumping over the moons, is it?" Lyla asked with grave concern in her voice.

I looked at my watch and realized we'd already gone over the half hour and announced we had to leave while assuring Lyla and her mother that the party would be in the yarn department at the table the Hookers used.

"So, did you teach her to crochet?" I asked Adele as we walked to my car.

"You're kidding, right?" Adele said. "I think she mastered the slipknot."

"But that's just the first thing you do. It's not even a stitch." This was not a good sign for the party.

CHAPTER 13

"MOLLY," BARRY CALLED OUT TO ME JUST AFTER I turned the corner onto Ventura Boulevard. I was on my way into the bookstore from the parking lot. Adele had already rushed on ahead since we were late in coming back. Barry was walking toward me with a man in a suit who I assumed was another detective.

Barry's detective face gave way to a smile as we stopped, facing each other. He said he and his detective friend were just coming from lunch at Le Grande Fromage down the street. I expected him to walk on after that, but he seemed to hesitate, like he was hanging onto the moment.

"Well," I said, finally. "I have to get back to work." I nodded toward the bookstore.

"Where are you coming from?" he asked. I noticed he caught himself and tried to soften his interrogation voice.

"It's a long story," I said and took a step away.

"I'd like to hear about it." He called to his companion to go on ahead. Then he walked me the rest of the way to the bookstore.

"I don't suppose Mrs. Shedd would let you get a cup of coffee with me." He sounded hopeful. "Then you could give me all the details of your long story."

"Are you feeling all right?" I said.

"Why?" He seemed puzzled.

"Because you aren't exactly acting like yourself," I said. Normally, Barry might have stopped in during the day to see how I was, but then he was out the door in a flash.

"Maybe I've changed," he said, and his smile grew warmer as it lit his dark eyes.

I assured him Mrs. Shedd wasn't going to want me to take a break, but that didn't seem to deter him.

"Do you want something? Information, maybe?" I said, still not trusting the way he was acting.

"Why? Do you have some? You have been spending a lot of time with Thursday Fields. She must be confiding in you."

"I thought so. That's what this is all about. You're on an information hunt." I walked through the bookstore, letting Mrs. Shedd see that I was back, and then I headed toward the yarn department. Barry kept pace with me.

"I was joking about the information," he said. "Of course, if you have any, I'd be glad to hear it." He pulled out one of the chairs and sat down while I straightened up the yarn bins. "It's just that I never get to see you alone."

I reminded him of our upcoming evening to see Jeffrey's play. He started to fiddle with one of the hooks on the table. "I know I screwed up and was undependable and everything else when we were together. I miss spending time with you."

"But we're still friends," I said. "We can still spend time together."

He didn't say it, but I knew what he was thinking—that it wasn't the same, and of course, he was right.

"So, tell me the long story." He'd leaned back in the chair and stretched his legs out.

"Are you sure you really want to hear it?" I said, and he nodded.

I told him about the Parties with a Purpose idea and that we were arranging the first one. He started to grin. "It's not going to be like the author events. No smoke alarms going off, or floods when a Mr. Fixit turns out to be Mr. Breakit. It can't be that way. If it is, there goes the business, and Mrs. Shedd is counting on me and Adele."

Now Barry laughed. "Adele's involved and you think it's going to go smoothly?"

"You wouldn't recognize her," I said. "Your fellow cop Eric has had a big effect on her. Well, maybe it's more the fact that his mother is visiting." I filled Barry in on Leonora and the change in Adele.

He was enjoying hearing about it all, even though he didn't buy that Adele had changed or that the party would come off without a hitch. I did remind him that even though most of my events had some kind of drama, they were always successful, if success was measured by the book sales.

"I hope you're wrong or that Emerson is understanding if you're right." I told him that Emerson did the flowers for Thursday's wedding, including the arrangement on the wedding cake. "It's lucky she didn't see what happened to her work." I still had the image of Jaimee Fields sitting in the cake with the flowers Emerson had so carefully placed having turned into a bunch of crushed petals.

"Really?" Barry said, sitting up.

"Relax, she was only at the reception long enough to put the fresh flowers on the cake and make sure the flowers in everyone's lapels were fresh. When she left, everyone was still alive."

"How do you know?" Barry said.

"Because she told me she did. And because she didn't even know the groom or any of the wedding party. Jaimee Fields hired her and must have given her the go-ahead to leave the reception."

"You're probably right. Besides, I think Heather probably talked to her."

"How's the investigation going? Any suspects?" I asked.

Barry looked at me intently. "Maybe I should ask you the same thing."

"What makes you think I'm sleuthing?" I gave Barry an innocent shrug, but he responded with a deep laugh.

"Let me count the ways. You walked into the middle of it. Thursday is staying at your house, and you seem to enjoy playing Nancy Drew."

"You left out that I'm good at it," I said with grin. I waited to see if he was going to admonish me to stay out of it as he'd always done in the past. Maybe he really had changed because instead he suggested that we share notes. Though I knew the real meaning of that was I was to give up what I knew. He sighed when he glanced at his watch.

"I'll have to take a rain check on the information share," he said as he stood. "I have to see a man at the morgue." He didn't elaborate if the man was standing up or on a slab, and I didn't ask. "I don't remember what the rules of being friends are. Is a good-bye hug acceptable?"

I rolled my eyes and nodded. I expected a chaste hug that

was mostly arms, but Barry apparently didn't understand the different kinds of hugs, and the one he offered was full body and lasted long enough to be more like holding than hugging.

I was so stunned at his display of affection—Barry had always been very reserved in public when we were together—I didn't know how to react for a moment. I think Barry was as surprised at his actions as I was and suddenly dropped his arms.

"Sorry," he said and pulled away. "This whole platonic thing is still a little confusing." He gave me a wave good-bye as he headed toward the door. He looked back just before he went out. There was something in his eyes I had never seen before. He had let down his guard and finally opened the door to his soul. The look of regret and longing went straight to my heart.

I sighed to myself. And I thought just being friends was going to be less complicated.

I didn't get much chance to mull it over, because a moment later I heard Mrs. Shedd point me out to someone.

"You can give it to her yourself," she said. Ben Sherman was standing next to her at the edge of the yarn department. He certainly had the writer look down pat. The day-old stubble, the mass of slightly disheveled black curls and the messenger bag slung across his chest.

Mrs. Shedd walked away as he held out a piece of paper. "I wrote up a description of the workshop and a bio more aimed at an adult audience." I took it and read it over. No mention of *Janet and the Beanstalk* in this one.

"You're like an all-around writer," I said, noting that he'd listed a number of publications he'd written for and several television programs.

"Some people say credits are like money in the bank. Personally, I'd rather have the money in the bank. But it could all turn around. I just found out I'm in the running for a regular gig on a series." He held up his hands and showed off his crossed fingers. "Then no more juggling a bunch of jobs."

"Then what happens to the kids' group and the adult workshop?" I said. "It wouldn't look good for the bookstore if we set up these two workshops and suddenly had no one to facilitate them." I couldn't believe I'd said that pretentious word, but then that was how he was being listed for both groups.

"How about I guarantee I'll stick with both groups for six months, no matter what," he offered. I wondered if I was being foolish taking him at his word, since I really didn't know him, but I finally agreed. With that settled, I said I would use what he'd given me in advertising the adult workshop, and he ambled off, saying something about looking around to get some ideas for books he could suggest to the workshop people.

I took what he'd given me and headed to what now served as my office. Mrs. Shedd had come up with the idea that if I did all the work for the events in the customer service booth, I could help customers at the same time. I actually liked being out in the middle of things, even though it came with lots of interruptions.

Not that I minded the first one I got. "Sunshine," Mason said, smiling at me from the other side of the counter. I was surprised to see him in the middle of the day, and worried there was something new wrong.

"It must be the attire," he said, glancing down at himself. Instead of the beautifully tailored suits he wore for work, he had on a pair of khakis and a Hawaiian shirt. "I took the day off to help Thursday. Now that the funeral is over," he said with a heavy sigh. "She needs to move on, and she doesn't want to overstay her welcome. We went looking for a place for her."

The funeral had been several days earlier. Thursday had barely talked about it, other than to say that it was small and terribly sad. Mason and Jaimee had gone with her, and I was glad I hadn't been invited along.

I asked him about the outcome of their search, and he said they'd looked at a few places, but hadn't found anything yet. "It will still be a while longer, if that's okay," he said. I assured him it was.

Mason leaned on the counter and looked around the bookstore with a grin. "I wouldn't want to get you in trouble with your boss. Should I pretend to be asking for help in finding something?"

I rolled my eyes. "Mrs. Shedd knows who you are. So, you were saying?"

"Thursday's mother was going to help her, but my daughter didn't want to have a film crew traipsing behind them, so I stepped in." He shrugged as if it was no big thing. It was to me. I was so impressed at what a caring father he was. It wasn't so much what he did, but how he did it. All from the heart.

"We stopped by on the chance you were ready for a break and we could treat you to something." He put his hand on my arm and ran his finger over my skin. "There's no way I can thank you for what you've done." He stopped and chuckled. "But wait, maybe there is. If you want to be friends with the detective, okay, but I say we step things up with us to the next level, and then I can properly show my appreciation." He got a naughty grin and wiggled his eyebrows.

I was glad to see that Mason was back to his fun self. "Thanks, but no thanks for now," I said.

"Like I told you before, I'm a patient man," Mason said.

"And persistent," I said. "For now, I'll take you up on a coffee. Did you say Thursday was with you?"

I made a scan of the bookstore and then stopped when I recognized her stylish lopsided haircut. She was standing at one of the display tables at the front of the bookstore, looking over the selection of Halloween merchandise. Ben Sherman was at the same table, examining the candles and plastic skeletons. There seemed no connection between them, but then I noticed a slight shake of her head that was clearly a response to someone. And since there was no one else there, it seemed obvious it had to be Ben.

"Does Thursday know him?" I said, trying to be discreet as I gestured over Mason's shoulder.

"Who?" Mason said, picking up my cue and turning. But by then, Ben was already out the door and Thursday was walking toward us.

She seemed happy to see me and greeted me with a hug. She repeated what Mason had said about getting a place and getting on with her life. Mason put a supportive arm around her and said how well she was doing under the circumstances.

"Maybe when you get settled, you'll want to join the writing workshop we're going to have at the bookstore," I said, watching Thursday intently. "Ben Sherman is going to be the facilitator," I said, keeping tabs on her expression. "I think you know him. He was just at the front table with you, and I saw you talking to him before."

I was hoping she'd break into a smile and say something like, "Oh, him. Sure I met him at a party or we went to high school together." Instead, she seemed nonchalant as she said, "You must be mistaken. I wasn't talking to anyone."

Uh-oh.

CHAPTER 14

"I can't tell Mason that I think his daughter is lying," I said to Dinah. When my day at the bookstore had finally ended, Dinah and I had gone up the street to Le Grande Fromage to get some dinner. I was glad for the company as I needed some help in processing everything that had happened. Dinah was a whiz at dealing with students that were all over the place, and I hoped she could do something with my day.

It was past dinner hour, and there were only a couple of tables occupied in Le Grande Fromage. We picked an empty one and left our things before heading to the counter to order. I didn't realize until we were at the front counter that the person being waited on was Isa Susberg.

She was talking to the counter help. I ate here often and saw she was talking to a fellow named Matt Kearns. I knew she didn't want to commit to having the shower at the bookstore yet, but I thought it would be a good idea to be friendly. I'd wait until she was finished with her order and then say hello.

I heard the tail end of their conversation and almost let out a groan as I realized they were talking about Thursday's wedding. How long was it going to take before it wasn't the topic of conversation all over Tarzana?

"I'm certainly not putting that on my résumé," the counter guy said, shaking his head. "I think you guests got off easier. It seems like the cops took your statements first. When they got to me, it was strictly my name and I didn't see anything."

"My husband was very upset. All those questions about who had invited us and his connection with the groom's family." Isa looked past Matt to the cook in the back who was putting together her order. She asked for extra sauce for something before turning back to the counter guy. "It was very awkward because my husband is a business associate of Jackson Kingsley's, rather than a friend or family." I couldn't see her face, but the counter guy seemed to react to her expression.

"And I'm guessing he wasn't a big fan," Matt said. It seemed like he was going to add something, but then shrugged it off as he noticed me standing behind her and said he'd be with me in a minute.

As Isa picked up her order, I greeted her. Before I could say anything, she brought up the shower and said she would let me know soon. As she left, Dinah pretended to be looking over the menu, but I knew she was giving me a moment to talk to Matt.

"I couldn't help but overhear," I said. "So, you worked that reception." He nodded.

"I saw you come in," he said. "You were with the homicide detective." He said it half as a question and half as a statement. "He's the one who took my statement." Matt gestured toward the menu and started listing the daily specials, clearly trying to move things along. Dinah and I ordered and then went to our table to wait for the food.

"How come you didn't ask him anything?" Dinah said in a low voice when we'd sat down.

I lowered my voice even more to whisper. "He said he saw me come in with Barry, and Barry took his statement." I mentioned that he'd told Isa that he'd only told the cop who questioned him his name and that he knew nothing. "Do you think he would tell me anything else?"

"You're right," Dinah said.

"Besides, I'm more concerned with Thursday." I repeated what I'd thought I had seen earlier and her reaction.

"Maybe there's an explanation. Suppose she just ran into him those two times and they started up a conversation, but there were no names attached."

"I'd agree, except that the second time, it was obvious they were trying to appear like they weren't talking to each other. That implies hiding something. And she said she wasn't talking to anybody."

"You'll just have to confront her," Dinah said. "Use some of the interrogation tricks in the *Average Joe* book."

I rocked my head with discouragement. "This is so awful to say, but Thursday is pretty clever. And she is a lawyer's daughter. I think she understands that all she has to do is deny knowing him."

I went back over the rest of my day, and by the time I got to Adele and the crochet lesson, which amounted to Lyla learning how to do a slipknot, Dinah's eyes were almost going in circles. "Though I have to say, Adele seems to be okay as a teacher." I was going to go into more detail, but Dinah stopped me.

"Enough about her, can we go back to the Detective Barry encounter?" my friend said. Just then Matt showed up with our tray of food. Had he heard her? I couldn't tell by his expression. It didn't matter anyway. I'd already figured he wasn't about to confide anything in me. He put the onion soup down in front of Dinah. I had only a croissant and some brie cheese. We were sharing a green salad. It wasn't until he'd headed back to the front with the empty tray that we resumed our conversation.

"I wasn't going to say anything about Emerson doing the flowers. I just sort of blurted it out," I said, figuring that was what she meant about the Barry encounter.

Dinah stuck her spoon through the layer of soft bread and melted cheese to the steaming soup. "I was thinking more about that hug you say he gave you. It sounds like it left you a little weak-kneed."

"It doesn't matter. And it doesn't matter that Mason isn't happy with the state of affairs." I giggled at my word choice. "Or that there aren't any. Nothing is changing." I took a bite of the buttery croissant and creamy cheese. I was glad they'd added some baby lettuce to cut the richness. "I'd rather talk about Jonah's murder."

Dinah gave me a knowing look. "Sure, if that's what you want to talk about. I bet he's not the only one who just gave their name," Dinah said with the hint of a gesture toward Matt, who was back behind the counter.

"It seemed like Isa's husband wasn't very forthcoming, either," I said.

"And with all those guests and servers wandering around,

how they'll ever figure out what evidence goes with the killer is beyond me," Dinah said. "You should really ask Thursday about Paxton Cline. Maybe she knows why he got bounced as best man. Think about it. He could have known about the robot-looking servers and figured out he could blend in and leave before anybody knew what happened. And his alibi of going to a baseball game. Puleeze. Talk about lame."

"Wouldn't Barry be surprised if I not only told him about Paxton, but handed him all the evidence he needed?" Then I deflated. "But Paxton seems so nice and he works for his grandmother's yarn company."

Dinah rolled her eyes. "Nice people can do bad things." She spooned up the last of her soup.

"It's going to be pretty hard to ask Thursday about Paxton if I'm trying to corner her about knowing Ben." I pushed my plate away and wiped my mouth with my napkin. "I hope it turns out that I'm just seeing bogeymen under the bed, and there's a simple explanation. Or she misunderstood. It has to be something like that, doesn't it?" I looked to Dinah for confirmation. She just put up her hands and shrugged. Then, good friend that she is, offered to come with.

"It's better if I do it alone," I said. "And there's no time like the present."

We walked back to the parking lot, and Dinah wished me luck before continuing on the short distance to her house.

As was becoming all too common, things didn't turn out as I had planned. When I walked into my kitchen, I noticed two things right away. No dogs and cats met me at the door as they usually did, and there was the sound of voices coming from my living room. I slipped to the doorway and took a peek. Thursday and her mother were sitting on the couch, talking. Maybe *talking* was the wrong word. It sounded more like arguing. Not the yelling kind of arguing, more like terse voices coming through gritted teeth.

I didn't want to get in the middle of it and just wanted to get across the house to my room. But the only way was through the living room. Could I manage without getting caught up in their tussle? I paused a moment, listening.

"Thursday, you can't just avoid dealing with it," Jaimee said.

"Yes, I can," Thursday countered. There seemed to be a momentary standoff, the perfect time for me to make my way across the house.

As I stepped through the doorway, Jaimee looked up. "Good, you're here. I've been trying to tell Thursday she can't just walk away from the condo where she and Jonah were going to live." Even at this distance, I could see that Jaimee was perfectly outfitted in a turquoise pants outfit with a lot of gold accents. After the day I'd had, I felt tired and grubby in comparison. I was also stunned to hear that she seemed happy to see me, until it became apparent why. She thought I would take her side in the argument and make it go in her favor. I already knew the condo situation, but I let her explain in detail anyway. The condo itself was in the Kingsleys' business name, and she agreed that Thursday had no claim to it. Jaimee didn't care about most of the furnishings. It was really only a few things. "I know your father is all for you just walking away from all of it, but we picked those things out for you and you should take them." Jaimee turned back to me. "You were there when we picked them out."

I had to laugh that she was trying to make that a reason why I should side with her. Yes, I'd been with Mason and her when they'd bought the gifts, but she'd done her best to make me feel like an unwelcome third wheel. Could it be that she had changed?

Jaimee's face did seem softer as she looked at me. "Don't you think she ought to have them?" Jaimee continued to plead her case to me. "I understand Jackson Kingsley is grief-stricken," she said, "but blaming our family for the tragedy is ridiculous. You would think they'd be trying to embrace Thursday as their son's widow instead of acting like she's the enemy. You should have seen them at the funeral." She leaned forward and dropped her voice as if her daughter wasn't sitting right next to her and could hear every word even if she whispered.

"We didn't even sit with them. There was a lunch afterwards at Brae Mar Country Club. The atmosphere was so cold I got the chills. Now that I see what kind of person Jackson Kingsley is, I'm glad Thursday isn't going to be part of their family." She waited for a nod of understanding from me. I could see her point.

"I was mortified when that man insisted that the police detain me," Jaimee said. "I bet if he didn't have that deep voice that made him sound like he's some kind of authority on everything, the police wouldn't have listened to him. Why in the world would I have wanted to kill Jonah? I was very happy that Thursday was marrying him. I thought they were a nice family and he was a solid young man. Just because I was holding the knife." She cringed thinking about it.

"If I hadn't been able to show them how my shapewear made it impossible to lift my arms high enough to stab anyone, who knows what would have happened?" She let out a big sigh. "The only good thing that came out of that horrible trip to the police station was that the producer of *The Housewives of Mulholland Drive* decided to make me the focal character. Cerise is the only other housewife that came close in the drama department." Jaimee rolled her eyes. "As if getting caught stealing the salt and pepper shaker, jelly dispenser and vase off the table at a deli is even on the same planet of what I went through."

"It must have been terrible," I said in a compassionate tone. I admit it was a little calculated, but I had never heard Jaimee's version of what had happened at the wedding. Her face softened even more, and she pointed to the spot on the couch next to Thursday and urged me to join them, which was pretty funny considering it was my couch.

"You have no idea," she began, looking at me as if I was her new best friend. "I was going to check on the cake. The florist was supposed to add the floral decorations to the cake at the last minute, and I wanted to make sure it was right."

"Wasn't she supposed to hand out fresh boutonnieres, too?" I said, interrupting. Then I explained how I knew Emerson.

Jaimee flashed me a surprised look, then made a face. "Everybody thinks I'm too fussy, but redo the boutonnieres? No." I don't think she appreciated the interruption and went back to her story.

"The cake was on a long table at the edge of the tent. Right away I saw that the knife was missing. As I went around to the back of the table, I saw that it was on the ground. What I didn't see—" she stopped and took a few breaths before continuing, "was that Jonah's foot was sticking out beyond the end of the table. I picked up the knife and saw the blood on it, and then I at the same time, I saw someone was lying on the ground. I guess I stepped backwards in shock and that's when I tripped over his foot. I tried to catch myself, but every time I tried to move my arms, that shapewear made them snap back to my sides." She rocked her head in dismay as she relived the moment. "I couldn't keep myself from landing in the cake."

With her story finished, Jaimee let out her breath. Thursday started to speak in a shaky voice.

"When I saw Jonah on the ground, I thought he must have had some kind of attack," Thursday said. "My first thought was to help him up. But when I did—" She paused to suck in her breath. "It was horrible." Her voice quivered for a moment as tears welled up in her eyes.

And then the dam broke. Thursday began to cry, then sob, until her shoulders shook. Jaimee and I leaned toward her from either side, cocooning her as she wrapped her arms around herself, finally letting out all the emotions that she'd been holding in. The sobs turned to spasms of hiccups as she tried to calm herself. Then the three of us leaned back into the couch, exhausted, and in my case, relieved. Finally, Thursday had shown a normal reaction to the death of her groom.

"Maybe we should get you some tranquilizers. We need to get you something," her mother said, sounding a little frantic. But Thursday shook her head. I had to give Jaimee credit, at least she was trying to do something.

What happened next surprised and warmed my heart. Still having an occasional hiccup, Thursday leaned toward the coffee table and picked up her crocheting, and as she began to work her hook through the cream-colored cotton, her breathing evened out and the anguish left her face.

I offered them some tea and cookies. There was a sound of banging coming from the door to my wing of the house. I looked at Jaimee and shrugged to myself. This was my house, and there was no reason for my animals to be locked up. Without making any sort of statement, I opened the door and the two dogs and two cats rushed out.

While I made the tea, Cosmo and Blondie went out in the yard, but the cats—there is something curious about cats. They seem to know when someone doesn't like them. I don't know if it was to try to win her over or to punish her, but Holstein and Cat Woman positioned themselves on the back of the couch on either side of Jaimee. I noticed she kept looking straight ahead as if her not seeing them meant they weren't really there.

I brought in a tray with cups of Darjeeling tea and a plate of the cookie bars that Bob, our cafe's barista, had given me to try to get the party-food business. Jaimee accepted both with gusto. I guess she forgot she'd told me she never ate anything with sugar in it. Thursday set down her crocheting and took a cup of tea. For a little while, the three of us sat there in silence.

Jaimee set down her empty cup and hesitated before leaning back on the couch, seeing that the cats were still there and staring at her. She stood up instead. I could see there was still something on her mind.

"Thursday, honey, I wish you would reconsider," she began before turning to me. "The *Housewives* people are pressuring me to get some kind of mother-daughter thing. Like us shopping. The way it is, it looks like I have no family." She explained that her other daughter had gone back to San Diego. She was talking directly to me now.

"But I thought the point of reality shows was they just followed you on your regular day."

Jaimee touched my shoulder for emphasis as her eyes went skyward. "That's what they want you to think. There may not be a script, but they create situations." She glanced back at her daughter, who had picked up her crochet work again. "Thursday, I wish you would at least think about it. I really need your help."

CHAPTER 15

J AIMEE KNEW JUST WHICH BUTTON TO PUSH WITH her daughter. Asking for Thursday's help was what finally got her to agree to be part of the *Housewives of Mulholland Drive*. Thursday told her mother that it was just a onetime thing and she insisted that I come along.

Why did I agree? I didn't want the responsibility of ruining the peace between them, I had the morning off, and, well, I was curious to see the housewives in action. I dressed all in black, including the tote bag with my crochet stuff, hoping it would make me invisible, or at least hide any lumps and bumps.

"I can't believe I let her talk me into this," Thursday said, the little rasp in her voice made her words sound less serious than she probably meant them. She adjusted the blue-and-white-striped loose top she wore over white jeans. I knew she'd picked an outfit that would please her mother. We were walking through the mall to the center court where we were supposed to meet up.

"The only way to do one of these reality shows is with a sense of humor," Thursday said as she looked up ahead to the clump of people with her mother in the middle. "And you may have noticed my mother has none. She can't even see the absurdity of using too-small shapewear on her arms as an alibi."

I knew the rules. She could say negative things about her mother to her heart's content, but if I were to say anything, she would come to her mother's defense. I only responded with a nod to show I was listening. Thursday's meltdown had seemed to clear the air for her. Now that it was out, she really could start moving on, or so I hoped.

Even though Thursday seemed to know I was an amateur sleuth, I'd never mentioned anything about me investigating Jonah's death. I was glad that Jaimee and Thursday had told me the details of what had happened at the wedding without me having to ask. It wasn't that either one of them were suspects as far as I was concerned, but I didn't really want them to know what I was doing. Despite my past successes in solving some cases, it made me seem like a Nancy Drew wannabe. But when I saw Paxton Cline on the other side of the walkway, I thought I might have to come clean.

This was my opportunity to ask her about him. I tried to come up with some reason to point him out and bring up his former status as best man. Nothing came to mind, so I finally just steered her toward him, hoping they'd see each other and make contact. Then I'd ask her about him afterward.

He looked in her direction and I could see recognition in his expression. He'd opened his mouth to speak, just as her gaze rested on him. Her eyes stayed on him for another moment, and then she quickly looked away and turned her attention to a display window we were passing.

It was not what I'd expected and I wasn't sure what to do. "Did you know that guy?" I said at last. She looked at me with a blank expression before looking around as if to see who I was talking about. "Which guy?"

I mentioned his name and she kept the confused expression. She was so convincing, I began to think I might be wrong. I searched for a casual way to bring up her late groom's former best man, but any chance for that ended abruptly as we reached the group from the reality show. Jaimee walked toward us, closely followed by a man with a handheld camera. A small throng of people were behind him. They all seemed to be trying to blend in with the mall crowd.

If I'd dressed to be invisible, Jaimee had done the opposite. The golden tan fitted pants and fuchsia top were hard to miss. Her blond hair looked professionally styled, as did her makeup. She crossed the space between us and embraced her daughter.

The embrace looked like the hug version of an air kiss—all arms with no real contact. "I can't smudge the makeup, Thurs," she said, keeping her head away from her daughter's. "Thank you for doing this for Mommy."

A woman who appeared in charge joined us and explained the scene was going to play out in a shoe store up ahead. "It's just a mother-daughter shopping trip," she said as somebody handed Jaimee a zebra-print tote bag with a tiny dog's head sticking out of the top. Its fur was gathered into a topknot with a fuchsia bow that matched Jaimee's shirt.

"You got a dog?" Thursday said, her face lighting up as she lifted the tiny dog out of the tote bag and nuzzled it.

"It's just rented." The woman in charge retrieved the dog and placed it back in the bag and instructed Jaimee to hold the bag close to her.

The employees were waiting in a reception line when we got to the high-end shoe store. We'd been joined by two women who looked like Jaimee. Blond hair, lots of makeup and clothes that drew attention. I didn't need an introduction to figure out they were two more of the housewives.

"Okay, then, remember conflict, conflict, conflict," the woman in charge said as she ushered the group into the store with the camera guy in close pursuit.

I sat down out of camera range in one of the chairs as did the rest of the throng while the action took place across the store. The setup seemed to be that the two housewives had run into Jaimee and Thursday. Jaimee set her bag on the floor and the group stood talking. It seemed as if there were just introductions going on at first, then the two other housewives surrounded Thursday.

"We heard about your wedding. How terrible. You were there right in the middle of everything, so you must know what really happened." Thursday reacted by stepping back and turning to her mother. Before she could say a word, Jaimee put her arm around her daughter protectively and turned to the woman in charge.

"You said it was just a mother-and-daughter shopping trip. You promised no one would ask her about the wedding." Jaimee had become the mother wolf protecting her cub. "You want conflict." She pointed toward me. "She's my ex's girlfriend."

The black outfit did nothing to make me invisible as all

eyes turned my way. The two other housewives' eyes lit up with malevolence, and they actually took a step toward me.

"Not girlfriend," I said, trying to keep my voice from warbling. "More like friend who is a girl, well, it really should be woman. That whole girlfriend-boyfriend thing for adults sounds ridiculous." I nodded to them, hoping they'd agree with my point.

But then the rented dog got me off the hook. A whirl of fur flew between me and the others with a red stiletto heel in its mouth. The shoe was almost as big as the dog, and it was amazing how fast it managed to run. It turned out rental dog had gotten bored sitting in the bag and jumped out while all the talking was going on. He was like a kid in a candy store, only it was shoes. He'd already left bite marks on a whole row of display shoes before he'd chosen the red one. While the shoe store owner complained that somebody was going to have to pay for the damage, the three housewives chased after the dog with the cameraman running behind them.

When the dust settled, it was agreed that the shot of me would be edited out, and pretty much the whole scene would revolve around the dog shoe thief. Thursday was awed by her mother's defense of her, and the two of them went off to have lunch, with no cameras watching.

And I was on my own. As I crossed the center court, a flicker of color caught my attention. I looked and did a double take when I saw that the bronze statue of the girl and boy dancing through the large fountain now seemed to be wearing colorful ponchos. A smattering of people had noticed the change in the statues and stopped, too. As I stepped closer to get a better look, two mall cops on Segways zoomed up and began to circle the fountain. One of them had a man in a suit riding with him. I gathered that he was the mall manager, and he seemed very upset about the addition to the fountain. By now, I'd gotten a close enough look to ascertain that the ponchos were more of the random acts of crochet that had been popping up around Tarzana.

Two uniformed cops joined the group. One of them was the heavyset officer with the olive complexion I'd seen before. They looked at the fountain and began to talk among themselves. "The yarn bomber seems to be stepping up the targets," the one I'd seen before said. The mall executive stepped off the Segway and joined them, saying rather loudly that while they were standing there discussing it, the yarn graffiti artist could be getting away. Meanwhile the two mall cops on Segways started circling the group.

The mall executive looked over the people watching the action. "Maybe it's one of them." He mentioned how arsonists like to watch the fire they set because they got some kind of thrill out of seeing the results of what they've done. "Maybe the yarn bomber is like those firebugs."

Now they were getting ridiculous, trying to equate somebody who started fires with someone who'd merely added a little color to a couple of bronze statues. The familiar cop looked in my direction. His gaze fixated on me and I got a bad feeling. I recognized him from the other two yarn bombings and it seemed like he might have recognized me. Time to go. I turned quickly, but as I tried to make my exit, my tote bag caught on something sticking out of the shopping bag the woman next to me was holding. I tried to pull my bag free and keep going, but I lost my grip and it went tumbling to the floor—bottom up. The hooks fell out with a clatter, followed by balls of red and royal blue yarn.

Before I could make a move, I felt myself surrounded by uniforms. "We got our yarn bug," the cop said who'd been staring at me. "Here's the evidence." He put his foot on my J hook before I could pick it up. When I looked up, the two mall cops were doing figure eights around me on their Segways, high-fiving each other as their paths intersected.

"YARN BOMBER?" MASON SAID, TRYING TO CONtain a grin as he crossed the lobby of the police station to the bench I was sitting on. I showed off my non-handcuffed hands and got up to go. Mason was just there to give me a ride. I'd talked my own way out of it. It wasn't that hard, because I don't think the cops really wanted to go through all the paperwork that came with an arrest. I'd been given a stern warning that I'd better not do any yarn graffiti. I answered with a perfectly free conscience that I was telling the truth when I agreed. I mean, it's not like I was the yarn bomber.

"Talk about making a fuss about nothing," Mason said, shaking his head with disgust. I think he was sorry he didn't get to use his attorney skills to free me. He would have had fun making mincemeat out of them for detaining me for having a few hooks and some balls of yarn. "They ought to give the person a prize for brightening up those dull statues."

"Not according to the cops. It's right up there with spray painting. Worse because the taggers never actually go inside a mall." I slung my tote bag and purse on my shoulder and got ready to leave. The door whooshed open and Barry came in. His brow was furrowed as he glanced around the lobby, then his gaze stopped on me.

"So you're already sprung," he said, before explaining that one of his cop friends had recognized me and called him. Apparently, whoever it was didn't realize Barry and I weren't a couple anymore. His glance moved to Mason. "No reason to keep you from your lawyering. I can give her a lift."

Mason had taken my arm and was holding on to it. "It's no problem, you can go back to keeping our streets safe."

I thought it was going to turn into a standoff, but Barry's phone buzzed. Just before he answered it, he looked at me. "I just want you to know, I dropped everything to get here." Before I could react, he was on the phone and back to his homicide detective persona. As Mason and I went toward the door, Barry glanced up from his cell and our eyes met. His eyes flared with warmth as he mouthed something I couldn't quite make out, but I assumed was some kind of farewell. I was stunned. Barry had never interrupted a work call like that before.

If Mason noticed, he didn't let on as he ushered me out the door into the warm sunlight. By now, it was late afternoon. I took a deep breath of freedom and thanked Mason for coming.

"I was looking for an excuse to leave early," he said. "After what you've been through, you need a treat. Or maybe a medal of valor for dealing with my ex." When I seemed surprised that he knew, he said Thursday had called him. "She rented a dog?" he said with a laugh.

Just before we got to his car, he turned to face me. "I am sorry that you have gotten sucked into my family's drama."

I told him I preferred it to the way things were before, when he'd kept his family separate from his single life. "I guess it turned out okay, at least on my end. Thursday is very fond of you," he said. I assured him, I was fond of her as well.

"The treat sounds like a good idea," I said. "Preferably something sweet."

"How about going to Caitlyn's?" Mason said, starting the engine.

A few minutes later we were standing in line at the cup-cake emporium. As usual, it was crowded.

"I have so much to talk to you about," I said.

"I hope it's about the murder," Mason said, trying to get a clear view of the cupcake cases as we moved forward. "Maybe you can figure out who stabbed Jonah Kingsley. The cops certainly aren't getting anywhere."

"Next," Kirsty said in a tired voice from behind the counter. When no one answered, she waved at me to get my attention. "It's you," she said. "Are you here about the party order? We need to know what kind of cupcakes you want and the number."

Oh, no, I realized I hadn't brought that up to Emerson, or more accurately, Lyla. I told Kirsty that I'd have to get back to them on the party platter and that Mason and I were still trying to choose what we wanted. I suggested she take the customer behind us.

While Mason and I went back and forth between the German chocolate, chocolate with a caramel surprise and the vanilla ones with buttercream icing, the person behind us stepped forward.

"What do you have that's dietetic? You know, sugar-free, low cal," she said. I was surprised at her request because the woman was very thin, almost too thin.

"We only use real ingredients here. No fake food, artificial sweeteners, and no no-fat sour cream," Kirsty said in a harsh tone. I thought she might have overreacted.

"Well, you should. All those calories. You must be crazy," the woman said. Just then, Caitlyn came out of the back carrying a tray of fresh cupcakes. Diet woman was on her like cream cheese on a bagel, complaining about Kirsty and saying they ought to carry a dietetic line.

The woman next to me had been watching the whole thing. I nodded at her and said, "Caitlyn ought to talk to Kirsty. Doesn't she get it that she's supposed to help the customers?"

The woman turned to me and in a low voice explained why Kirsty had overreacted. "That woman hit a sensitive spot with all that talk of dietetic foods and calories."

"Oh," I said, assuming Kirsty took it as some kind of rebuke about her own curvy figure.

MEANWHILE, MASON HAD SOLVED THE PROBLEM of choosing and simply picked a selection of different cupcakes. "Make that to go," he said, and Kirsty packed them up in a pink box.

"How about a nice espresso to cut all that sweetness?" Mason offered when we got outside with the package. When I nodded, he gestured toward his car. "I know the best place," he said.

"Your house?" I said as he pulled into his garage. He responded with a devilish chuckle and said he made a mean espresso.

We walked out of the freestanding garage and into the backyard. I looked over the green expanse and the free-form pool, amazed that the tent had covered it all. It was the first time I'd been back to his house since the wedding, and it was hard to picture where Thursday and I had crossed the backyard. The tent had created a corridor along the back of the yard that led right into the narrow walkway between the garage and the back fence. Mason followed me as I went to a spot near the fence.

"That's where the shirt was," I said, pointing at a spot on the sidewalk that ran along the garage. A thin strip of dirt ran along the back fence and was planted with a row of neatly trimmed bushes.

"The shirt is a key piece of evidence," Mason said. "If you hadn't found that, the cops wouldn't have gotten the idea that someone slipped in dressed as a server."

"I'm sure they would have found the shirt themselves," I said. "It's too bad it was such a mess. I'm sure it has made it hard to connect it with the wearer." I stood staring at the spot for a few minutes, as if some new evidence would pop out. It didn't happen and we went inside. Spike ran in to greet us. He gave me the once-over, but the toy fox terrier caught up with Mason as he headed to the kitchen.

I kept thinking back to when I had found the shirt. Something was nagging at me, and I told him I wanted to go outside again. Mason shrugged and followed me back to the walkway behind the garage. I retraced the path Thursday and I had taken, then I stopped and took off the black gauzy shirt I had on over my tank top. I heard Mason make a surprised sound.

"You want to take off your clothes?" he said. He was behind me, but I was sure he was grinning.

I dropped the shirt and looked at where it landed for a long time.

Mason joined me looking down at my shirt. "Okay, what are we looking for, Sherlock?"

"I was just thinking," I said as I picked up the shirt and put it on again. I turned as if to go back into the house and dropped the shirt again. This time the collar was vaguely pointing toward the back gate. "Don't you see, the way the shirt falls might show the direction the killer went."

"And?" Mason said.

"And," I said. "My foot was hurting, so I took off my shoes, that's how I noticed the shirt in the first place. I was standing on it." I stopped and closed my eyes, trying to re-live the moment. "When I picked it up, I was holding the collar and I was facing the back gate."

"Meaning?" Mason said. I think he knew what I was going to say, but he was letting me play detective.

"That the killer might not have dropped the shirt and then headed out the gate, but rather went back into the re-ception like nothing happened." My shoulders sagged. "Just when I had a good suspect, too."

"Suspect?" Mason said. "How is it I'm so out of the loop?" We went back inside. I took out some plates and opened the pink box of cupcakes, while Mason opened a cabinet reach-ing for something. "I guess we haven't spent much time together, alone," he said, answering his own question.

I suddenly wished I could take back my words. I had de-cided not to tell Barry about Paxton Cline until I had some evidence to go with it, but after the episode at the mall when Thursday pretended not to know Paxton, I couldn't really tell Mason about him, either.

"Did I say suspect? What I meant to say was scenario. A scenario that the killer was a stranger and not a worker or guest at the wedding."

"And that's what I think happened," Mason said, sounding happier that he wasn't left out. I didn't feel better, though. I was still wondering why Thursday didn't want me to know she knew Paxton.

I glanced over the elaborate kitchen for the evidence of some kind of fancy espresso maker, but there was none. Mason took out two demitasse cups and then reached back in the cabinet and came out with a small metal pot.

"What's that?" I said.

"This is the old-school way to make espresso. I certainly regret now that I didn't get to know Jonah better." He began to add coffee and water and screwed the top and bottom together before putting the small pot on the stove. "Then I might have been some help in finding his killer."

"Tell me again what you thought of him," I said. Mason repeated the statement about wondering if anyone would seem good enough for his daughter. "He was always cordial when we met. I understood he worked for his father, but Thursday mostly kept him separate from me."

"What about his family?"

Mason's expression darkened. "It's hard for me to separate how they were before the wedding and how Kingsley has acted since." He shook his head with anger, which was rare for Mason, and I knew he was thinking of how Jackson Kingsley had tried from the very beginning to blame Mason's family for his son's death and wanted to cut Thursday out of their family. "We had an engagement party and a few dinners. I just talked to Kingsley about sports. It was a safe topic. My main aim was just to keep things peaceful, so I didn't bring up any issues that could stir things up."

I started to say something about the current Mrs. Kingsley, but stopped, reminding myself that Mason didn't know about Thursday's and my trip to the Kingsleys', which is how I knew that she wasn't Jonah's mother and not that many years older than him. I really didn't like all these secrets.

The pungent smell of the espresso filled the air as the water made its way up through the coffee grounds into the top of the small pot. He put everything on a tray, and we took it into his den with Spike following close behind.

After all the commotion of the day, it was nice to sink into his ultracomfortable couch and enjoy the peaceful moment. Mason inched a little closer to me. "Can you remind me what happened to the plan for us to be more than friends?"

CHAPTER 16

"SO THE COPS THINK YOU'RE THE YARN BOMBER," Adele said, sounding a little too happy after I told her about my episode at the mall. I don't think it was so much that she wanted it to be me as much as to have the spotlight off of her, particularly where Eric and his mother were concerned. Though with her crochet obsession and natural flamboyance, it was hard to believe it wasn't her work.

I responded to her comment by rolling my eyes. We were sitting at the worktable together, crocheting. I was trying to get a head start on holiday gifts and working on a scarf in yarn that created its own stripes. Adele was immersed in her jewelry making, but then she'd turned it into a side business. She had set aside using wire for a while and was using hemp cord and beads to make lovely chokers. She had even started making her own beads out of polymer clay.

Adele pulled the newspaper out of her tote bag, laid it on

the table and pointed out a photograph on the second page. It must have been a very slow news day for yarn bombing to get such a prominent position. The statues showed up really well, and, frankly, I thought the colorful ponchos jazzed them up. I examined the picture again and laughed. "It looks like these signs giving directions in the mall are sticking out of their heads," I said.

Adele pointed out that the article mentioned that a suspect had been taken into custody. "Now I get it. I guess that means you."

"You do realize I didn't do it," I said.

"But it sounds like the cops think you did. They've seen you at two other bombing sites, and then to catch you with yarn and hooks at the mall . . . ?" Adele gave me a disparaging shake of her head. "As long as they don't think it's me," she said, checking the chair next to her to make sure her boyfriend's mother hadn't slid in when she wasn't looking.

"What happened to your need to find out the truth about who was really doing it?"

Adele shrugged. "That's when they thought it was me."

I had let Adele get away with any number of outrageous statements, but this time she'd gone too far.

"I see how it is. When you're on the hook, you want everybody to help you get off it, but when it's somebody else, you step back."

Adele's mouth fell open and she looked like she was about to object, but then she got a guilty look. "Pink, I think you might be right." She paused and seemed to struggle as if what she was going to say was really hard. "I, ah, I—well, take this as an apology."

"You can't say the words, can you? You can't just say, 'I'm sorry'?"

"Pink, my motto has been never surrender. Never show your underbelly and be vulnerable. Saying the actual words 'I'm sorry' counts as that for me."

Only once had Adele let down her guard and told us something that explained why she was the way she was. It was all about a wicked knitting stepmother who made fun of her and a father who wasn't impressed with her crocheted gift.

Maybe Eric's mother was having an effect on her. Certainly her clothing choices were different, but I was beginning to miss her wild outfits. She was blah in all beige today. Not even a beanie with a flower to add a little pizzazz.

I supposed I should be grateful that she sort of admitted she was wrong, and let it go. I was about to say something along those lines when she leaned into me and grabbed my shoulders in an awkward hug.

"Okay, Pink. You did it. You got me to say the words 'I'm sorry,' even if it was out of context." She seemed stunned. "There, I just said it again. I've shown you my vulnerable side. Go ahead, take your shot." She closed her eyes as if preparing for the worst. When nothing happened, she opened her eyes a slit. "I'm waiting. The anticipation is killing me. Say whatever you're going to say."

I touched her shoulder and told her to relax. "All I was trying to say was that since you wanted my help when you thought you were in jeopardy, it would be nice if you returned the favor since I'm the one in the crosshairs now.

"You want *my* help? I thought you had so many people who would rush to your aid. Dinah, Barry, Mason and all the Hookers."

By now, I was regretting saying anything. Adele with her defenses down was more difficult to deal with than when she was being outrageous. And I began to wonder what kind of help she'd really be. Maybe more of a hindrance. But I'd gotten myself in a corner and said yes. I was relieved when some of the other Hookers started to show up and the subject got dropped.

Mrs. Shedd came by the table and pulled me aside. "Everything settled for the party?" She sounded a little nervous. What had seemed easy at first was turning out to be more complicated. I still hadn't come up with a project, and there was the yarn and supplies, and the food. I did my best to make it seem like it was all under control, but when I rejoined the Hookers I told them the truth.

"Pink, I'm handling the crochet lessons," Adele said. She stopped to check her calendar. "Even though I'm having an important visitor at story time that morning." Leonora was sitting next to her knitting a pale blue baby blanket. Adele almost bowed to her. "Maybe you've heard of Kate Moore, author of *Pig Tales*." Leonora barely reacted, but several other people did, particularly Dinah.

"That's a classic," Dinah said. "I read it to my kids. And again to my ex's kids when they came to visit." Then Dinah steered the subject back to the upcoming party. "I'll be glad to help in any way you need," my best friend said.

"Yes, dear," CeeCee said. "Tell us what you need." I ran down the list of things that still weren't settled and reiterated that if this first party didn't come off, there wouldn't be any more. CeeCee acted as leader and spoke to the group, reminding them of Mrs. Shedd's generosity in letting us meet at the bookstore and how she always supplied the yarn for our charity ventures. "The bookstore needs to take in money in new ways and the Party with a Purpose is an excellent way. So let's all pitch in to make this first party so fabulous that everyone in Tarzana, Encino and Woodland Hills will want to have one themselves."

Rhoda spoke up first. "Give me a little time and I'll come up with a project," she said. Rhoda was a very direct person, and I knew she wouldn't make a promise she couldn't keep. I gave her a relieved nod before explaining the criteria.

"I've made kits before," Elise said, reminding me we sold her vampire scarf kits every time a new Anthony book came out. "I'll give them to you almost for cost." Despite her wispy birdlike voice, Elise had a tough core. The table erupted into shock. Finally she conceded and said she'd do them at cost, but she'd need help in putting them together.

Sheila said she'd help Elise with the kits. Eduardo put down the lacy doily he was making. He'd begun using them for display items in his old-fashioned drugstore. "We have penny candy," he said with a laugh. We all knew why he laughed—the name should have been changed to "many penny candy."

"I can make up little goody bags for the kids," Eduardo added.

"I'll help with paper goods and set up," Dinah said.

Leonora looked up. "I'm not really a member of your group, but if there's anything I can do." What she didn't see was that Adele was standing behind her shaking her head vehemently, waving her arms and mouthing *no*.

I let out a sigh of relief and went back to crocheting. Peace settled over the group for a minute.

"What happened to Thursday?" Rhoda said. Leonora's head shot up with a puzzled expression.

"Nothing happened to it," Leonora said. "It's only Tuesday."

A chuckle went through the group and Rhoda explained that Thursday was a person. Of course, she didn't stop at that. She went on to explain my connection to the bride and how her husband of one hour had been stabbed at the wedding reception.

"Oh," Leonora said. "I did hear about that from Eric. He was one of the first responders," she added with a touch of pride. I assured the group Thursday wanted to come again, but she'd just gotten back to teaching. I told them how we'd had a dinner together on Sunday night before she went back. "We cooked together and then we sat around crocheting. She's getting really good."

Rhoda went right back to talking about the murder. "What's with the cops? With all those witnesses, how can they not have arrested somebody?" she said in her matter-of-fact voice. "What about you, Molly?" She turned to me. "I can't believe that with Thursday staying at your house and Mason being a 'friend' and all, that you aren't up to your elbows in investigating." It was the first Leonora was hearing of my sleuthing skills. By the squinty look she gave me, I don't think she was too impressed.

"Maybe that's the problem. Between the guests and the servers, there were so many people, it was hard for anyone to notice anything. And it isn't like anyone was expecting something like that to happen. The cops' scenario still has someone coming in dressed like one of the servers, doing the deed and leaving. But I'm not so sure." No one picked up on the last part of my comment and asked what I meant.

"What about the Kingsley family?" CeeCee said.

I shook my head sadly. "They've cut themselves off from Thursday. They're treating her like the enemy." I paused.

"Or as if she had something to do with Jonah's death." There was a moment of silence and I knew what some of them were thinking. Maybe she did it.

"Talk about crime," Elise said, cutting into the dead air. "You should have been at the mall the other day. I saw the mall cops racing on their Segways toward something. Probably a bunch of shoplifters."

"Not exactly," Adele said, unfolding the newspaper and putting it in the middle of the table. Of course, then I had to explain what had happened to me.

"You were in the police station again?" CeeCee said. "They ought to have a special chair with your name on it."

"It doesn't matter," Adele said, making her voice sound important. "I'm going to help Molly prove her innocence by working with her to find the real yarn bomber."

I was stunned. Maybe a leopard could change its spots, or in Adele's case, stop wearing them.

"Why didn't you tell them about Paxton Cline?" Dinah asked when we were alone. After the group broke up, Dinah and I had headed for the café. When we'd gotten our drinks, we had taken them to a table in the window. It was surrounded by displays of items the café sold, and it offered the most privacy in the place.

"I was thinking about it, but Leonora is Eric's mother. Eric is a motor cop, but still his path crosses Barry's."

Dinah nodded knowingly. "So you still haven't told Barry about him."

"My plan was to deliver Paxton with some hot evidence, but so far I've got nothing more than we got the other day." I put my head down and rocked it with dismay. "It gets worse." I told her about all the secrets I was keeping from Mason, including the whole Paxton thing, too. "How could I tell Mason about Paxton being a possible suspect and then tell him that his daughter pretended not to know him?" Dinah understood and gave me a reassuring pat on the arm.

"You said something to the group about not being sure the killer was some stranger who had slipped in and out." Dinah poured equal amounts of steamed milk and coffee into her mug.

I gave her the details of my experiment with the shirt in Mason's backyard. "When I went back to the spot where I had found the shirt and relived it, suddenly I remembered that the collar was closest to the gate. As if someone had taken off the shirt, dropped it and gone back into the reception." My red eye was almost gone, and I considered having another.

"Did you tell Mason about that?" my friend asked.

"He was standing with me when I did it." I turned to Dinah. "His daughter and his ex are still loosely in the suspect pool. I don't know how seriously they're being considered, but I have a feeling that Mason would just as soon the cops stick with the idea that someone came in from the outside in a revenge plot. And someone they'll never be able to track down."

There was so much to tell Dinah. The whole meltdown with Thursday and her mother's version of what had happened at the wedding. As I was talking to Dinah, something nagged at me. It took me a few minutes to remember. "This is probably nothing, but Emerson made a point to me that she stayed to arrange the flowers on the cake and hand out fresh boutonnieres to the wedding party But when I mentioned that to Jaimee, she looked at me like I was nuts and said that she had not ordered a second round of lapel flowers handed out."

"Maybe Emerson confused it with another wedding," Dinah said.

"Must be," I said, relieved that there seemed to be a reasonable explanation. "And there's more. I just remembered that I saw Paxton Cline at the mall. His family owns a yarn business. Maybe he's doing the yarn bombing as some kind of advertising."

"And what about Ben Sherman? Did Thursday admit to knowing him?"

By now, I had my head in my hands and was rocking it with frustration. All I had were a bunch of loose strings.

CHAPTER 17

I CAME HOME TO A QUIET HOUSE, BUT IT WASN'T empty. There were a bunch of boxes and a fountain and some metal cherubs holding a banner saying, "Love Forever." A note from my son was attached. Someone had delivered them earlier.

I let Cosmo in the yard and went across the house to encourage Blondie to do the same. It was too late in the day to let the cats have some outdoor time, so I filled their bowls and let them follow me around. It seemed like forever since I'd had my house all to myself. The options were overwhelming. Should I have an ice cream dinner and watch a comedy DVD? Or sit in my yard and crochet with the help of the outdoor lights?

The front doorbell rang, interrupting my thoughts. I considered ignoring it, thinking it was somebody collecting for something, but it rang again. A double ring, like the person was a little impatient and would keep ringing until someone answered. I pulled the door open and looked out.

"You shouldn't just open the door," Barry said. "I could have been a home invasion robber." I did a double take. This wasn't end-of-the-day Barry with a five o'clock shadow and his tie pulled loose. I could smell his cologne and see that his hair was a touch wet from a shower. The shirt was fresh, and he was wearing a sport coat over slacks instead of the suits he wore for work. He noticed my perplexed expression.

"I'm right on time," he said, showing me his watch. Then he started to smile. "Hmm, look who's not ready."

"Ready for what?" I said.

"Dinner and Jeffrey's play." He seemed to be amused at my surprise. He took out his cell phone and showed me that it was turned to off. "Remember, I promised there was no way I wouldn't show up or be called away in the middle of things. I even reminded you when I saw you at the station."

"You did?" Then I remembered his mouthed message. "That was about tonight. But it's a weeknight. I assumed the play was on a Saturday."

He was enjoying this way too much: I was the one who wasn't ready and who'd forgotten. "Am I going to have to make excuses to Jeffrey about why you didn't come?" he said with a teasing lift of his eyebrows.

I couldn't do that to his son. He was probably used to his father not showing up to things, but I'd always been the dependable one.

"Give me a few minutes," I said, inviting him in. He did a double take at the stuff in the front hall.

"It belongs to Thursday," I said, explaining they were things her parents had bought for the condo she was supposed to have shared with Jonah. "She has no stake in the town house or most of the furnishings. But then, you probably know all that," I said. I left the comment hanging to see what he'd say, but all he did was tell me I'd better hurry and that we'd have to eat after the play.

Ten minutes, well, maybe it was more like twenty minutes later, I reappeared. I'd dumped the khaki slacks and shirt I always wore for work, showered and put on a black dress and ballet flats. I'd finished the look with a shawl I'd made in a whisper-soft cream-colored mohair.

Judging by the uptick in Barry's expression, I must have looked pretty good. This was all too weird. Barry was acting very formal. He opened the door of the Tahoe for me and even helped me step into the SUV.

The parking lot was full at the middle school. Even though Jeffrey was officially in high school now, the play was from the drama group that had met over the summer at the middle school. The auditorium was already crowded when we walked in. We'd gotten there just in time. I saw Jeffrey in full Captain Hook costume peeking out from the wings as we found our seats. When I saw how his face lit up seeing us there, I was glad I'd come.

I was about to sit when I heard someone call my name.

"Emerson?" I said, surprised as the dark-haired woman got out of her seat and came up to me. Lyla turned around in her seat and waved.

"I'm glad I ran into you," the event florist said. "You probably realize Lyla didn't get very far with the crochet lesson. Could we do another one?" She paused as if there was something else on her mind.

"There's something else I'd like to run by you," she said.

"I was thinking how nice it would be if the mothers, or in one case, father, got in on the crochet. They could stay and learn, too."

My mind was ticking. It would be more people to teach how to crochet, but if the parents had a positive experience, it would help spread the word about our new venture. "I think that's a great idea," I said. She seemed relieved by my answer. I understood why when she let it slip that she'd already told one of the parents they could join the party.

"Then I'll need a crochet lesson, too," she said. She was agreeable to coming to the bookstore this time, and we set up a time.

"Lyla is very excited about her birthday party. She's been telling all her friends. The RSVPs are coming in fast and furious," she added with a smile. "I'm glad we're doing this." The lights went off and on, indicating the play was about to start, so Emerson went back to her seat.

I saw Barry's eyes lock on her and then back to me, questioning. I promised to explain later because now the lights had gone off and the curtain was opening. No matter how much Barry fussed about his son's acting aspirations and name change to just Columbia, he was all pride as he watched his son's big moment. Even if his wig was a little crooked, and the hook almost fell off.

"He was great, wasn't he?" Barry said when the last curtain call had ended. I nodded in agreement and Barry took my hand, squeezing it. Then he dropped it like he'd done something wrong. "Am I overstepping?" he said. I thought he was being facetious, but I checked his expression and he seemed serious. "I don't want to screw this up," he said finally.

We waited by the backstage entrance until Jeffrey joined

us, floating on a cloud from the excitement and the applause. But he only stayed long enough for us to get a picture together. After hugging me and thanking me for coming, he announced that the cast was going out for pizza and somebody would drop him off at home, if that was okay. As Barry nodded, a bunch of voices said, "Hey, Columbia, hurry up."

"Hmmm," Barry said, watching as his son joined his group without looking back. Barry looked bereft.

"It's hard letting go, isn't it?" I said. I heard Barry let out his breath as he nodded with a touch of sadness. "If you just want to call it a night," I started, thinking the whole point of the evening had been Jeffrey. But Barry shook his head, insisting that the plan had been the play and food.

"A promise is a promise," he said. I knew he was referring to all the plans in the past cut short because of something with his work. He really did seem to have changed his priorities.

I let him pick the place, expecting he'd choose somewhere local for a quick bite. That way he could live up to his word and still be on call soon. I could only imagine all the messages with leads to follow up on collecting on his phone. I was getting nervous just thinking about it. He caught me by complete surprise when he suggested a place probably ten miles away in Studio City.

Traffic was light on the 101, before he turned off onto a friendly-looking side street. The residential street gave way to a block of appealing retail places. The café was in what had been a house back in the day. Most of the seating was on a brick-lined patio that surrounded the small structure. We went inside to order at a counter that was flanked by a display case of mouthwatering pastries and cakes. Barry saw me eyeing the princess cake and before we'd even chosen our food, he ordered a piece for us to share. I couldn't help my surprised expression. Barry had never been a share-a-piece-of-cake kind of guy. It was almost too much when he pointed out their extensive tea selection and fondly remembered the cups of tea we'd shared at my place. I asked for coffee, dark and strong.

It had gotten chilly outside and we chose a table next to a patio heater in a secluded corner of the backyard, though by now, the crowd had thinned out. With the flickering candles on the table and the night sky as a ceiling, it was very atmospheric or, should I say, romantic.

Our food was delivered shortly. I fidgeted with my silverware and napkin, feeling awkward. This had become too date-like. I was almost relieved when Barry checked his phone once, but then he put it away without a word.

"It's been a long time since we've been out like this," he said, picking up half of his sandwich. "So, tell me what's going on in your life?"

A long time since we'd been out like this—how about never?

I started to talk about putting on the crochet parties and all the parts to them I hadn't considered, and all the stiffness went away. "So, then you won't be doing author events anymore?" Barry said with a friendly smile.

"It's in addition to, not instead of," I said. "I have an author event coming up in a few days. Dr. Chopin Wheel. He wrote a book called *Cheap and Natural Cure-Alls.*" I went back to talking about the crochet parties and mentioned that the woman I'd talked to at the play was my first client. "She's the event florist who did Thursday's wedding."

Barry nodded. "That's why she looked familiar. I think Heather and I talked to her."

"She's a suspect?" I said, surprised.

"No. There are so many people involved with this case. We're still trying to find out who was at the reception and left before you and I got there." His mouth settled in a straight line. "Between dealing with the caterer—" He shook his head in dismay. "At least if all the workers hadn't been dressed like unisex robots it would be easier. Whose idea was that?"

"Mason's ex," I said. There were more head shakes. Jaimee seemed to inspire that reaction in people.

Barry finished his bite of sandwich and took a sip of his beer. "So, how's it going?"

"How's what going?" I was confused. Hadn't he just asked me about my life?

"Molly, I know you. With Thursday living at your house, you have to be nosing around the case. You want to share?"

"You're really asking what I know?" I said with a surprised laugh. I was still getting used to this new him. Barry had always told me to stay out of things and had never taken my investigating very seriously. Paxton Cline crossed my mind. I wasn't ready to tell Barry about him. I still wanted to get some more information, well, really, evidence. But there was something I could share. I told him about the shirt and that I'd remembered an important detail—the way it was positioned on the ground. I even described how I'd figured it out by dropping my own shirt on the ground when I faced different directions. "It seems to me that when the killer dropped it, they were facing the house. Why would they be facing that way unless they were going back to the reception?"

Barry listened and nodded, seeming impressed. "Good thinking, babe, I mean, Molly. You did all this shirt-taking-off at Mason's?" he said, his eyes narrowing. Barry seemed to have forgotten about my evidence and was more focused on me being shirtless at Mason's.

I realized how it sounded and explained it was an over-shirt I'd been dropping. Barry still didn't look happy. "What were you doing at his place? Nothing's changed between you, right?"

I laughed and said we were all just friends. That word was starting to grate on me. Why not just be straight. It was a relationship with no serious touching.

"Right," Barry said. Something about the tension in his expression made me believe the word was starting to grate on him, too. But whatever it was, he dismissed the mood as he pushed his plate away and pulled the piece of cake between us.

"The first bite is yours," he said. His hand brushed mine as he handed me a fork. He waited until I had a piece of cake in my mouth and watched my smile. Since the frosting was a pastel green, you would expect it to be lime or mint, but it was actually a thin layer of marzipan, giving it a sweet almond flavor. The yellow cake had lemon, whipped cream and raspberry between the layers.

Barry cut off a piece with his fork and made an *mmm* sound as he tasted the combination of flavors. We both kept working on the cake, smiling at each other with each bite. I'd never noticed how intimate sharing food was.

The café help had long since deposited a to-go box with the half sandwich I couldn't finish, and they were sweeping up by the time we'd finished and headed to his Tahoe. When Barry pulled his SUV into my driveway, I thought he was just going to leave me off, and I prepared to open the car door. I was surprised when he cut the motor and got out.

"What kind of escort would I be if I didn't make sure you got in all right?" he said, following me across my back-yard. My mind was ticking away. How was I supposed to end this evening? Should I kiss him like the old days? No. I could just imagine his reaction if I went to shake his hand. Maybe a kiss was the way to go—a kiss on the cheek or the forehead.

It ended up being a nonissue. I opened the kitchen door and before I could do anything, Thursday called out a greet-ing. She was in the midst of working on a project for her class on my kitchen table.

"Are you here to question me again?" Thursday said in a tired voice when she saw Barry. I quickly told her about Jef-frey's play, but her expression said she wasn't buying it. "It's awfully late for a play on a school night."

Barry seemed amused that I had to answer to someone. I was thinking how ridiculous it was that I had to answer to anyone. I mentioned we'd gotten something to eat after-ward. I thought she was going to comment on that, but she didn't.

Cosmo had already run past and gone out into the yard. I went across the house to get Blondie and encourage her to come outside. As I was bringing her back, I heard Barry and Thursday talking. Was he interrogating her again? I leaned closer to hear what they were talking about—it wasn't what I expected.

"I'm glad to hear you and Molly are just old friends. My

dad really cares about her. I'm not sure if either of them realize it, but they're made for each other," Thursday said.

When I walked into the kitchen, Barry's cop face had returned, but I knew the blank expression was hiding his reaction to her comment. He followed me as I went outside with Blondie. He'd become so quiet and withdrawn, I couldn't help it. I leaned up and kissed him. It wasn't on the cheek, either.

CHAPTER 18

BY THE TIME I GOT UP THE NEXT MORNING, THURSday was already off to work. It was one of the days when I worked the afternoon and evening because I had an author event. I took care of the animals and looked forward to sitting down at the table for a leisurely cup of coffee. Samuel's door was shut, which probably meant he was in there asleep, so I left him alone. We both did our best not to infringe on each other's lives.

I made the coffee, thinking about what I'd overheard Thursday say to Barry the night before. Were Mason and I made for each other? I quickly switched to thinking about the shirt I'd found in Mason's backyard the day of the wedding, wondering how I could figure out who'd dropped it. It was more comfortable to think about clues than relationships. I'd just sat down and was about to have my first sip of the dark brew when the phone rang. With all the gizmos on phones now, there was no secret to who was calling, so I knew it was Mason before I even clicked Talk.

"Good morning, Sunshine," he said in an upbeat voice. "There's something I want to talk to you about." He gave it a moment to sink in before continuing. "I was thinking we could discuss it over dinner tonight."

I explained my work schedule, and he sounded a little disappointed. "Why can't we talk about it right now?" I asked. It had sounded like Thursday might think Mason and I were made for each other, but she wasn't going to tell either one of us directly. Still, I wondered what she might do to stir the pot.

"I could do that. I was working from home this morning. We could get breakfast or I could come over there."

I made another attempt to keep it to a phone conversation, but he held firm to the plan of us meeting in person to discuss it. Breakfast was my favorite meal to have out, so I agreed.

"Where are we going?" I said after Mason had picked me up and had gotten on the 101 heading west. I was expecting Le Grande Fromage or some local place.

"You'll see," was all he would say. Barry's choice of restaurants had been a surprise since he usually went for less atmosphere and more convenience. However, grand gestures were common with Mason. I made sure he wasn't planning something like driving somewhere up the coast, because I really couldn't be late for work.

Even though he'd said nothing, I knew he knew about last night and was trying to counter it. Not that there was that much to last night. Barry had seemed surprised by the kiss, obviously not in a bad way, but at the same time, he hadn't tried to prolong it or turn it into anything more.

He seemed to be accepting the new phase of our relationship, I thought with a sense of relief. Mason, on the other hand, was always pushing at the restraints. I bet if I kissed him the way I had kissed Barry, he wouldn't have sauntered off with just a wave good-night.

Mason got off at Topanga Canyon and headed up the windy road that led through the long canyon all the way to the beach. I said a trip to the ocean sounded appealing, but he chuckled and said that wasn't his plan. While we drove, I also tried to get him to discuss what he wanted to talk about, but he refused, instead urging me to enjoy the scenery.

His silence was only making me more tense, and I did my best to concentrate on the passing view. We'd gone from the busy Valley floor to a rustic wilderness in a few minutes. The houses on either side of the twisting road were mostly a little offbeat. I could barely see the creek that ran below the road on one side. The water was only a trickle now, which made the quirky bridges some of the homeowners had built seem like overkill. But when the winter rains came, the creek could become a dangerous torrent. We passed some small businesses and went through the actual town of Topanga, which looked like a throwback to the '60s with its hippie feel.

Still Mason refused to tell me where we were going or to talk about the information. "Enjoy the adventure," he said with a sly smile. "It's always an adventure with me."

Eventually, I caught Mason's vibe and began to enjoy the feeling that I was running away from everything for a little while. No worries about crochet lessons, the bookstore, or the book signing. It was like playing hooky from school, though I really wasn't.

Mason turned off the main road and drove on a bridge over the creek. There were a few more twists and turns, and he pulled up to a valet stand in front of a rustic-looking restaurant with a poetic name.

It was early and the place was empty. Mason spoke to the host and we were led to a table outside. When I say outside, I don't mean some wooden deck patio. I mean a table on a rocky ledge with dirt as the floor. Below, the lazy creek made its way through rocks and plants, and the whole area was shaded by big, old trees.

Mason's eyes were dancing as I looked around the place. He must have known where Barry and I had gone, and he'd found a way to outdo it. Then I knew. The box from the café had its name on it and was in the refrigerator. Thursday must have seen it and told Mason.

I was still surprised that she was trying to put something together between me and her father. I thought it was always the dream of kids, no matter how old, that their divorced parents get back together. But then maybe that dream didn't factor in Jaimee.

The menu said lunch, but Mason got them to make us omelets, sweet potato patties, fruit and toast made of the homemade whole-grain bread they baked on-site. Coffee was served in a French press pot.

"Well?" I said expectantly, when we'd gotten our food and started in on it. I looked across at Mason and expected his cheerful expression, but instead he appeared dead serious and I felt my heart rate quicken.

"I need your help," he said. "You know how Jackson Kingsley has said repeatedly that he thinks Jonah was stabbed to get back at me." There was a long pause before Mason continued. "I blew it off and just took it for what it was, a grieving father looking for someone else to blame. You don't know, but Detective Heather, er . . . Gilmore raked me over the coals about the revenge motive, too. I insisted it was ridiculous . . ." He let his voice trail off.

"But I began to wonder if it could be true. I went through the past few years of cases to see if there was anyone who might be holding a grudge against me or blaming me for something."

I was going to say something reassuring, but Mason wanted to keep on going. "There's someone I got off for a DUI hit-and-run. The car jumped the curb and just some daffodils and marigolds died." To make sure I understood, he explained more fully that the tires had crushed the flowerbed in front of a home.

"But that's nothing," I said. "Who would come after you for that?"

"There's another chapter to the story," Mason said. "Two weeks later, the same person got into another accident and this time it wasn't flowers that died." Mason's whole expression seemed to sag. "The family of the victim knew my client had been in a previous accident and had kept his license and gotten off. You see where they could blame me?"

I had lost interest in the food by then. "You were just doing your job," I said, reaching across to touch his arm.

"That's what I try to think. My job is to defend my clients. But I have to tell you, I wish I had never taken that case."

"You said there's something you want me to do," I said.

"I need to know if some member of the victim's family was one of the servers at the reception. I can't get through to the caterer. She isn't happy with my family and claims the murder and all the discussion about the way she had the servers dress has hurt her business. Actually, she said it killed her business." He looked toward me.

"We all know you have rather unconventional ways of doing things. Could you try to get a list of who worked at the reception?"

Of course, I agreed. Then Mason went out of his way to lighten the mood, and we went back to eating our brunch. On the way back through the picturesque canyon, I looked over at him. "It was a lovely place, but wasn't that a long way to go for an omelet?"

Mason smiled. Maybe that was the point. He drove in silence for a few moments, and it was obvious he had something else on his mind. "Was this better than last night?"

"I'm taking the Fifth on that," I said with a laugh. I knew no matter what I said, it would probably come out wrong.

CHAPTER 19

"Thanks for meeting me," I said to Dinah. We were parked next to each other in the parking lot behind the bookstore. I had called her when Mason dropped me off at my house, and I explained what Mason wanted. She offered to be my Watson right away. Since I had some time until I had to get to work, and Dinah had a break in classes, we decided to move on it immediately.

"What's the plan?" she said, rubbing her hands together in enthusiasm. "I hope there isn't sneaking around involved, because I'm not dressed for it." That was the truth. Dinah was wearing a burnt orange cotton pantsuit with a white shirt. A long scarf in a lighter shade of the orange trailed in the wind behind her. She was definitely jazzed by the idea we were teaming up to investigate. "I'm so glad to be in the middle of things again. I feel like I've been out of the loop."

"No sneaking around, so your outfit is fine," I said, gesturing for her to get into my car. "I decided to go directly to the caterer. I even made an appointment to see her." I started the engine and we took off out of the parking lot.

"Wait a second, if Mason can't get the list from her, how can you?"

"I haven't exactly worked that part out yet."

It was only a short drive to our destination, and I told Dinah about the dueling meals I'd had with Barry and then Mason. "Men are too much. They'll try to one-up each other on anything—even romantic restaurants," Dinah said with a merry chuckle. But when I told her what I'd overheard Thursday say to Barry, she almost choked on her breath. We both agreed that Thursday's reaction was surprising.

Just before I parked, I had an idea about how to approach the caterer. "It's obvious. I'm planning a party and that's her specialty."

"You're going to talk to her about Lyla's birthday party?" Dinah said.

"I might leave out a few details. Just go along with whatever I say or do."

Laurie Jean's Party People was located in a storefront on Ventura. We had to ring a bell to get in. Laurie Jean greeted us and took us into a small room in the front. It had comfortable armchairs and a table in the middle.

"Have a seat, ladies," the caterer said. I checked out the rest of the place as I was choosing a seat. I noted a small office on the other side of the entrance, and the whole back seemed to be given over to a kitchen and food storage.

She waited until Dinah and I sat, then she took a seat across from us. I noticed she had a pad and pen and started to scribble some notes. She had long, blond hair and a smile that was a little too bright to be real. It looked like the kind of smile that was going to give her a headache if she didn't let it fade soon.

"What sort of event are you planning?" she said. When I said it was a birthday party, her smile deflated a little, but she assured me they could do birthday parties. Her next question was how many guests I expected.

Dinah played the silent partner and just nodded along with the conversation. I did the politician thing and didn't answer her questions, but took the conversation where I wanted it to go. "I'd really like to use those servers who worked that wedding you put on a couple of weeks ago. They all looked the same, which I think is very professional." I stopped as if I was considering something. "In fact, I want those exact servers."

Laurie Jean did a double take. "You're putting on a birthday party for two hundred people?" she said. I noticed her manner changed, and she suddenly became more interested. Dinah was trying hard not to laugh. She knew we'd have maybe fifteen people at Lyla's party.

Laurie Jean immediately turned the subject away from the servers to the menu. I tried to gloss over the menu, saying I was more concerned with the look of the party and brought the subject back to the servers.

"How many servers were there at that wedding?" I said.

"You don't have to worry about that," she said. "That's why you hire a caterer. It's much more important that you choose the type of party and the food. Once we take care of the paperwork, we can set up a tasting."

Dinah threw me a worried look as Laurie Jean produced

a bunch of forms and mentioned the word *deposit*. This wasn't working. I had hoped to be able to get what I wanted by talking, but it was time for plan B.

"I wonder if I could use your restroom?" I said. I threw Dinah a nod, hoping she realized I needed her to stall. Laurie Jean graciously gestured toward the hall and said there was a restroom just before the kitchen.

I walked into the hall slowly, checking to see that I was out of sight. I heard Dinah begin talking to Laurie Jean. My friend always came through, and I knew one way or another she'd keep the conversation going.

I went across the hall to the small office, hoping to get a quick look around. Whatever records she had were probably in there. The first thing I noticed was the absence of a computer. I glanced over the desk, and there didn't seem to be anything there resembling what I was looking for. A credenza sat against the wall and I noticed a row of plastic bins. When I looked closer, I saw that each had a label, presumably for some event. I also noticed that just about all of them had a line through them and the word *Canceled* written above. Wow, it really did look like her business had been killed. The one on the end said *Fields/Kingsley*. I noticed a handful of papers in it. I listened for a moment and the drone of conversation was still coming from across the hall. I'd just have a quick look through the bin.

I'd already figured I would take a picture of the list with my phone and hope that Mason could read it. I began to thumb through the sheets. I was encouraged when they seemed to be checklists of supplies and such. I got a little too interested in examining the sheets as I went through them. I had no idea about all the stuff she'd had to bring. It made me think of Lyla's party and stuff I hadn't thought about, like a first aid kit. I was almost to the bottom of the bin. My phone screen had gone dark, and I got it back on and made sure it was set to camera. Just as I went back to the bin, I heard a rustle and then a voice.

"What are you doing?" Laurie Jean yelled.

CHAPTER 20

LAURIE JEAN CAME RUNNING AFTER ME AS I MADE a move toward the door. I signaled Dinah to get going. Laurie Jean was faster and rushed ahead of me and blocked the exit. And then she burst into tears.

"I finally thought I was getting a client," she wailed, "and you're just some snoop after information. What are you, reporters? P.I.'s?"

Dinah and I traded guilty glances and I came clean. When she heard it was Mason who wanted the list of servers, her eyes went skyward, and then she got up. "You want to see a list of who worked the reception. I'll show it to you." She marched into the office and came back with the bin I'd been looking through. She dumped the container on the table and ruffled through the papers before pulling a clump of pages that seemed stuck together and covered in a brown ooze. She pushed it toward me.

My first impulse was to go *ewww*. "Go ahead, look at it if you want. Good luck getting the pages apart." Laurie Jean gave me a moment to pick up the clump of pages before she continued. "I pay the servers in cash as though it comes directly from the client," she said. "I don't keep records on them other than a handwritten list of who is supposed to work. They sign in as they come. I don't know how it happened, but the sheet was on the table in the service area of the tent." She pointed to the thing in my hand. "We think the brown stuff is balsamic vinegar glaze. Just before each tray of caprese appetizers went out, each one was given a squirt of the glaze. I don't know how it ended up on the list. I don't know who worked the wedding. All I know is that it was a disaster all the way around."

Laurie Jean began to cry again. "The cops think I put the glaze on the papers and that I'm trying to cover up who was there. Everybody is calling my business Calamity Caterers." Dinah found a tissue in her bag and handed it to Laurie Jean, and I felt terrible for leading her on and sneaking around. It all ended with a group hug and me offering to try to get her the food gig for a future crochet party. I waited for her to calm down before we left.

I called Mason when we got outside.

"It's okay, Sunshine. You did the best you could," he said when I finished telling him the whole story. Then I heard a low chuckle. "Sunshine, you always surprise me."

"I SHOULD HAVE ASKED LAURIE JEAN ABOUT THE shirt," I said as Dinah and I headed down the street toward my car.

"Do you want to go back?" my friend said, but I shook

my head. I had to get to work, and I didn't want to do anything to bring up the wedding again to Laurie Jean. "Are we
talking about the shirt you found outside the reception?"
Dinah asked. I started the car and pulled out into traffic.

I said it was and reminded her of my discovery, which
took longer than I'd expected because this time she had the
same reaction Barry had and wondered why I was taking my
shirt off in Mason's yard.

"That's not the point," I said. "I think the direction the
collar was facing means the killer came out of the reception,
dropped the bloody shirt, and then went back in as if nothing had happened." Then something troubling occurred to
me. "Except for one thing—what were they wearing? I'm
sure if someone came in without a shirt, they would have
been noticed."

"I bet they would have," Dinah said with a giggle. We
talked back and forth about it for a moment before my
friend had an idea. "Didn't you say you were giving a crochet
lesson to Emerson. She was there and wore one of those
white shirts. Maybe you can slip in some questions while
you teach her the chain stitch."

I pulled into a parking spot behind the bookstore. Dinah
got out of the car and rushed to hers so she could get back
to Beasley Community College for her class. I moved at the
same speed to the bookstore, suddenly realizing the time.

Mrs. Shedd was glancing down at her watch when I skid-
ded into the bookstore. Normally she didn't keep tabs on
my exact hours, because I always worked more hours than I
got paid for. To me it was all about getting the job done. I
saw that some of the Hookers were hanging out at the worktable. Before heading back there, I mentioned to Mrs. Shedd

that Emerson and her daughter were coming for a pre-party crochet lesson. I also told her about Emerson's idea for expanding the party. No surprise, my boss was thrilled.

I didn't get quite the same reaction from Adele. She was hunkered down in the children's area, finishing up a sign about her upcoming story time event. Usually we just had a photograph of the author, but she'd added a picture of a cute little pig. "Pink, you should have checked with me before you agreed to the lesson. I could have had plans."

"Why the pig picture?" I said.

"That's Hamlet, the mini pig," she said, shaking her head and rolling her eyes as if it was a ridiculous question. She pointed to the title of the book, *Pig Tales*. "The tales are about him." She brushed off some crumbs of rubber cement and set the sign on an easel in the entrance to her area.

"So, are you going to help me with the crochet lesson or not?" I asked as I prepared to go to the yarn department.

"You're lucky I just finished putting up the sign and can help." She joined me and we went across the store to the back area. Adele pulled out a plastic bin we kept stowed in one of the cabinets. It had a supply of different-size hooks and some odd balls of yarn. I was glad to see Rhoda and Elise were both at the worktable, even though it wasn't a regular meeting time. Rhoda was finishing a brown scarf to send to a group that sent them off to soldiers. Elise shoved her project into her bag and pulled out a skein of black-and-white variegated yarn, saying she'd come up with a new vampire style. "Instead of exact stripes, this yarn creates the impression of stripes."

"The plans for the party have changed a bit," I said before explaining the addition of the parents. I told Rhoda we'd need either two separate projects for the adults and kids, or one that would work for both groups, and I told Elise we'd need more kits.

Elise said she had made up a list of items to put in the kits. She began to search through her bag for it. Ever since she'd started selling the health products, she'd replaced her cloth tote bag with a big thing on wheels. She began to empty its contents on the table. As she set a small shopping bag with a label on the table, she looked toward Adele. "I brought your reorder of the diet powder." She pushed it to Adele, who seemed a little surprised.

"Leonora was concerned you were going to run out," Elise explained. At the sound of the name, Adele jumped, looking around as if the woman she was hoping would be her mother-in-law had suddenly appeared. At least she was dressed appropriately. Ever since Leonora had come for her visit, Adele had stayed with the plain look, even when the woman wasn't present.

Adele snagged the paper shopping bag and went off to put it with her things as the two Hookers packed up their yarn and hooks and left.

Emerson and Lyla showed up just as Adele was returning. I let Adele take the girl down to one end of the table and then directed her mother to a separate spot. I gave her a size J hook and some worsted-weight yarn in an easy-to-work-with beige color. I demonstrated how to make a slipknot, followed by chain stitches. Emerson picked it up easily. It took some doing to segue from helping her do her first row of single crochet stitches to the white shirts at the wedding. I began by commenting on how nimble her fingers were, which was no surprise since she was used to working with her hands on all the event floral arrangements. I commented on how lovely the table arrangements were at Thursday's wedding, deliberately not mentioning the havoc with the blooms on the wedding cake. From there I took a leap and said how it seemed unfair that she'd had to dress like a server.

Emerson shrugged. "It wasn't just me. The DJ was dressed that way, too, and the bartenders, even the caterer." She held up the tail of stitches and admired them. "What's the project for the party going to be?"

"We're still working out the kinks on it," I said quickly before returning to the shirt subject. "Me, I never wear white. Whenever I have, something always gets on it. I wonder what the workers at the wedding would have done if something had spilled on their pristine shirts."

Emerson seemed irritated as she looked up from her crochet work. "Did somebody say something to you?" It seemed like she was going to wait for me to respond, but then she continued talking. "I was leaving anyway. I can't believe anybody saw the wine stain on my shirt."

"Red or white?" I asked.

"What's the difference?" she said with a hint of annoyance. "If I'd been staying for the whole event, I'd have brought a backup shirt. And the white gloves—" She let out a snort. "None of the servers were used to wearing them and lots of them were getting soiled. The caterer supplied them and brought a big box of them."

"So when you left, did you go out the back gate?"

"I'm trying to file that wedding reception in the back of my mind and forget about it," she said. "But yes, I did go out the back gate. My van was parked down the street. I told the police all about it."

She sounded like she thought that was the end of the

subject, but I wanted to ask her one more thing. "Did you see the groom when you were leaving?"

Emerson seemed to pause as if she was thinking about what she was going to say. "I probably should have told this to the police." She paused and blew out her breath. "When I left, Jonah Kingsley was gripping Thursday's wrist. I couldn't hear the conversation, but their body language made it appear they were arguing."

I opened my mouth to ask more, but she shook her head. "I said I wanted to file it away. If we can get back to my crochet lesson and Lyla's party."

I apologized and dropped it. "Let me show you how to start the next row." I showed her how to make a chain stitch at the end of the row, turn her work, and start doing single crochets into the stitches of the preceding row.

She picked it up easily, and her hook began to move in an even rhythm. "You haven't mentioned the menu yet?"

"Menu?" I repeated.

"The lunch menu for Lyla's party. Now that the parents are going to be there, it might need some adjusting."

"Lunch? I thought we were just serving cupcakes."

"That's okay," she said, totally surprising me. "First times are always hard. I remember the first wedding I did." She explained how nervous she'd been and how she'd felt she had one chance to do it right. "There are no do-overs for events."

"What about pizza for lunch?" I suggested, but she nixed the idea. Every party had pizza, and the point of this was to have a party that was different. She looked around at the surroundings.

"You don't want anything too messy or with too strong a smell." Then her face lit up. "Finger sandwiches. Fruit pieces with toothpicks. Maybe some carrot sticks with hummus. Lyla will love it. So sophisticated."

I let out a sigh of relief with that settled. No problem. I would be able to give Laurie Jean a job faster than I had thought. "You need to pick out the kind of cupcakes you want," I said and handed her the list I'd been carrying around.

Emerson chose the basic yellow cake with buttercream icing.

"Lyla is very excited about her birthday party," Emerson said, glancing at her daughter. "She loves the idea of learning how to crochet. I should warn you that once the party is over, I bet she tries talking you into starting a kids' group."

An interesting thought and one Mrs. Shedd would jump on. We'd sell more yarn and supplies, and kids were always hungry, so the café would get more business.

"Strike that. Not a kids' group. Change it to young adult group," Emerson corrected. "She hates it when I call her a kid. The writers' group was a wonderful idea. She spent a lot of time picking out her journal. I think she has a crush on the leader, oops, I mean facilitator. You have to watch everything you say today. When I met Ben, he corrected me." Emerson got to the end of the row of her swatch and looked at me. I repeated the instructions I'd given her at the end of the first row, and she was already doing it before I finished explaining.

"I had this feeling I'd seen him before, but I couldn't place it until he brushed back his hair and I saw the birthmark on the side of his face," Emerson said. I was only half-listening, thinking about the finger sandwiches Laurie Jean would make. No peanut butter and jelly; we'd have them English tea–style. Egg salad, cucumber and watercress. "I was so surprised when I realized where I'd seen him." What Emerson said next cut through my mind fog and made me sit up abruptly. "Even though he kept denying it, I know he was at the Fields-Kingsley wedding."

"What? Who are you talking about?" I asked to make sure I was getting it right.

"Ben Sherman, the writer facilitator." She looked me in the eye to make sure I understood. "He was one of the servers in those white shirts you seemed so concerned about."

What? The person Thursday claimed not to know, even though I'd seen them talking together twice, was a server at her wedding. I couldn't wait to tell Dinah. We'd be doing some Sherlock and Watson investigating for sure.

CHAPTER 21

WHEN THE MOTHER-DAUGHTER TEAM LEFT, ADELE and I went to the café for a break. I got a coffee and one of Bob's baked oatmeal squares. They were delicious and almost counted as real food rather than a sweet snack. Adele took out one of her diet powders and sprinkled it in a glass of water. The greenish brown powder slowly descended in the water, turning it a pond color as it did.

Finally, she stirred it and took a sip. She didn't make a face, so I guessed the taste was better than the color. But she also didn't seem to be enjoying it, and more than once looked toward my oatmeal square as she grumbled that I hadn't consulted with her before I agreed to include the parents in the party.

I didn't want to remind her that the crochet-themed parties were my idea, and Mrs. Shedd had told me to handle

them. Adele was just supposed to help with the actual crochet lessons.

She took another gulp of the drink and looked back at
the glass and then at the envelope it came in. "It says all
natural ingredients, but does that mean it's safe? Cyanide
occurs naturally in apricot pits," Adele said.

"Why don't you ask Dr. Chopin Wheel," I said, reminding her of the author event that evening. "He's one of those
alternative medicine guys."

"Pink, that's an excellent idea," she said, dumping out
the contents of the glass. I let her go on into the bookstore
ahead of me. Bob made another pitch for the birthday cookie
as I went by. I had to give him credit for his persistence.

I started putting out the folding chairs for the event and
glanced out the window that faced Ventura. As darkness
was settling, the sky had turned a soft translucent blue. I
wasn't worried about the turnout. Dr. Wheel was like a rock
star in the world of alternative medicine, and I knew he'd
draw a crowd.

I'd done this so many times—it was almost automatic. I
set up a table at the front with a display of his latest book
and had all his others displayed nearby. For the event, Bob
brought in pots of Dr. Wheel's special oolong tea and chia
seed crackers. When I was worried about the turnout for
an event, I always talked the Hookers into coming. Not tonight. Sheila was the only one who showed up, and that was
completely on her own.

Sheila was always looking for some new help for her
anxiety.

The seats were all full by the time Dr. Wheel came in
with his handler. It was funny to see the handler dressed
in business attire, escorting the man wearing loose dark-

wash blue jeans and a teal blue T-shirt. The escort had neatly trimmed dark hair, while Dr. Wheel's was mostly gray and done in a long braid. There was a soft roundness to his body, and he had a glowing smile only partially hidden by his neatly trimmed gray moustache. He wore a bunch of bracelets made from different stones, which I knew from his book were supposed to have healing properties. I think the silver-and-turquoise necklace was just for looks. Despite his hectic travel schedule, he seemed mellow, which made you think maybe there was something to his theories.

I noticed that Adele had slipped into the first row, right in the middle. Since she seemed confident that she wouldn't be seeing Leonora, she'd jazzed her outfit up a bit with a necklace she had crocheted out of silver wire and colorful clay beads, and a natural-color beanie-style hat with a row of bluish lavender flowers.

I'd barely introduced Dr. Wheel when Adele's hand shot up. His smile was warm as he nodded for her to speak. It was times like this that I wished we had a big hook so we could grab Adele by the arm and take her out of the picture. But all I could do was cringe as she popped out of her seat, faced the crowd, and began to ask about the diet powder. "I'm asking this for all of you," she said in her this-is-important tone of voice.

"I was actually going to take questions at the end," Dr. Wheel said, "but I'm also not one of those people with a rigid plan." He walked over to Adele, took the envelope of powder, put on a pair of half-glasses and began to read it over.

"The ingredients listed on here are all considered safe," he began. But he cautioned that since the ingredients were imported, they weren't always trustworthy. "You don't always know what you're getting." Adele's eyes opened wider as he mentioned that there had been a problem in the past with that company. Though he said the product had since been discontinued, a banned substance had been found in one of their products that had been linked to the deaths of some consumers.

A rumble of conversation went through the crowd. "I'm glad that——" and he looked toward Adele to identify herself. As soon as she gave her name, he added it to his spiel while gesturing for her to sit down. "I'm glad that Adele brought this powder up. I am a bit of a renegade in that I tell people not to take supplements. I think you should get your vitamin D from some safe sun exposure, your vitamin C from oranges, and, of course, we can't forget all those antioxidants you get from a daily dose of chocolate."

The crowd loved what he was saying because as he pointed out, it was all easily accessible and cheaper than pills and potions. He went on about a few cures like ginger candy for an acidy stomach and tart cherry juice for arthritis. He didn't just talk to the crowd, he interacted with them, asking about their problems and then bringing up how various chapters in his book had just the information they needed.

When someone asked how to beat the blues, the friendly-looking doctor smiled. "One of the best cures is laughter. I have a whole chapter on busting a bad mood. It includes my list of go-to movies. They're all comedies and available on DVD." Then he let several people express issues they had without his offering a solution.

"What I'm hearing from you, and what I know to be the basis of most problems, is stress. I have devoted a whole chapter to a solution so elegant, it makes me smile every time I think of it."

Someone shouted out from the crowd in a tired voice. "I know. It's all about meditation. But do you know how stressful it is to try to meditate?"

Dr. Wheel nodded in acknowledgment. "I do mention meditation, but without the stress." He stopped talking, and I thought he was going to leave it at that, just a tease to get people to buy his book. But it turned out just to be a pause to build up the tension.

I heard Adele yelp when she saw what he took out of his shoulder satchel. He held up a wooden hook and a ball of undyed cotton yarn. "In case any of you don't recognize this, it's a crochet hook that I carved myself," he said, showing it off. "The store-bought ones come in all different materials, but I like wood the best." He went on to explain how easy crochet was to learn and that his book included a basic lesson and directions for what he called a meditation washcloth. The point was that working on it made meditation easy. All you had to do was focus on the movement of your hook.

Adele's eyes were shining with adoration, and when someone asked why not knitting, I thought she was going to swoon when he gave his answer. "I personally find knitting stressful. All that worry that you're going to drop a stitch or make a mistake. Mistakes in crochet are easy to fix, so there's no worry about making them. I start with the most basic easy pattern. You can just keep repeating that or move to more challenging ones."

He laid out a whole series of meditation washcloths in different colors and variations of stitches. "And you can clean your face with them when you're done. How often is something so win-win. And in the case of weight loss," he looked at Adele, "so often stress is the basis for eating problems.

So instead of eating a bag of potato chips, make a potato chip scarf." In sync with what he said, he pulled out a long cappuccino-colored ruffly scarf that did indeed resemble a stack of chips.

Adele popped back out of her seat and said she couldn't agree more. I was concerned she was going to turn it into a personal conversation with him, so I stepped in and used my arm as a hook to remove her.

She started to fuss until I told her I needed her help with the signing. While he took questions, I set up the signing table. When Dr. Wheel took his seat there, Adele positioned herself next to him, opening the books to the signing page, so all he had to do was write his name. I'd never seen Adele so gushy, but Dr. Wheel seemed to appreciate her help and complimented her when she showed off her crocheted necklace. There was worship in her eyes as she gazed at him, and when there was a lull in people she leaned closer. "I'd love to talk crochet with you later," she said in a seductive voice.

By now she was acting flirty with the washcloths, naming the stitches in the more complicated one and bragging about all the stitches she knew and could teach him. But a sudden pause in the background din of conversation caught my attention and out of the corner of my eye, I saw people parting to make way for someone.

None other than Eric Humphries came striding through the crowd in full motor cop uniform, right down to the shiny black shoes with boot tops. He was a head taller than most people in the crowd, and his barrel chest and ramrod-straight posture made him even more imposing. In his hand he held something that looked like a pair of bright-colored crocheted mittens. His gaze moved over the top of the crowd and then focused on Adele, who was holding one of the washcloths as she leaned on the table and talked to Dr. Wheel. Eric's expression went from upset to horrified. He held up the striped tubes in front of Adele. "These were on the handles of my motorcycle. Do you want to explain?"

The way Eric's eyes were flitting back and forth between the crocheted mittens and Dr. Wheel, I had the feeling his question had taken on a new meaning.

Adele stood up with a dramatic sigh. "Eric, I wasn't expecting you to stop in," she said. "How can you even think I'm the yarn bomber? I wasn't the one taken into custody at the mall." She waved her arm in my direction.

"Maybe we should talk about this outside," Eric said, glancing back at Dr. Wheel. Adele told her boyfriend to go on ahead and that she'd be out there in a minute.

With Eric on his way out the door, she turned back to our author guest. "I will treasure these few moments we spent together. I hope I didn't give you the wrong impression when I accepted your heartfelt offer of one of your handmade hooks. I can only accept it if it comes with no strings attached."

CHAPTER 22

IT HAD BEEN QUITE A DAY, AND FOR ONCE THERE was no circus going on at my house when I got home after the Dr. Wheel event. Thursday had left a note saying she'd gone out, but had let the dogs out and fed all the animals. She'd also left a pot holder she'd crocheted. Samuel's room was dark.

I let the dogs out in the yard again, anyway. Cosmo bounded out and rushed off into the dark yard to chase something in the bushes, but as usual, Blondie had to be coaxed outside. The two cats looked longingly toward the dark yard, but I only let them out during the day when I could watch them.

Since I had gotten some of Dr. Wheel's special oolong tea, I measured out some of the loose leaves into a tea strainer. They were certainly different-looking, long and thin, almost like tiny twigs. I was about to add the hot water when the phone rang, startling me. The robotic voice announced it was Dinah.

"I heard there was some excitement at the bookstore. I was going to come to the reading. Now I'm sorry I missed it. Sheila called me, but she was kind of sketchy on the details. So spill," she said in a merry tone.

I told her about Dr. Wheel's love of crochet and how Adele was all over him when her boyfriend showed up. "Eric was upset to begin with. The yarn bomber put some mittens on his motorcycle handles. Apparently he had left it parked outside when he went into Le Grande Fromage, and when he came out, the handlebars weren't bare anymore. You could see where he would think it was Adele," I said. "And then to see her leaning all over Dr. Wheel."

"I bet Adele loved it," Dinah said.

"Not the yarn-bombing accusation, but I think she enjoyed giving her speech to Dr. Wheel with an audience." I told Dinah the details of it.

"I'm sorry I missed that. No one can do drama like Adele. Do you think Dr. Wheel really liked her?" Dinah asked.

"Who knows? Maybe," I said. "I got the answer about the shirt." I told her what Emerson had said about people bringing a spare one. "And there's more. She told me that Ben Sherman, the person I saw Thursday talking to twice who she claims not to know, worked as one of the servers at the wedding."

"The writing teacher?" Dinah said.

"Right, and there's more besides. Emerson said she saw what seemed like an argument between Thursday and her late groom at the wedding reception just before she left."

I heard Dinah suck in her breath. "That doesn't sound good. Are you going to talk to Thursday about it?"

I said I'd hoped to, but Thursday wasn't home. "I'm not sure how I could ask her about any of it anyway without it seeming like I thought she was guilty of something. And she would probably just deny knowing Ben again. Claim it was a coincidence that he worked at the wedding."

"What about talking to Mason?" Dinah suggested.

"No way. It would be a lose-lose thing. He'd be upset that I was implying anything about his daughter. And remember, he's a criminal attorney, so he'd just say something like it was all a misunderstanding."

"What about telling Barry?" Dinah said.

Dinah couldn't see it through the phone, but I was shaking my head vehemently. It didn't matter that he and I had a personal relationship. He would handle the information as Barry the homicide detective. "I'd only do that if I knew for sure . . ." I let my voice trail off. I couldn't even say the possibility out loud.

Dinah realized I was right and started saying it was an impossible situation, but I stopped her.

"I have an idea. Maybe Thursday won't admit to knowing Ben, but how about we switch it around? We could see if Ben would admit to knowing Thursday." I finally added the hot water to the tea and let it start steeping. "Even though I really hope there is some other explanation. Aside from her being Mason's daughter, I like her."

"I know, and she's the first person you taught how to crochet." Dinah started to add the part that Barry had said about just because you liked somebody didn't mean they couldn't be a killer.

"I got it," I said, cutting her off and going back to my plan for approaching Ben. "I found out from Mrs. Shedd where Ben works as a waiter. I say we show up at the restaurant and see what we can find out."

"I like it," Dinah said. Before we signed off, we made arrangements to meet the next evening, and I made my way across the house and fell into bed.

THE NEXT MORNING AS I DROVE TO THE BOOK-store, I was thinking about how Dinah and I would handle Ben. But the subject ended as soon as I walked in Shedd & Royal Books and More and remembered that everything had been left out from the night before. I went into the event area, prepared to break down the setup. Adele was sitting next to the signing table, crocheting. When she looked up, I saw the upset in her eyes.

"He gave me this," she said, holding up a wooden hook. "He carved it himself." She stopped and ran her fingers along the smooth surface. "Pink, what am I going to do? I thought Eric was the yin for my yang, but Chopin is my crochet soul mate. Eric doesn't understand. He accused me of being the yarn bomber, as if it was something terrible. Chopin looked upon spreading the word of crochet as something of honor."

"Are you the yarn bomber?" I asked.

"Of course not. I'm just saying that if I was, Eric wouldn't understand." She took out the colorful mittens that had been on Eric's motorcycle handles. I took a moment to look them over because it was a chance to see the yarn bomber's work up close. They were nicely crocheted in a variety of different colors.

"I wonder if this is a clue," I said, pointing to what

appeared to be the letter P done as surface crochet in a series of chain stitches on one of them. Adele looked at it with new interest and seemed upset with herself that she hadn't noticed.

I started to fold up the chairs and put them on a cart to be rolled into the back storage room. Adele had set aside the crochet-bomber pieces and put a little shopping bag on the table. "Thanks to Chopin, I see the light. No more of this diet stuff for me. I'm sticking with the crochet plan."

It turned out she had another plan, too. She wanted to take the diet powder back to Elise for a refund. Apparently, while Leonora had ordered it for her, Adele had to pay for it.

"I thought I'd bring it along when we go over to her place to see the kits she's made up," Adele said. "You could back me up. You heard what Chopin said about some problems with that company in the past."

What had I gotten myself into? But I agreed to take Adele with me to Elise's because I thought that with Adele's crochet mania, she could tell if the kits were complete. We were also going to Rhoda's to see some sample projects she'd come up with.

Adele got up and helped me with the chairs and with putting together a display based on Dr. Wheel's appearance. Little by little, we'd started putting displays together that were more than books. Adele and I arranged one with his latest book in the center, surrounded by some of the dark chocolate he'd mentioned and an array of hooks and cotton yarn. Adele had already crocheted several of his meditation washcloths and added them to the display. Of course, she rushed off to the computer and made up a sign saying who'd made them.

As we finished putting it together, she touched one of the

cloths tenderly. "It's like a connection between us," she said wistfully.

I really didn't want to get twisted up in Adele's social life, but at the same time I hated to see her mess up something good. As we drove to Elise's, I tried to get her to see that she should let go of her infatuation with Dr. Wheel and stick with the bird in the hand, Eric.

"Pink, you're so wise," she said in an over-the-top dramatic tone. I almost choked. Had she just given me a compliment? "You're right, I should just accept the moment Chopin and I had and let it go. I'll always have this," she said, showing off the hook again.

Elise lived in a development called Brae Mar. The houses were on twisty roads that ran along the slopes of the Santa Monica Mountains. They had great views of the Valley, but paid the price by having steep yards that were mostly unusable.

Elise was waiting for us. One of the features of houses like hers was they had an upstairs den. She'd turned hers into a combination crochet room and supply room for her side business. The health-products side of the room had stacks of boxes and a long table she used to put together the orders. The yarn side had bins of yarn arranged by color, though one bin was a hodgepodge with single skeins. She also had a wall unit she'd turned into a shrine to Anthony, the fictional vampire who crocheted, with all the books, samples of all her vampire-style crochet projects, and a life-size cardboard cutout of Hugh Jackman, who'd played the part in the movie. CeeCee had been in the film, and she'd gotten the cutout signed for Elise. I walked over to admire the display, but Elise suddenly stepped in front of me and ushered me over to a long table she'd set up.

"I made up a couple of sample kits for you to pick from," she said in her wispy voice. Between the voice and her fly-away frizzle of brown wavy hair, she gave the impression of being a bit scattered. I looked through the kits. She had used different types of tote bags and varied the contents accordingly. At one end of the spectrum, there was a small bag made of recycled plastic bottles with just a skein of yarn and a hook, and at the other, an unbleached cloth tote that had "Lyla's Birthday" written in pink glitter glue across the front and was outfitted with yarn, a hook, scissors, tapestry needle for weaving in the ends, and a small ruler that measured gauge. There were several levels of tote bags in between.

Adele was being no help and wasn't even looking at the samples, so I started to point out the most basic one, when I saw that Adele was pulling out the small shopping bag from her own large cloth tote. She laid it on the table and pushed it toward Elise.

"Molly will tell you why I'm bringing this back."

Elise turned to me, and I gave Adele an annoyed stare. My idea of helping her bring the stuff back was just being there as moral support, not doing the dirty work. I explained about Dr. Wheel's appearance and that Adele wanted to stick to using crochet as a weight-loss tool because it had only good side effects.

I could see resistance building up in Elise. Adele must have seen it too because she stepped in front of me and took over. "I know that some people died because of some products from this company. I'm not taking any chances." She pushed the shopping bag closer to Elise.

Elise merely pushed it back toward Adele. "I'm sorry, I can't take it back. You'll have to take it up with the company directly." Elise's voice didn't have a trace of its usual flighty quality and was all business. "I'm sorry," she said again, softening a little, "but I can't take it back. It's company policy." Adele didn't take this well and went storming toward the door. I told Elise I wanted to talk to Emerson about the prices of the kits, and I'd let her know.

"They're up in Chatsworth," Elise said as she walked us to the door. Adele wanted to go right there, but I insisted we stop at Rhoda's first.

I hadn't realized it before, but Rhoda lived across the street from Emerson. Only instead of living in a town house, Rhoda and Hal had a small stucco house that looked like it had been built in the 1950s, which was old by Tarzana standards.

Like Rhoda, her house was straightforward. She took us into the small den where she kept her yarn and supplies. There were no plastic bags of yarn lying around or hooks hiding under chairs. She had everything arranged neatly in a cabinet with doors that closed.

Adele seemed distracted as she followed behind me, and I knew her mind was on taking back the diet stuff. Rhoda brought out several projects and set them out on the coffee table.

She had a beanie all done in single crochet, a flower pin and a skinny scarf. None of them were too exciting. I picked up the skinny scarf while Adele told Rhoda about Dr. Wheel's appearance. I described the ruffly potato chip scarf and said it was too bad we couldn't do something like that.

Rhoda's face lit up. "I'll work on it." Rhoda offered us something to drink, but Adele was so anxious to take back the diet stuff, she had one foot out the door. I declined and we stood by the door making small talk for a few minutes.

"I didn't realize you lived across the street from Emerson,"

I said, pointing out the front bay window toward Emerson's town house. *Across the street* was a loose term. It was more like catty-corner, and the wide street between them had two lanes in each direction.

Rhoda seemed surprised. "I wonder if she's the one I heard about," Rhoda muttered. "There was some kind of scandal, but I can't remember what it was."

Emerson with a scandal? It didn't seem likely. All the town houses looked the same, so I was sure that Rhoda was wrong.

"C'mon Pink," Adele said, moving to the door. "We have to go if we're going to get back to the bookstore on time." What Adele left out was that she'd planned a side trip first.

It was pointless to suggest that Adele return her stuff some other time or go on her own. She'd only make a fuss. The most efficient thing to do was just to go there and get it done.

Chatsworth was in the northwest corner of the San Fernando Valley. There were some ranches and big properties, and also an industrial area. I'd been there before when I'd gone to talk to Paxton Cline, the fired best man. Adele had gotten directions from Elise and was telling me where to turn. I was surprised when we ended up on the same street the yarn company was on.

"There it is," Adele said, grabbing the shopping bag and getting out of the car. I suggested that I wait in the car, but she insisted she needed me for backup. "You heard what Chopin said about how you could never be sure what was really in these products, no matter what the label said."

Adele took the lead and I reluctantly followed her. My plan was just to stand there and let her do her thing. It was only when we got to the double doors that I realized where we were. This was the building Paxton Cline had pointed out. This was the building where Jonah Kingsley had worked in the family business. I looked at the placard on the wall. It said Kingsley Enterprises, Inc., and below that the names of their divisions. One of them was MRX Health Products.

I was suddenly much more interested. Inside, there was a reception area with some seats and a table full of brochures and information about the company. The wall was lined with black-and-white photos. Adele went to the counter and set her bag on it. Before the young woman at the desk got to the counter, Adele was already doing her spiel.

I hadn't thought about what the Kingsleys' family business was until now. *Enterprises* could mean anything.

It was taking a while for Adele to get her story out, particularly since she had launched into telling the woman that if the company really wanted to make something that helped people, they'd make crochet kits. The woman looked as if she was waiting for Adele to take a breath so she could jump in and refuse the return.

I began to look over the photographs with new interest. I recognized Jackson Kingsley with his even-featured good looks. He was standing with another man, both in white coats, holding some dark bottles. Underneath, there was a caption saying it was their first product. Kingsley was much younger, but still recognizable. I started to gloss over the man standing next to him, but then I looked again. How could he possibly look familiar? The more I stared, the more I was sure that I'd seen him somewhere before.

I interrupted Adele and asked the receptionist who was in that photograph.

She gave me a suspicious look. I didn't really blame her.

It must seem rather odd to have Adele raising a fuss about one of their products and then me wanting to know the identity of someone in a photograph on the wall.

"That's Mr. Kingsley, the CEO, president and chairman of the board of Kingsley Enterprises." She seemed to want to leave it at that, but I pressed her about the man next to him.

"His name is Felix Rooten."

"What does he do?" I asked. She seemed even more hesitant to answer. "I'm not exactly sure. I think he was in charge of products."

"I wonder if I could talk to him?" I said. The woman swallowed a few times as if her throat had grown dry.

"Maybe I should get someone else to speak to both of you," she said, backing away and disappearing into what I imagined was a warren of offices.

I was surprised to see a familiar blond woman come toward us. Margo Kingsley. She didn't seem to recognize me and looked at both Adele and me with an arched eyebrow.

"This is our VP in charge of customer service," the receptionist said. Adele spoke first. She just cut to the chase and said she wanted to return the unopened products. The latest Mrs. Kingsley looked past her to me and asked what I wanted. I didn't think my connection to Thursday would help either Adele or me, so I didn't bring it up.

"I thought I recognized someone in one of the photos on the wall. I can't place where I know him from. I thought if I could pop in to his office and say hello, I could figure it out," I said.

The receptionist leaned in to Mrs. Kingsley. Her eyes went to the photo as she did. Mrs. Kingsley's expression darkened.

"I'm sorry, but Mr. Rooten doesn't work here anymore."

Their manner had gotten my curiosity fired up, so I didn't leave it at that. I asked if they knew where I could reach him. Mrs. VP of Customer Service pursed her lips in hesitation, then must have decided just to be direct.

"I'm afraid nowhere. Mr. Rooten is dead."

CHAPTER 23

"WHO IS FELIX ROOTEN?" I ASKED. I HEARD A chuckle come through the phone.

"How about a little small talk first, Sunshine?" Mason said. I guess I had been a little abrupt. It was just that it was really bugging me that not only had Felix looked familiar and I couldn't place him, but now he was dead. Words tumbled out of my mouth as I tried to explain my trip to Kingsley Enterprises. I'd called Mason as soon as Adele and I had gotten back to the bookstore. I didn't like to make personal calls from work, so to make up for it, I busied myself in the yarn department, looking at the samples of the different kits Elise had given me while I talked to Mason. He had access to all kinds of Internet search stuff and people who knew how to use it, so I figured he could help me.

"You went there? Why?" I began to tell him the whole story about Dr. Wheel and Adele wanting to return the diet stuff. "I had no idea what their business was." Mason was taking it all in without saying a word, though he started to laugh when I got to the part where Adele suddenly seemed to have a mission beyond returning the diet products.

"I should have some information about this Rooten guy in a few minutes." He explained he'd already passed it on to one of his assistants. "It's good to talk to you," he said and continued on about how much he'd enjoyed our lunch. "It finally feels like things are getting back to normal. In no time, Thursday will be living in her own place, and Jaimee will get on with her *Housewives* show, and we can get back to having fun." He let it hang in the air. I looked at the three sample kits I had chosen to show Emerson. "Are you still there?" he said after a moment. "I was expecting you to make some kind of comment about the prospect of us having fun."

"It sounds good," I said.

"Why wait? How about tonight. I have to go to a charity dinner. It would be easier to stomach the rubber chicken and the rounds of speeches and awards if you were there."

I'd gone with him to something similar in the past, and it had been fun, but Dinah and I had sleuthing plans. So I tried to say no without telling him why. There was no way he would take it well that I was questioning what his daughter had said.

"Dinah and I made plans to have an evening together."

"That's fine. Just bring her along," he said. I wasn't expecting that and didn't have an answer at first. Then I said that neither of us wanted to have to get dressed up and hoped he'd drop it. But he didn't. Suddenly he turned into Mason the Interrogator.

Where were Dinah and I going? What time were we

meeting? I tried to laugh it off. "You almost sound like you don't believe me," I said finally.

Mason let down his defenses. "Sorry, I just thought you might be meeting the detective."

"If I was, I would tell you. Remember, we're all just friends."

Mason let out a laugh. "Is that what he's saying? At least I'm up front with my intentions."

Inwardly, I sighed. Being able to keep both Barry and Mason at arm's length might have just been wishful thinking on my part.

"I've always said you and I are after the same thing. A casual relationship not leading to anything more," Mason continued.

"But I like things just the way they are now. I can go out with Dinah or whoever and not have to answer to anyone."

"I'm a patient man, Sunshine. I know you'll come around." I thought he was going to say good-bye, but instead he told me he had the information on Felix Rooten. "I don't see anything here that shows how your paths would have crossed," Mason said.

He read me the notes his assistant had made. "Felix Rooten was the product supervisor at Kingsley Industries for a long time." Mason made a surprised sound. "No gold watch for him. I'm surprised they have his picture. He was convicted of embezzling from the company and went to jail."

"Well, I couldn't have seen him at the wedding, that's for sure," I said.

"Excuse me," a voice said behind me. "I really need some help with this sock yarn."

"Do you want to know the rest of it?" Mason asked.

"It'll have to wait," I said, turning to a woman holding several skeins of yarn. "I have a customer."

DINAH WAS WAITING OUTSIDE THE BOOKSTORE when I finished my day. She was bristling with energy and excitement. "You have no idea how I need this. My freshmen class is particularly bad this semester. They're all addicted to their phones. I insist they turn them off, but they still need to have them in view." Dinah had on a camel-colored blazer over some black jeans. It looked like she'd re-gelled her short salt-and-pepper hair into the spiky style that gave her a contemporary fun look.

I looked down at my outfit and suddenly felt underdressed. I was still in my work clothes. As usual, I was wearing khaki-colored pants and a shirt. Today's was a teal blue, and I had added a crocheted cowl in a complementary shade of blue.

In anticipation of the evening chill, I'd brought along a shawl in beautiful shades of blues, greens and lavenders that Sheila had made for me.

"C'mon, Watson, time to talk to Ben and see what we can find out."

"What's the name of the restaurant where he works?" Dinah said as we walked to the greenmobile.

"You don't know what I had to do to get the information out of Mrs. Shedd," I said. "Apparently he gave the Storybook Cabaret as a reference, but said he didn't want anyone to know he worked there. I can see his point. Just like not wanting to admit to working as a robo server at the wedding. I'm sure he tells people that his profession is writer not waiter."

"But he's working in a public place. It's pretty hard to stay incognito," Dinah said. We got into the car and I headed down Ventura Boulevard to Sherman Oaks.

Neither of us had been to the Storybook Cabaret, and we weren't sure what to expect as I handed my car over to a valet. I remembered the place as being an old-time supper club, but the freestanding building had been redone to look like a castle, complete with a drawbridge over an inky-looking moat. Inside it was dark and noisy. A woman dressed like Alice in Wonderland was manning the reception booth.

Before I could speak, Alice asked if we had a reservation. When I said no, she gave me an ominous shake of her head and said there was a two-hour wait. I looked around the interior of the restaurant hoping to catch sight of Ben, checking each male face that went by with a tray. He wasn't the Great Gatsby, Prince Charming or Tom Sawyer. But in my sweep, I noticed the bar.

"How long for the bar?" I asked Alice.

"Immediate seating," she said, holding out her arm in a welcoming gesture.

"It'll give us a chance to figure something out," I said as we walked along the edge of the restaurant to the long bar. We went to the far end, away from the other people seated there.

"Food or just liquid refreshment?" the bartender said in a strangely formal tone as he approached us. I glanced at him. The lighting was very dim, but he appeared nice-looking in a model sort of way. He was dressed in a black shirt and black slacks. Without waiting for our answer, he stepped closer to the bar. "We're having a special on Bloody Marys," he said with a strange emphasis on the bloody part. His face was caught in the light coming from the recessed lamps in the ceiling, and it began to sparkle with iridescence.

"You're in a costume, too," I blurted out. "I didn't notice at first. But who are you supposed to be?"

He let down the aura he'd been trying to project and took something out of his shirt pocket. The recessed lighting glinted off a crochet hook, and he had a pretty sad-looking swatch of red yarn coming off it. "I told them, even with the fish-scale powder it was too subtle." He gestured toward his sparkly face. "I'm supposed to be Anthony, the vampire who crochets," he said before reeling off the titles of the books in the series. I stopped him and told him we were familiar with the books and that I worked in a bookstore. He instantly seemed to relax.

I turned to Dinah. "I wonder if Elise knows about him," I said. The bartender overheard. "If you mean Elise Belmont, she's been here, a lot. She even made this for me, though management said it isn't part of his official costume." From below the bar, he produced a long black-and-white striped scarf with a bloodred tassel. I asked him if he knew how to crochet.

"Anthony" rolled his eyes and said no. "This is just a job until I get my big break. I'm reading for a new sitcom next week," he said, letting go of the weird speech pattern. We both ordered boozeless Bloody Marys, and he gave us a basket of peanuts to go with them.

"Do you know a waiter named Ben?" I said as Prince Charming brought a tray of food to some people at the end of the bar. The bartender surveyed the restaurant and pointed in a discreet manner. I almost choked when I saw which of the costumed waiters he'd pointed out. Now I understood why Ben wasn't worried about being recognized. He was dressed as Pinocchio, complete with the pointy hat, shorts, tunic and long nose. Dinah and I exchanged stifled grins, thinking of how serious he was at the bookstore.

"I wonder if his nose will grow if he doesn't tell the truth," Dinah said under her breath.

"Could you call him over?" I asked the bartender. "I'd like to say hello." The bartender shrugged and waved Pinocchio over. When Ben saw it was me, his eyes got big.

"Ben, I know it's you," I said. Though to be honest, if "Anthony" hadn't pointed him out I don't think I would have.

"Ah, hello, Mrs. Pink," Ben said with a look of doom. "I hope this doesn't make you change your mind about adding the adult writing group. I assure you, nobody knows it's me."

"I'm not here to out you," I said. "I had Anthony here call you over because I want to order some food to go for my houseguest, Thursday Fields Kingsley." I watched him for a reaction, and there was a long pause as if he was thinking about something. I didn't wait for him to come up with an answer. "I know you worked as a server at her wedding."

"Right," he said, "I did work that wedding." He looked up at me, almost poking me with the long nose. "I'd appreciate it if you wouldn't mention either of my jobs to anyone. They're only temporary. Like I told you, I have a bunch of things in the works, and if I get a go on anything I have out there, then this all ends." He made a sweeping glance across the restaurant. "But in the meantime . . ." He handed me a menu.

Before I opened it, I tried to get the subject back to Thursday and asked him if he knew her.

"I just do my job and never pay much attention to the guests."

"So I guess that means no," I said, and he nodded in agreement.

"I'd love to stay and chat, but . . ." He pointed to the menu he'd handed me before giving "Tom Sawyer" a nervous glance. "For now, I need this job and I'm getting the evil eye from my boss. So if you could order the food."

I looked down at the menu. "I think I'll get Thursday a burger. I wonder which one I should get," I said, noting that there was a long list of them. By now, Ben was in a hurry to get back to his station. He tapped his finger on one at the bottom, and I ordered it to go.

"I guess that was a bust," Dinah said a little while later as we walked across the drawbridge to the street. The smell of the burger and fairy-tale fries wafted up from the to-go box I was carrying.

"Not at all. Ben tipped his hand. No matter what he says, he knows Thursday very well," I said, not able to contain my smile. While we waited for the valet to bring the greenmobile around, I opened the food container and lifted the bun. Dinah still didn't get it until I explained that Thursday had been very quiet about her food choices; even her father didn't know she was a vegetarian.

"But Ben knew to get her a veggie burger," Dinah said. "Excellent work, Sherlock!"

"Yes and no," I said. "It doesn't make me happy to know they're lying. And it's one thing to know they know each other, but it's another thing to prove it."

CHAPTER 24

"WHEN WERE YOU GOING TO TELL ME ABOUT PAX-ton Cline?" Barry asked.

"What?" I said, looking up startled by Barry's sudden appearance and his question. It was the next day, and I was working in the yarn department, putting away some yarn that had come in. Truth be told, I was lost in admiring the gorgeous shades of pumpkin, rust and brown as I separated the skeins into their own sections.

As I set down the yarn, Barry repeated the question. I checked his expression. There was definitely an edge to it.

"How did you find out about him?" I said, disgruntled. I had been so proud of how I had found the dropped best man, but didn't want to turn the information over to Barry until I had more evidence. Barry stopped, closed his eyes in resignation.

"You've been hanging around me too much—answering a question with a question," he said.

"Actually, I learned it from *The Average Joe's Guide to Criminal Investigation*. Remember, you didn't used to share information about cases." I hadn't even thought about it, but just automatically answered that way. I was so pleased with myself, I wanted to give myself a high five.

Barry muttered some disparaging remarks about the book I viewed as my own personal bible when it came to learning sleuthing. "We're getting off the subject," he said. "Or was that your plan?" I was relieved to see he was cracking a smile. I looked closer and saw he had a five o'clock shadow. His tie was pulled tight, and he was wearing his suit jacket, but his shirt showed some wrinkles.

"You've been up all night, haven't you?"

"That's beside the point," he said. "So, you still haven't answered my question."

"And you haven't answered any of mine," I said. I moved a skein of rust-colored yarn away from the edge of the table. "Your question was really more a rhetorical one, while mine was a real question. And your answer would be much more interesting. It's a chance for me to see behind the curtain of your superior investigative skills."

Barry rolled his eyes. "You don't really think I'm going to fall for that, do you? I mean, you really laid it on thick. I just want to know why you didn't tell me about Paxton Cline."

"Okay," I said, finally capitulating. When all else fails, go with the truth. "I haven't found out much yet, and I wanted to have it all tied up before I gave it to you."

Barry had his arms folded now and was looking at me

out of the corner of his eye, as if he didn't quite believe me. "So then, why not just tell me what you know." His tone had lightened into something almost playful.

This was a whole new-and-improved Barry as far as I was concerned. I liked that he seemed to value what I had to say.

"I know that Paxton was supposed to be the best man, but something happened and Jonah changed his mind and gave the job to someone else. Paxton said he was at a baseball game when Jonah got killed," I said.

"Do you know why Jonah fired him as best man?"

I shrugged. "We didn't get that far. That could be an understatement. He denied even knowing Jonah Kingsley."

Barry seemed distressed that that was all I had.

"I know he lied," I said, "but he seems like such a nice guy and he works at his grandmother's yarn company."

Barry was rolling his eyes and shaking his head. "None of which exclude him from killing somebody."

"Did you find out why he got dropped as the best man?" I said.

Barry seemed to be contemplating whether to share. "It took a while to get him to admit that he knew Jonah Kingsley. But when I told Paxton I knew for a fact that he was supposed to be best man, he caved and admitted he knew the groom and was supposed to be best man. He apologized for lying about not knowing Jonah. He insisted he had nothing to do with Jonah's death and was just trying to stay out of the whole thing."

"That's what I thought," I said. "So then it doesn't matter that I didn't mention him to you."

"Not so fast," Barry said. "I'm just telling you what he said, not what is necessarily the truth, anymore than the reason he gave for his not being best man. He claimed it was all for financial reasons, but I have a source who said there was a big argument between Jonah and Paxton and that they'd almost started throwing punches. According to my source, Jonah told Paxton he didn't want him to be his best man."

"Did you confront Paxton with that information?" I asked.

Barry rolled his eyes at me. "What kind of detective do you think I am? Of course. I used all my tricks, but he wouldn't budge. He said there was no fight, that he and Jonah were just playing and insisted it all came down to his not wanting to spend the money on a tuxedo, hosting the bachelor party and the rest of the stuff that went with being best man."

"Except for one thing. If it was just about the money, and he was on such good terms with Jonah, why didn't he come to the wedding as a guest?"

"Very good, Molly. I asked him that very question. He didn't miss a beat and said he was embarrassed about having to step down from the position and thought it was better if he skipped the whole thing." Barry sighed. "I don't care what he says, I think he's a definite suspect. I think there was bad feeling between them. From the start, we've thought it was someone who wanted revenge. Maybe it was Paxton. He's a bland-looking guy and would have no problem blending in. How hard would it have been for him to find out about the servers' outfits?"

"But what about his alibi?"

"Molly, I can't believe you would fall for that. A baseball game, really? And by himself. Nancy Drew would be horrified."

"So, you arrested him?" I asked.

"I need some concrete evidence. We're combing through

all the photographs of the wedding, hoping to find one with him in it. Is there anything you've forgotten to tell me?"

"That sounds like you think I'm holding something back," I said.

Barry laughed at my response. "You've gotten way too good at not answering questions."

"I'm going to take that as a compliment," I said with a little smile of pride.

"Well, are you going to tell me how you found out about Paxton?" I said.

Barry mumbled something about how he shouldn't be encouraging me by giving me lessons. But I guess his pride in his skill won out because he explained, "I talked to the tuxedo-rental guy. The whole blowup between Jonah and Paxton happened when they went for a tuxedo fitting."

"Wow," I said impressed.

"I'm glad you approve," Barry said. He put on a stern expression. "Now don't keep information from me again. Ever hear of interfering with an investigation?" He patted the handcuffs on his belt and made a mock snap of them on my wrists.

"You wouldn't," I said, not sure if he was serious or not. He had his cop face on again, which was enigmatic, and I got it. He wasn't going to answer.

"DID YOU TELL BARRY ABOUT THURSDAY AND BEN?" Dinah said. The words were barely out of her mouth before she looked around with a worried expression. It was Saturday morning and she had come by since we both had the day off. The weather was soft and clear, and we'd brought our coffee outside.

I'd let the cats out for some yard time, and both dogs were lying in the grass soaking up the sun.

"I don't think she's up," I said, but even so I'd dropped my voice to a whisper. We both looked toward the house with our ears cocked. After hearing silence for a moment, I continued. "Tell Barry what? That I believe there's something going on between them based on a veggie burger? And there's no proof it has anything to do with the murder."

"You're really hanging onto that, aren't you?" Dinah said. I nodded and reminded her that Barry was focusing on Paxton as a suspect anyway.

She was about to say something more when we heard some noise coming from the kitchen.

Dinah abruptly changed the conversation to my encounter with Barry. "So how did you say good-bye?" my friend asked. When I didn't answer right away, she offered me a multiple choice of answers. Did we hug? Did we kiss? Did he give me a Great Aunt Gertie kind of kiss on the cheek or something better?

Dinah was laughing at my consternation as Thursday came outside and joined us.

I noticed her face was clouded over and wondered what it was in response to. She was dressed in jeans and a white T-shirt. Her short chestnut hair was still damp from her shower. It was her day off, too. "What a beautiful morning," she said, looking at the orange trees and then up at the sky.

Dinah nudged me. "Molly and I were just making plans for the day. You're welcome to join us." Dinah was living up to her Watson title by trying to snare Thursday into a day of us trying to get the truth out of her without her knowing it.

It didn't matter. Thursday declined. "Thanks for the offer, but I already have plans," she said.

"With your father?" I asked, but she shook her head. I got the same response when I asked if she was seeing her mother. "I suppose you're getting together with some of your friends," I offered. She seemed to hesitate. She had certainly learned how to avoid answering questions—a skill she had probably picked up from her lawyer father. If it had been me, I would have been blabbing all the details of what I was going to do. But then, I also never would have denied knowing Ben.

Trying to be subtle about it, I kept offering her answers, and when I suggested it might be connected with her search for an apartment, she finally nodded.

"That's it," she said. "I'm going to look at some places in Encino and Sherman Oaks." I noticed that she was looking away as she said it. "I can't keep accepting your hospitality forever." She headed back toward the kitchen, saying she was going to get a cup of coffee to take with her and go.

A few moments later, she came back out. I nudged Dinah and used my elbow to point to the gray hoodie that Thursday was carrying. Dinah nodded with recognition. The jacket meant that either Thursday was going someplace cooler, like the beach, or she was going to be gone for a long time, probably into evening, since it was too warm for a jacket at the present. Something was up.

Dinah and I traded glances. "Are you thinking what I am?" I said. "That a little ride might be nice?"

We rounded up the animals and took them inside. Quickly grabbing jackets and our bags, we rushed out to the driveway, just as Thursday was pulling her lime green Volkswagen bug away from the curb.

We jumped into Dinah's silver Honda, zoomed back out of the driveway and pulled into the street. Whenever we were shadowing somebody, we always took Dinah's car. It blended right in with the cars on the road, unlike the green-mobile, which stuck out.

I hung onto a shred of hope that Thursday was telling the truth when she said she was going to look at apartments. Some people always took a jacket, and she might have been reticent about answering questions because she'd been grilled so much lately. But when she got on the Ventura Freeway going away from Encino and Sherman Oaks, the shred of hope was gone.

We stayed several cars behind her and followed her when she got off at Las Virgenes Road and headed toward the mountains.

We zipped past some housing developments before the vista opened up into empty meadows with mountains as a backdrop. We left a car between us as the road began to go up and wind around between steep mountains and a drop-off to a creek. The view was now all jagged mountains and wilderness. We went through a tunnel and passed signs warning of falling rocks and deer crossings before we got to the place where we got our first panoramic view of the blue of the ocean dancing in the sunlight. As the road wound down, we passed the huge green lawn of Pepperdine University and were back in civilization with the beachfront mansions and fancy shops of Malibu.

We followed Thursday as she drove up Pacific Coast Highway. She passed an area of open beach and pulled to the side of the highway and parked. Dinah found a nearby parking spot, and we watched as Thursday got out of the car. The beach was big and relatively empty. She began crossing the sand toward the water.

"It looks like she's meeting somebody," I said, wishing

I'd brought binoculars. There was no choice; we had to get out of the car and follow her if we were going to see who she was meeting. Thursday seemed to feel confident she was unobserved as she walked toward a figure standing near the water.

I took out my smartphone and set it to camera as we followed at a safe distance. From the distance, I couldn't recognize who she was meeting. All I saw was that the person was wearing some kind of loose light-colored pants that flapped in the wind and a big floppy hat.

As Thursday got closer, she picked up speed and must have called out to them because I noticed the figure turning. Dinah and I were straining our eyes, and I had my smartphone ready to push the button.

When the floppy hat blew off, I knew right away who it was. Those unruly black curls were like a trademark. I was about to say something to Dinah when we both stopped in our tracks and just watched as Thursday threw herself into the arms of Ben Sherman.

"I guess she really does know him," Dinah said deadpan as they kissed.

I snapped a whole bunch of pictures with my smartphone. They seemed so involved with each other that it was easy for us to get close enough to grab clear shots of them together.

"Now what to do with them?" I said, looking at my phone as we headed back to the car. Dinah ran through the multiple choices. Show them to Mason, show them to Barry, show them to Thursday. None of them sounded good.

CHAPTER 25

"WHAT ARE YOU FIDGETING WITH?" MASON SAID
as I fiddled with my BlackBerry. The thing had a mind of
its own, and with no help from me was displaying the contents of its camera. I was trying to get the screen to go dark.
Mason had come by to take Thursday and me to Sunday
brunch, and we were standing in my living room waiting for
Thursday.

"Nothing," I said as I quickly put my smartphone in my
purse. I still hadn't done anything with the pictures of
Thursday and Ben, other than look at them numerous times
myself. I kept hoping that when I looked at them again, I'd
realize I'd followed the wrong person and that it was two
strangers in the pictures. But there was no denying it was
them. There was also no denying their relationship was a lot
more than two people just casually talking, either. As Dinah

and I had watched them, the phrase "get a room" had come to mind.

Once we got the pictures, Dinah and I had given up trailing Thursday and driven on to the outlet mall. Thursday was already home when we finally got back. We found her sitting in the crochet room with a big hook moving through three strands of colorful yarn.

She held up her work and explained she was making one of the pet mats like CeeCee had been making. How could I say anything? Not only was she crocheting, but she was making a pet mat. A girl who'd never had a pet. She even insisted on making dinner for us.

Apparently she hadn't exactly been lying about checking out places to live, because she announced that she'd found a place—a guesthouse on the edge of Tarzana.

I snapped back to the present as Mason smiled at me. "This is nice," Mason said, "taking two of my favorite people out together." A moment later, Thursday came into the room all smiles as she hugged her father. "I thought we'd go to the beach," he said.

It felt vaguely familiar as Mason steered his Mercedes through the canyon on the way through the mountains. Only he took Topanga Canyon. But all the canyon roads that led to the beach had one thing in common, you felt like you'd gone off to some wilderness instead of being a few minutes from a freeway traffic jam.

I kept looking at my purse, thinking of the bombshell in there. As Mason and Thursday talked about her getting on with her life, I knew she was leaving something major out. She had something going with Ben, and I was pretty sure it wasn't something new. I didn't even want to think about the fact that he'd worked at the wedding as a server and would have known where a knife was going to be.

The last part of the ride, when the view of the ocean suddenly appeared, was always like opening a present. I never got tired of looking at the sun glinting off the water or of searching in the distance for the Channel Islands sitting offshore.

Mason had chosen a restaurant that sat right on the beach, and he'd scored a table by the window. I tried to lose myself in the view and stop thinking about the phone in my purse. The conversation had been mostly between Mason and his daughter, though I'd been included enough not to feel left out.

"I knew you would bounce back," Mason said to Thursday as we sat down at our table. "You take after me." Thursday looked up and made eye contact with her father.

"What else could I do?" she said.

The brunch was served buffet-style, and the three of us went to fill our plates. I couldn't help but check out Thursday's plate. She had eggs, potatoes, French toast with fruit sauce, fruit salad and a mélange of vegetables.

"I'm afraid this case is going to get filed away. It seems impossible to believe with all those witnesses, that nobody saw anything. But the cops seem to have nothing beyond a shirt that was messed with enough to ruin any evidence it might have held."

He looked to me. "What about you, Sunshine? Have you found anything? I know you, and you must have been doing your own investigating. We all might just be depending on you this time." He explained to his daughter that my methods were hardly traditional. "But fun," he added with a chuckle.

"Actually, Barry does have his eye on someone." Barry hadn't said anything about keeping it quiet, so why not tell them. Was it my imagination or did both of them jump?

"Who?" Mason said quickly. Thursday had set down her fork and had her hands in her lap as if she was ready for bad news.

"Paxton Cline," I said. Thursday blew out her breath and Mason looked mystified.

"Who?" he repeated. I explained who Paxton was and his connection to Jonah.

Mason turned to his daughter. "You must know him. What do you think?"

I remembered that Thursday had pretended not to know him when we'd passed him in the mall, so I was curious to see how she would respond.

"I forgot about him," she said. "He was a friend of Jonah's from the time they were kids. I really didn't know him that well, and I don't know what happened with him being best man. It was all between Jonah and him. He could have had a grudge against Jonah."

She had given the perfect answer, which even went along with her reaction at the mall. If she didn't know him that well, she easily could not have recognized him.

"He sounds like a suspect to me," Mason said.

"But maybe not the right one," I said. "I know he lied, but my gut says it will turn out not to be him. He has an alibi, though it's kind of flimsy." I mentioned the baseball game and Mason laughed. Whatever I said, they both seemed to want to think that Paxton was the guy.

It wasn't too hard to figure out why. Mason was worried the revenge motive was aimed at him for getting off a client. And as for Thursday—could she be worried that Ben might come under Barry's scrutiny if he wasn't busy looking at somebody else?

The mood lightened and we all went back to the buffet for seconds. But I was left wondering what was going on with Thursday and Ben. As I sat back down, I put my purse in my lap. Instinctively, I held on to it, feeling the outline of my BlackBerry.

"Sunshine, why are you clutching your purse so tightly?" Mason stood up and reached for it, saying I'd be more comfortable with it sitting on the empty chair. If only the strap hadn't caught on my arm. I tried to make a save, but the bag opened up and everything started to tumble out.

Mason, ever the gentleman, rushed to help me. Thursday went after the rolling coins. My BlackBerry hit the floor, bounced and landed by Mason's foot. I could see the screen had gone to some application, and since the last thing I'd looked at was the photo display, I was sure that was what was on the screen.

I tried to make a grab for it, but Mason picked it up before I could. Since I was notorious for my phone issues, the first thing Mason did was look at the screen.

I heard my breath suck in with a loud noise. Any second he would start asking about the photograph. Would he recognize his daughter? Would he show it to her, and I'd have to explain why I'd been following her?

Mason kept looking at the screen and shaking his head.

"I can explain," I stammered, hoping an explanation would suddenly appear in my mind, because I really didn't have one at all.

"I should hope so," Mason said. His usual grin was gone, and his mouth was drawn up into an unhappy straight line. Visions of having to walk home went through my mind as

I imagined him thinking I was trying to incriminate his daughter and the two of them making a hasty exit without me.

In the midst of this, a waiter came by offering skewers of chicken satay. He obviously had no idea of what he'd walked into and held out the tray.

"We're just testing them," the waiter said. "I'm supposed to find out what you think." My stomach was doing flip-flops, and I wanted to make a grab for my BlackBerry now that they were distracted, but Mason was holding it tight. He shrugged at the waiter and took three skewers, putting one on each of our plates. Mason tasted the chicken on his skewer and said it was okay.

Meanwhile, the waiter looked to Thursday and me. I tasted mine, even though I was so tense I could barely swallow it. Now all eyes were on Thursday. She stared at the hunk of meat on her plate.

Finally she rocked her head in dismay and looked up at the waiter. "I'm sorry I can't help you. I'm a vegetarian."

"What?" Mason said from across the table. "Since when? Why didn't you tell me? Does your mother know? What do you eat? And what about vitamin B12?"

I was happy to see Mason was acting like an irate father and hoped I could use the distraction to make him lose his train of thought. The delay had caused the screen of my phone to go dark, and if I could just get the phone and put it away, I was sure he'd be so lost in grilling his daughter about her eating habits, he'd forget all about what he had seen.

But there were two problems. Mason never let go of my BlackBerry, and Thursday had the same distraction idea I had.

"Dad, you were upset about a photograph on Molly's phone." She waved her hand toward the object in his hands. Mason's attention snapped back to my phone, and he ran his finger across the rolling ball until the screen came back on. I checked my shoes for their comfort level and thought there must be a bus that would take me back to the Valley, even if it took forever.

As soon as he saw the picture again, he started shaking his head in dismay.

"I don't understand." He held up the squarish phone so the screen was visible to his daughter. She had a reaction similar to his. I took a deep breath as he moved it in front of me. "Do you want to explain?" When I saw the image I almost choked on my own breath. The phone had gone to camera mode and displayed a photograph. But instead of the beach scene with Thursday and Ben I was worried about, the display had gone to a photo that was from the night I'd gone to Jeffrey's play. Barry, Jeffrey and I were all standing together with our arms around one another, looking very much like a family.

"I suppose there are more?" Mason said. I saw his finger going toward the roller ball in the middle of the phone. Just a slight touch and it would start scrolling through the rest of the photos on the phone. I snatched it before he could touch it.

"It's for Jeffrey," I said. "It was a big night for him." Mason seemed a little less upset with the explanation.

"I'm sorry I overreacted, but it just looked like there was more going on with Barry than you were letting on." I felt a giddy laugh coming as I buried the phone in the bottom of my purse. This was horrible. Mason had always been the one I could open up to. And now I was keeping this terrible secret from him.

Whatever I did, I would lose. If I told Mason about his daughter and Ben, he would blame the messenger—me—for the message. If I didn't tell him and he found out, he would be forever angry with me for not telling him. One way or the other, I was going to have to confront Thursday. But I wanted to do it when we were alone.

CHAPTER 26

THURSDAY MUST HAVE SENSED SOMETHING BE-
cause she made herself scarce. When we went back to my
house, she immediately left, saying she had to pick up some
supplies for a class project she was doing the next week. I was
glad Mason and I only had a few minutes alone before I said
I had to leave for the bookstore. Having this secret about
Thursday had become overwhelming, and I knew he'd pick
up that something was wrong and start asking questions.

I was in such a hurry to get away from Mason, I'd actually left early for the bookstore. I used the extra time to stop
by Emerson's to show her the sample kits. Time was running out, and I needed to know her choice so I could get
them put together.

I was surprised when a man answered the door. Lyla
came up behind him, and when she saw me, she explained
the whole party idea to him.

"Dennis Lake," he said, putting out his hand before inviting me in. He explained that Emerson wasn't there. "She's working a fiftieth anniversary at the Four Seasons in Westlake."

It came back to me that Emerson had mentioned her husband worked in Silicon Valley and was home on the weekends while she was off handling the flowers for events.

"I have some samples of crochet kits to show Emerson," I said. He seemed confused until I described the format of the party and that each of the guests needed some tools and yarn for the project. Lyla stood next to her father as I took out the three kits Elise had made up. "I suppose I could just leave them and she can get back to me."

"I can pick," Lyla said to her father. Lyla reached out for them, but I wasn't sure what to do and I looked to her father.

"Could you give us a minute?" Dennis said. He invited me in and took his daughter into the dining area. I could hear them discussing, which sounded more like arguing, and I tried to pretend I wasn't listening by looking around the condo living room, moving around as I did. With Emerson's husband there, the mood was slightly changed. The TV was tuned to some sports game, and it was obvious by the setup of two paper plates and take-out containers that Lyla had been watching it with her father.

They'd gotten to the point of discussing the merits of one of the kits I'd brought. Lyla liked the one that came in a cloth tote with her name inscribed on the front in glitter glue. "I'd be famous," she said and went on to describe how everybody would be carrying a bag with her name on it.

I tried to distance myself more as her father picked up on the obvious: That kit cost the most. Lyla kept working on her father, showing off the tote and its larger amount of supplies. I tried to step away from their conversation and ended up next to the fireplace. Dennis was the analytical type and kept asking his daughter questions about what was really necessary. I moved further away and pretended to be interested in the contents on the mantelpiece.

It was hard to appear really interested in a pair of candlesticks and a stack of somebody else's mail. I had examined every inch of the candlesticks by the time I heard their conversation wind down. After a moment, the two of them rejoined me in the living room. "This is the one I want," Lyla said, holding up the cloth tote with her name in glitter glue. Her father seemed less certain, but nodded.

Was that a yes? If I questioned it, Lyla might throw a fit. But if I just went ahead without talking to Emerson, she might be upset I didn't consult her. Oh, the politics of it all. I thanked Lyla, but made a mental note not to do anything until I also got the go-ahead from Emerson.

The street was Sunday peaceful as I drove to the bookstore. There was a leisurely feel to the day, so I was surprised to see a small crowd along with a cop car and a motorcycle on the street in front of Le Grande Fromage. Everyone was looking up. I walked down the street to find out what was going on.

When I got closer, I recognized Eric in full uniform. He saw me and stepped away from the crowd. He was all business as he reached me.

"There's been another yarn bombing," he said in such a serious voice I wanted to laugh. He said it as if the yarn really was going to make something explode rather than just offering a surprise. His arm shot out straight as an arrow, pointing at a striped socklike shape that had been pulled

partway over a sign that pointed out there was parking behind the building.

"You have to do something," he said. "Maybe she'll listen
to you. But this yarn stuff has to stop. They all think it's
her. Doesn't she get it? She's making it look like I can't control my woman."

Did he just call Adele *his woman*? Like his possession he
couldn't control? It was lucky Adele wasn't there, she would
have reacted like a bull to a red cape. I pulled Eric aside.

It was none of my business, but I stuck my nose in it
anyway. "If you plan to have any future with Adele, I'd suggest you drop the caveman act. She's not your woman. She
might be your partner, your girlfriend, your lov—, no cancel
that. She could even be your Cutchykins, but not your
woman." Eric took a moment to process the information.

"Let me rephrase that. What I was trying to say was that
I can't have someone of the female persuasion who I am see-
ing on a consistent basis going around leaving yarn graffiti.
She's making me look like a fool."

I did my best to try to convince him he was jumping to
conclusions about Adele. But he wasn't buying it.

"Who is always standing up for crochet? Who tends toward flamboyant gestures? And who doesn't always know
when to quit?" he said.

I had to admit, he had a point.

He pleaded with me to do something. "It's only a matter
of time before she gets caught in the act if she doesn't stop.
Look," he said, pointing to a security camera being installed
in the front of Luxe, the lifestyle store. "I won't be able to do
anything to help her. The department thinks the yarn
bomber is thumbing their nose at us cops, and cops don't
like that."

I promised to do my best and headed back to the bookstore. After the three encounters I'd had, I welcomed the peaceful dullness of Shedd & Royal. I helped some customers with the Halloween costumes. Mrs. Shedd had convinced everybody they were going to sell out in a hurry, so they actually were selling in a hurry. I sold a Sherlock Holmes costume with its deerslayer hat and capelike coat, and a Hard Luck Harry outfit from the series about the hobo who traveled on freight trains in the forties.

When I took a break, I sat down at the worktable in the yarn department. I was surprised to see CeeCee sitting there alone. CeeCee was one of those people who didn't function well without an audience. She was weaving in the ends of another pet mat.

"Hello, dear," she said when I slid into a chair. "They're painting at my house," she said by way of explanation. It turned out *painting* was not quite the right term. She was having a mural painted in her dining room. "It's me as Ophelia," she said with a proud trill in her voice. "I have news. They're making a sequel to *Caught by a Kiss*. And I'll be reprising the role."

CeeCee tended to be self-absorbed, so I was surprised she noticed that I seemed a little snowed under. CeeCee asked for details. I only got as far as my concern about the details of the upcoming birthday party before CeeCee's eyes began to glaze over, and she stopped me.

"I know about parties," she said gaily. "There's nothing to worry about. The group has already said they would help."

I brought up the kits. "The one the little girl seems to want has her name on the front of cloth totes. It's written in glitter glue, and I have a feeling it's done by hand."

"No problem, dear. We'll make a party of decorating the bags at my house. It will also be the unveiling of the mural. Maybe you can bring some of those finger sandwiches you're doing for the birthday party. I love finger sandwiches. Maybe we should have a sample of the birthday cupcakes as well." She added the finished pet mat to the others and said something about taking them to an animal shelter. "Is there any word on who stabbed Thursday's husband? Are you going to bring her back to the group? I hope so, she's such a lovely girl."

I was glad that CeeCee didn't wait for an answer about any of it before she left.

"I'm hanging up my sleuthing shoes," I said to Dinah. After the bookstore closed, I had shown up on her doorstep with a bag of food from Le Grande Fromage. "I don't think Paxton is the guy, but I don't know who is." I flopped down on her chartreuse couch while she dished up the croissant sandwiches and salad. "I think I've reached the end of my rope for everything." I went on about the yarn bomber and how Eric had dumped it in my lap. And how the parties had seemed like such an easy idea, but I didn't even know what the project was going to be. "And I have an okay for the expensive kit, but it's from a kid."

Dinah calmed me down and assured me I was just having a black moment. "It's all because you don't want to confront Thursday about the photographs, isn't it?"

I nodded and my bleak mood lifted. I was so grateful to have a friend like Dinah who knew me so well.

CHAPTER 27

SEVERAL DAYS LATER, I CAME HOME CARRYING grocery bags with the fixings for finger sandwiches. I was going to make the sample sandwich platter to take to CeeCee's. I'd hired Laurie Jean, the caterer from Thursday's wedding, to do the sandwiches for Lyla's party, but she was having so many problems, I wasn't about to suggest she make up a sample platter. Getting Caitlyn to supply a tray of cupcakes was another matter. She actually offered before I could even ask.

I noticed there were folded boxes next to Thursday's fountain and cherubs in my front hall. Since it was supposed to be only temporary, I'd left the wedding presents from her parents there. I had gotten some weird looks when the mailman brought mail to my door and checked out those cherubs. Seeing the boxes made it real that Thursday would be moving into her own place soon. Once she left, I wondered if I'd see much of her. I had confused feelings about her. I'd taught her to crochet and we'd spent time together. I cared for her, but she wasn't being honest with me. I knew for sure she'd lied about knowing Ben, which made me wonder what else she'd lied about.

I had put off talking to her when I came home from Dinah's and the nights after. I could make a lot of excuses, like she was busy working on a poster for her class, or that it was late, but the reality was I hadn't wanted to know the truth yet.

But now I was ready. There would be no more excuses or delays. When she came home, I'd confront her.

I unloaded the bags in the kitchen and went right to making the sandwich fillings. I felt a little more on top of things, at least as far as the party was concerned. Rhoda had come up with the perfect project. I'd gotten a confirmation from Emerson on the kits with the glitter-glue name on the bag. I'd helped Elise get the supplies together for the kits. Eduardo had his staff making up bags of so-called penny candy. And CeeCee had repeated the invite for everything to come together at her place.

I was cutting the crusts off the bread when the phone rang. The robotic voice didn't give a name this time, so I didn't know it was Barry until I picked up.

"Jeffrey and I are at your back door," he said after the hellos. He had called earlier to arrange their arrival. It was all because of Cosmo. The black mutt had technically been their dog, though they'd gradually relinquished him to my care. Apparently part of the new Barry was taking back the responsibility of their dog.

I opened the door and Barry walked in carrying a case of

dog food. Jeffrey had a brush and some dog toys and immediately went looking for the dog.

"Thanks for being so nice about taking care of Cosmo. I'm sorry it's taken us so long to get our act together," Barry said as Jeffrey and Cosmo came through the kitchen together. Jeffrey went for the leash and announced he was taking him for a walk.

"You aren't taking him with you, are you?" I said in a worried tone. I'd gotten attached to the little dog. Barry seemed relieved by my question and said that even with Jeffrey giving the dog regular care, he was better off staying with me.

Barry leaned against the counter and looked at what I was making. "Help yourself," I said, gesturing toward a plate of triangular-shaped sandwiches. The plan was to get everything ready to assemble just before I took it to CeeCee's, but I'd made up one plate of finished sandwiches to see what they looked—and tasted—like.

Barry took several and smiled with approval as he bit into a watercress and butter sandwich. I'm sure he hadn't a hint about the rock I felt in my stomach as I thought about talking to Thursday.

My company had left, the kitchen was cleaned up, and I was in the yarn room crocheting when I heard Thursday finally come home. I called out to her and invited her to join me. I was tense about talking to her and decided it was a good time to try one of Dr. Wheel's meditation washcloths. I was using some organic cotton I had and the most basic pattern.

"Not much longer until you have your house back," she said, plopping down on the love seat that had become her regular spot. She had a basket next to it where she kept her works in progress. She hadn't gotten like me, with countless half-done projects. So far, Thursday had only two projects she was going back and forth between.

She left the scarf and picked up the pet mat she was working on with the odds and ends of cotton yarn I'd given her. It didn't seem like a good idea to just confront her with what I knew, but rather try to draw her into conversation. I let her crochet in silence for a few minutes before I said anything.

"It must be a relief for you to know the police at least have a suspect," I said. "I'm sure it's just a matter of time before they gather up enough evidence. If they can find Paxton in a photograph at the reception, there's a good chance he'll just confess." Thursday nodded. "You didn't happen to see him at the reception?" I said. "That would probably be a clincher."

Thursday seemed to be considering something. She looked up and seemed about to speak, but stopped herself. "No, I can't do that. I can't say I saw him at the reception," she said finally.

"But then why would you be paying attention to the servers on your wedding day? You must have been wrapped in a cocoon of happiness after marrying the man of your dreams."

Thursday's head came up abruptly, and her expression was pained.

"I'm so sorry," I said. "I didn't mean to hit a nerve. I wasn't thinking. I can only imagine how hard it is to think about the joy of your wedding when you realize it went to black so fast."

I watched as Thursday crocheted. Usually she had an

even rhythm and uniform stitches. But she seemed to be stabbing her hook into the stitches, and her tension was all over the place, a tight stitch followed by a loose loopy one.

I borrowed a line I'd heard Barry use when questioning people, even though when I'd heard the line, it was because he was using it on me.

"Why don't you just tell me what happened?" I was going to add more. Barry said things like he could help straighten things out if he knew the truth and more stuff to imply he was on the same side as the suspect. Thursday finished the row she was on and started to turn her work. She seemed determined to keep on crocheting and not look up. So far her MO had simply been not to talk, or if she did, to say she didn't know.

Her stitches were getting more and more erratic as she picked up speed. Finally, she threw down her work and looked up. "I can't keep it in anymore."

I continued crocheting, though I was paying more attention to her than the washcloth. I'm afraid it didn't look like meditation, but more like an anxiety attack. Thank heavens, crochet was so easy to rip out. I would fix it all later. For now I was trying to appear receptive and calm.

It took several deep breaths and sighs before she spoke. "I haven't told anyone this, but I wanted to call off the wedding." She seemed to be trying to gauge my expression. I was doing my best to keep a bland face, but I couldn't help it. Her comment had caught me by surprise.

"Why?" I said.

"You have to understand how I got involved with Jonah. I was coming off a breakup." She tried to pick up the crochet, but then dropped it again, while my hook kept going. "I was heartbroken, and Jonah seemed to be just what I needed. He made me feel wanted and cared for. When he asked me to marry him, it felt like the right thing to do. He had a job and a future. I liked the fact that he seemed to know what he wanted and took charge." She had to stop to gather herself together.

"We'd only dated a few months when we got engaged. As it got closer to the wedding, I began to notice that what I thought was him taking charge was really him taking control. When I objected, well . . ." She looked down and sighed.

I was stunned with what I was hearing. "He wasn't violent, was he?"

"No, but he had these outbursts, then he would apologize. When I told him I thought we should cancel the wedding, he went nuts. He wasn't going to be embarrassed that way, and he insisted everything would be better once we got past the wedding. Paxton tried to talk to him about at least postponing the wedding, but Jonah wouldn't listen. Paxton said he had no choice but to refuse to be the best man."

"So, it was Paxton's idea not to be the best man, not Jonah dropping him from the position," I said. She nodded and said in typical Jonah fashion, he'd made it sound like the decision had been his.

"Paxton told me that Jonah had changed ever since he'd gone to work in the family business. I think he was under a lot of pressure. He didn't talk much about his work, but a few times he said he didn't like the way his father did things."

"And why is it that you pretended not to know Paxton at the mall?" I asked.

"He knew the truth about Jonah, and I was afraid he

would say something," she said. "I thought if I could keep Jonah's reputation intact . . ." She didn't finish, but I nodded with understanding.

I asked her if she'd told her parents about her desire to end it with Jonah, and she shook her head vehemently. "I was embarrassed and I thought I could handle it myself." She started to tear up. "And then at the reception, I saw someone." She was having a hard time talking, but she seemed determined to get it out. "Remember I said I'd been getting over a breakup when I met Jonah? His name is Ben, and I was stunned to see that he was one of the servers at the reception." She said that Ben hadn't realized he was working her wedding—the caterer had merely given an address and a time, and the dress code.

"He said he was happy for me, that I must have found somebody who could give me the life I deserved. Then he explained why he'd broken up with me. It wasn't that he wanted space as he'd said. It was because he was broke and struggling, working odd jobs so he could write. How could he suggest a future together when he didn't feel he could hold up his end of things?

"Jonah saw me talking to him, and he grabbed me by the wrist and pulled me away." She grimaced as if remembering the pain of his hold. "His grasp had been so tight, it left an imprint of his fingers on my skin. I didn't want to make a scene, so I tried to calm Jonah down and told him I'd just been asking a server to get me a glass of sparkling water. He began to back off and even tried to make light of what he had done. He was my adoring groom, who couldn't bear to see me talking to another man. He had his arm around me in a tight hold. I told him I was sorry, that I was all wrong for talking to the server. Jonah seemed to relax, and when I said I needed to greet some of the guests, he finally let me go."

Cosmo came into the room and the black mutt sensed an emotional upheaval was going on. He climbed up on the love seat next to Thursday, and put his head on her thigh. She looked down at him and started to stroke his head.

"When Jonah grabbed me like that, he crossed the line. Before, I'd been nervous about his temper, but it had only been a threat. I got it. Now that we were married, it felt like he viewed me as his property. And the comment about me not talking to another man. . . . All of a sudden I felt like I had to get away. I was going to bolt, be a runaway bride. But to be sure, I gave myself some time first. Then I saw my mother going over to check on the cake. I couldn't run off without telling her. And then—"

Her voice broke off.

What came next? Had she gone to see her mother and found Jonah on the ground, or had she gone to see her mother and in a panic picked up the knife and stabbed Jonah? Or had she told her mother about Jonah and her mother had gotten so angry, she stabbed Jonah? With great trepidation, I asked her to tell me exactly what had happened after that.

Thursday understood what I was saying. "I didn't stab Jonah, but I have to be honest and admit I was relieved when I realized I was free of him."

"But Ben saw him grab me," she said. "I can't ask him, but I'm so afraid. The cops have thought all along it was someone masquerading as a server or one of the servers." She had a pleading look. "You said the cops have Paxton in their crosshairs. Can't we just leave it that way for now?" She admitted that she and Ben had been seeing each other again, but no one could know. She said she was going to get up the courage to ask Ben if he'd stabbed Jonah. "If he did, I'll make sure he turns himself in. He would have just been trying to protect me."

I'd been wanting her to open up to me, but you know that saying about being careful what you wish for? It was true. Now I didn't know what I was going to do with all the information she'd just dropped in my lap.

CHAPTER 28

"HAVE YOU DECIDED WHAT TO DO?" DINAH SAID. We were sitting in my car outside of CeeCee's house the next afternoon. Everything Thursday had told me had been rolling around in my mind the whole night and on into the morning as I assembled the tea sandwiches. The only person I'd told was Dinah.

"No," I said, pulling the key out of the ignition. "I can't tell Mason. His daughter has to be the one to tell him the truth about Jonah and Ben. And I don't want to tell Barry yet. I agree that after what Thursday told me, Ben could be a suspect. Everyone seems to agree that the shirt I found belonged to either someone who slipped in dressed like a server or one of the help. Ben fits that. I understand some of the servers brought spare white shirts. He could have brought one, changed into it, and just blended in with the crowd. They've never found any bloody white gloves. He could have just put on clean ones and stowed the other ones in his pocket. I say he *could* have done it, but I'm not *sure* he did.

"I don't know if Thursday is sure Ben is the killer or she is just worried that he is. She's convinced that Ben will do the right thing and confess if he's involved. If it's true, it would be better for him if he came forward with a lawyer already in place. Maybe they could make a deal since she thinks Ben would have been trying to protect her after seeing Jonah manhandling her."

I turned to Dinah. "But for now I need to focus on going to CeeCee's where we can get everything together for the birthday party."

We went over a checklist. I'd brought the tray of sandwiches, and we'd picked up the cupcakes for all of us to taste. Kirsty was the one who packed them up and insisted that since they were samples, she didn't have to decorate them. Rhoda was bringing samples of the project along with sheets with the directions. Elise had all the stuff to make up the kits. Eduardo was bringing the party favors, and Sheila was coming to help. CeeCee, as always, was generous about offering her house. And I think Adele felt her mere presence was enough.

We all loved going to CeeCee's. Her house was set far back from the street in a mini forest and the stone cottage look of it made it seem like something out of a fairy tale. We got out of the car and gathered up our parcels and headed up the stone path that led to the door.

I could hear CeeCee's two Yorkies, Tallulah and Marlena, yapping at the door. As soon as CeeCee opened it, the two dogs starting dancing around my ankles. I don't think they were as happy to see me as the trays of sandwiches and the cupcake platter Dinah and I were holding.

CeeCee sniffed the air and smiled. "Goody, you brought the treats. You know I would have made something. . . ." She rolled her eyes and laughed in her musical way. "But we all know I could burn water."

We were the first to arrive, and CeeCee took us right into her dining room, which was the usual spot where we met. I started to set down the sandwiches on the dark wood treadle table when I looked up at the wall.

"Wonderful, isn't it?" CeeCee said. When she'd mentioned having a mural done, I hadn't realized she meant in her dining room. It was a scene from the *Caught by a Kiss* movie. CeeCee in her Ophelia evening garb was talking to Anthony the vampire. I noticed the artist had included a hook and some yarn in his hand. Dinah and I both commented on how good the likeness was of CeeCee and Hugh Jackman who played Anthony in the movie. There was an empty space in the middle of the mural, and it seemed unfinished. I brought it up to CeeCee and she explained.

"You all know about the Oscar buzz for my performance," she said, giving the picture a loving glance. "There's just enough space for the muralist to paint in an Oscar. Otherwise, she'll just fill it in with background."

Dinah and I set out the food and then made coffee and tea. When we returned to the dining room with the drinks, Eduardo had just arrived with a box with clear cellophane bags of candy. I was glad he was staying. Ever since he'd bought the Crown Apothecary, it was hard for him to make a lot of our get-togethers. Now that he'd mostly given up his cover model/spokesperson career, he was dressing more businesslike, which meant he had retired his leather pants. He complimented CeeCee on the mural and took a seat on the side of the table.

Sheila came in next. She was still dressed from her day working at Luxe. I practically drooled over the champagne-colored silk jacket covered in sunny orange embroidered flowers.

We all looked expectantly toward Rhoda when she came in. I'd already seen the crochet project for the party that we'd agreed on, but the others hadn't. Before Rhoda sat down, she unloaded her tote bag and laid a smaller bag on the table. She handed me a stack of papers with the directions.

"I can't tell you how much I appreciate this," I said. Putting on the party was my job, and here they were all jumping in to help.

"Molly, it's in our best interest to have this party succeed," Rhoda said. "We all know what shaky ground the bookstore is on. So we're glad to help. Besides, I think I would kill Hal if I didn't have someplace to go to and hang out."

"I'm sure this is just a onetime thing, anyway," CeeCee said. "Once Molly gets the parties going, it will all be more routine."

Rhoda looked at me. "I also brought a sample project for the shower. Has the woman committed yet?"

"She wants to see how the birthday party goes first. She was one of the guests at the wedding, so I can understand how she'd be concerned with things not going as planned," I said. There was no need to explain which wedding— everybody knew which one I was referring to.

"How are things going with that?" CeeCee said. "I don't recall hearing that the police have arrested anyone. Actually, I haven't heard anything about it lately."

They all looked to me and I didn't know what to say. Luckily, I was saved by the bell, or really the barking dogs, as they started a ruckus at the door.

But the commotion didn't end when CeeCee answered the door. Adele sort of embodied a frenzy as she joined us at the table. First she looked around in a frantic manner, then sighed with relief.

"I was afraid Leonora might be here," she said, sinking into a chair. We all knew Adele was just being her usual dramatic self. There was absolutely no reason why her boy-friend's mother would have come to our get-together. Adele made a big point that finally she could be herself and then went on about how overwrought she was, having to deal with the birthday party on the same day she was having a major children's author come to story time.

"You all know who Kate Moore is," Adele said. I was surprised when Eduardo nodded and said his mother had read him *Pig Tales* when he was a kid.

Adele jumped from her major author event to talking about the yarn bombings. "Pink, we have to do something. There's been another yarn attack." Adele brought out her cell phone and displayed a picture of a band of color around a street sign. Like one of the other bombings, the colorful piece seemed to have something done in surface crochet. It was hard to tell in the photo, but it seemed like one side of a square.

"Even though you were the one arrested at the mall, Eric thinks it's me doing the yarn bombings. No matter what I say, he just shakes his head."

There was a flurry of discussion about the yarn bomber and who it was. "Pink, if you're such a great amateur sleuth, why can't you find out who the real yarn bomber is?" Adele had a pleading look. She didn't have to say it, I knew what would follow. Eric was the yin to her yang, the one, etc., and she didn't want to mess it up. I said I would help her. I know, why should I care, considering how thoughtless she seemed to be? Maybe there was something in me that hated to see the wrong person accused of a crime, even if it was Adele.

I told Adele to send me any pictures of the yarn bombings she had and Eric's as well. I would look over all of them and see if there was some unifying element.

"Oh, Pink, ever since we had French toast together at your house, we are like French toast sisters now." She threw her arms around me as the dogs started to yip again.

Elise came in at the end, dragging a stack of plastic bins on a luggage carrier. She was a small woman who looked like the wind could blow her away, and I wondered how she managed such a bulky burden. Eduardo jumped up and took over.

"Sorry I'm late," she said with a happy smile, sounding cheerful. "I've been busy with my other business. Weight loss knows no season." Her gaze fell on Adele and her mouth went into a straight line. "All my customers adore the weight-loss powder and have shed lots of weight."

Adele put her hook on the table and brought out some cotton yarn. "I stand behind what Dr. Wheel said. Crochet is my cure-all." Then Adele repeated what Dr. Wheel had said about distraction helps to deal with assorted issues and how there were no side effects, except maybe ending up with a beautiful scarf or shawl. "And nobody dies from crochet," she added.

Elise gave Adele an exasperated glance. "I looked into it. It was a bad shipment and once they realized it, they recalled all the orders. There is nothing wrong with the ingredients. They are a proprietary blend of herbs, all recognized as safe," Elise said, sounding like she was reading from a script.

Dinah nudged me and said I ought to do something to calm everyone down. I snatched Adele's crochet and shoved it in the pocket of my vest and said, "Why don't we all try the food while Rhoda shows us the project she's come up with for the party?"

CeeCee took the lead and made a plate for herself with the others following. I watched as they tasted the sandwiches and cupcakes and was relieved when even Adele didn't have a criticism. When they were done and the plates cleared, Rhoda opened the bag on the table with a flourish.

"And here it is, the party scarf," she said, taking out a long red, ruffly scarf with red fun fur along the edge. As she held it up, the light caught in the metallic glitter in the yarn. She took out versions done in gold, black, and hot pink. The consensus of the group was "Wow."

They looked over the pattern and saw that it used the most basic skills and yet ended with something spectacular-looking. "The girls and the mothers will love it," Dinah said. There was one father in the group, but they said he could give it to his wife.

Elise, Dinah and I laid out the supplies and we made an assembly line. To speed things along, Elise had already done the glitter glue writing on each of the cloth tote bags. With us all working together, it took no time to get everything assembled. Elise packed them in the plastic containers for me to take.

"There's one more thing," CeeCee said. She disappeared

for a few moments and then came back. "I remember how the girl liked the pet mat I was making and said she wanted to do something for animals. I had an idea." She set a bunch of yarn on the table and the beginning strip of one of the mats. "What about them passing the mat around at the party and asking each person to crochet a row until it's done? Then we can add it to our donation. Maybe Lyla would even like to come with when we take the mats to the shelter."

We all agreed it was a great idea. "I think Emerson will be very happy with the party. Or at least I hope so," I said, holding up my crossed fingers.

As we were getting ready to go, Rhoda pulled me aside. "Remember when you were at my house to talk about the project for the birthday party, and I said there was some kind of scandal at one of the houses across the street? I asked Hal and he said it had something to do with embezzling money."

Why did that sound familiar?

CHAPTER 29

"WHY DON'T YOU PUT EVERYTHING ABOUT THE murder out of your mind until after the party," Dinah suggested. We'd gone to a party store to pick up the paper goods.

"I feel terrible, knowing what I know and not doing anything about it. Even if Barry hasn't found any concrete evidence, I'm sure he's still grilling Paxton Cline. I worry," I said, letting my voice trail off. "There is such a thing as false confessions and Barry is very persistent." I followed Dinah to the birthday section.

"But Paxton could be the killer," Dinah said. "If what Thursday says is true, her groom was a troubled person, and who knows what went on between him and his former best man."

On the way, we passed the wedding department. Seeing the brides and grooms for the tops of wedding cakes and all the flowery banners spouting eternal love gave me a chill. "'Troubled' is a nice way to put it. It's lucky for Thursday she didn't stay married to him. It sounds like his view of her changed as soon as that ring went on her finger. If Jonah grabbed her arm at the reception in front of all those people, you can only imagine what he might have done when they were alone."

I still felt bad that Mason didn't know what had happened between Thursday and Jonah, but I couldn't be the one to tell him. Dinah pulled me away from the wedding stuff. We passed through all the different themes in the birthday area, but none of them seemed right for Lyla.

Much as I'd said I wanted to put Jonah's death out of my mind for the moment, it just wouldn't go away. "I admit that Ben certainly could have had a motive. . . . From the sounds of the reason for his breakup with Thursday and what we saw of them together later, Ben definitely still had feelings for her. And then to witness her being manhandled for talking to him? It's not a huge stretch to believe Ben could have acted without thinking."

Dinah nodded. "But it could be somebody else entirely. There were a lot of servers and people dressed like them, and they're all from around here and some of them probably have a connection to the groom's family."

"You're right," I acknowledged. "And there was also the DUI case of Mason's. If his client hadn't gotten off and kept their license, they might not have caused a deadly accident. Mason worried one of the servers might have been a family member of the accident victim's who blamed him for it and wanted revenge. Mason never gave me any of the names of the people involved."

We ended up leaving the kids' party area and choosing

paper products in pale shades of pink that would go with the writing on the tote bags. We passed on decorations, thinking Lyla would find them too childish. After we'd checked out and headed toward my car, we both agreed that if Ben was the culprit, we wished he would just come forward.

Back at the bookstore, Dinah helped me stow the party goods in the yarn department.

"There's Ben now," Dinah said. He was standing near the table we'd set up with writer's reference books. I remembered that he was dropping off some materials to be copied for the kid writers' group.

"If he's involved, maybe we can convince him to do the right thing," I said.

Together we crossed the bookstore and surrounded him. He looked a little startled, particularly when we walked him into a quiet corner.

"Did you want something?" he said in a tentative voice.

I gave the floor to Dinah. With all her experience dealing with stuff like getting her immature students to admit someone really hadn't infected their computer with a virus that ate their homework, I figured she'd be good at talking to Ben. I knew her approach was to act as if the person were guilty, and she was in the know. It always seemed to flush them out.

Dinah stepped close to him. "We know what you did and we understand why. But you need to do the right thing. You need to face up to the facts and not keep hiding."

Ben appeared stricken. "It wasn't like I had a choice. I just took advantage of the situation. What's done is done. I don't see any reason to say anything."

"It's going to keep haunting you unless you face up to it,"

Dinah said. "I'm sure if you take the first step, you can make some kind of arrangements. Some kind of deal."

"I don't know," Ben said, looking woeful. "I think it might be better just to leave everything as it is. Nobody knows, except you two. What will it take to keep you from talking?"

"We're not going to keep it quiet," I said, jumping in. "It's better if you handle it yourself, but if you don't, I will." I looked him in the eye. "Now tell me you will take care of it."

Ben sighed and finally nodded. "Just give me a few more days of freedom."

When he walked away, Dinah and I looked at each other wide-eyed. "Did he just confess?"

CHAPTER 30

"NOW YOU CAN TRULY FOCUS JUST ON THE PARTY," Dinah said after Ben left the bookstore, and she was heading out for her afternoon class.

I tried to do as Dinah said and put all my attention on the party. Once again I went over the details in my mind. Laurie Jean was delivering the sandwiches the next day just before the party. It was only a small job, but she was glad to have gotten it. I was going to bring in the kits for the crochet project and party favors. Then I'd go pick up the cupcakes at the last minute.

Adele and I had both made a Party Scarf using Rhoda's directions, and they'd been as easy and fast to make as she'd said. I had called Isa Susberg and she was also going to drop by during the party. If all went well, she'd give me a deposit for the shower. Thursday promised to come by, too. I was almost glad that Mrs. Shedd wasn't going to be in the bookstore. If she was, she would be sure to hover, which would make everyone nervous.

It seemed like I had everything in order.

Mason was leaning against his black Mercedes when I came out of the bookstore at the end of the day. He hugged me in greeting and I felt uneasy, thinking of everything that he didn't know. I hadn't wanted to meet him for dinner, but he'd talked me into it.

"You have to eat," he said after I'd told him no the third time. One thing I'd known about Mason from the start was he didn't like to lose—at anything. So I just gave in and said yes. At least I'd gotten him to agree to someplace close. I didn't want to have a long car ride, worrying about what I said.

We walked down the street to the neighborhood Thai restaurant. Mason spent a long time looking at the menu. "This would be a good place to take Thursday." He pointed out all the vegetarian options. Then he looked at me. "You knew for a while, didn't you?"

I flinched with guilt and was having a hard time looking him in the eye. I was glad when the waitress came by to take our order. When she left, Mason went back to talking about Thursday being a vegetarian and how she had underestimated him. He would be accepting of what she ate or didn't eat and never say a word, but he had bought her a bottle of vitamin B12 just in case.

He didn't say a word about Jonah's murder, and I think he had just settled on Paxton being the killer. It was easier than thinking the murder was connected to a case of his. Instead, Mason described what Jaimee's reaction would be when she found out that her daughter was a vegetarian and hadn't told her. My mind had wandered back to the party and all that it meant. It had to go flawlessly. But something was nagging at me. I looked at the setup on the table, the condiments and the vase, for a long time.

CHAPTER 31

THE DAY OF THE PARTY FINALLY ARRIVED, AND DE-
spite all my careful planning, I was still rushing around my
house like a chicken with its head cut off. It was a cliché,
but also accurate. There were so many details to pull together at the last minute, and the pressure of having only
one chance to get it right was hard to manage.

The Hookers had gone above and beyond by helping
with the preparations, but now it was up to me and Adele.
I was pretty confident that since all Adele had to do was
teach crochet—and it was the one thing I had no doubts
about with her—it would be okay.

I loaded up the car with the kits, party favors and sample
scarves Rhoda had provided. Thursday had stopped what
she was doing and helped me.

"Remember, I'm going to come by," she said. "If there's

anything I can do, I'm happy to do it. You've done so much for me."

There was a moment of silence as I thought back to all she'd told me and what I'd done about it. I wondered if she knew we'd talked to Ben, but decided if she didn't, I wasn't going to say anything.

I got to the bookstore just in time to set up. I'd purposely waited until Adele completed her author event before I left, so, luckily, all the kids were already gone from story time when I arrived at the bookstore. Adele rushed out of the kids' department when she saw me. She seemed very agitated. Apparently Eric's mother had come to observe and things hadn't gone well. My mind was really on the party and since what she was saying really didn't have much to do with me, I tuned out most of it. I just got that the author was rather elderly and had gotten sick during the event.

"But I took care of everything," Adele said. I said something about going into the storage room to bring out a rack of folding chairs to put around the table, but Adele insisted on doing it.

I was thrilled that she had offered to help and thought maybe she was turning over a new leaf.

The storage room opened off the yarn department, and Adele pulled the chairs on their carrier near the worktable. When we'd unloaded them all, I started to push the rack back to the storage room, but Adele swooped in before I got very far and said she'd do it. It was almost too good to be true, but I wasn't going to ask questions.

Mrs. Shedd had said she wasn't going to be at the bookstore the day of the party, but she did stop in just long enough to give me a thumbs-up when she saw how we'd fixed the table.

Emerson and Lyla arrived first. They looked at every-thing and seemed to approve. The others filtered in after. Dinah and Rhoda came in, but stayed in the background to offer help if needed. I was surprised to see CeeCee walk in, until she explained that she wanted to handle the pet mat go-around herself. She joined the other Hookers off to the side.

At first, the girls and their mothers and the one father seemed a little unsure about the party plan. The idea of making something rather than being entertained was new to most of them. Adele mingled among them, modeling the sample Party Scarves Rhoda had made. Adele's over-the-top quality worked well for a party. In no time, she had every-one excited about the project.

When everyone had found a seat and checked out the stuff at their place, I stepped forward. "I want to welcome you all to a Party with a Purpose." I began to explain how this was different than most of the parties they went to. "You're all going to learn how to crochet and make one of these." I held up a handful of the red party scarves, and the girls and the mothers all let out a "Wow." Even the father was impressed.

We'd decided to crochet first and then have the food. Adele had brought a huge hook and some beige yarn that was easy to see. She held it up and demonstrated how to make a slipknot and then waited while they all did the same. Then Adele moved on and demonstrated how to make a chain. As soon as they had the chain down, she had them make enough chain stitches for the scarf. Adele patrolled the table while everyone made their chains. Dinah, Rhoda, CeeCee and I hung back just in case.

When they'd all done the chain stitches, Adele demon-

strated how to do a single crochet and said that was all they
needed to know to make the scarf. Then Adele made a mini
version of the scarf and showed them how to do each row.
She demonstrated how to add the fun fur for the last row.
Finally, she showed them how to fasten off and weave in the
ends. All of the instructions were on a sheet in their bags.

With the actual lesson done, the group began to work on
their own and we fanned out to give help where needed.

Since Emerson and Lyla had already learned how to crochet, they were the stars of the party and ahead of the others
with their scarves.

"This is going well," I said to myself under my breath.
Isa Susberg showed up and observed. I saw her nodding and
smiling as CeeCee started the pet mat around the table.

"I guess you don't need my help," Thursday said as she
came up next to me. I had forgotten that Isa had been at the
fateful wedding reception and was surprised when she and
Thursday began to talk.

I'd also forgotten that Isa knew Jaimee and Thursday,
until I heard Isa mention that she was inviting both of them
to the shower and joking that Thursday's mother might
want to bring the film crew from the *Housewives of Mulholland Drive*.

I did a tiny fist pump, realizing that meant Isa was going
to do the shower at the bookstore. When they had crocheted
for a while, Emerson suggested we take a break from the
crocheting and serve the food.

"This is going great," I said to Dinah. "We did it! We've
started a new business for the bookstore. This has gone
without a hitch." Dinah gave me a somber look, and I got
her message. Wait until it was over before taking a bow.

Was it my comment that angered the party gods, or was

it just that nothing I ever did would really go without a hitch?

I heard some noise coming from the storage room. It sounded like knocking or banging. Like somebody was locked in there. Lyla heard it too and ran from the table to investigate. Adele looked up from helping one of the parents, just as Lyla started to turn the door handle.

I heard a loud no, as Adele loped toward the door. Lyla opened the door a little, and suddenly something pushed it wide open and ran out. It was so fast, I couldn't figure out what it was. It seemed about small-dog size, but it moved differently, and the noise it made wasn't barking; it sounded more like snorting.

I rushed to grab whatever it was, but it was too late. It had climbed on the table and was running toward the birthday cupcakes.

I was still trying to figure out what it was. Maybe a pig? A little pig the size of a dog?

Everybody started to make a grab for it, but it was in the middle of the cupcakes before they could catch it. Finally the father got hold of it and lowered it to the floor amid squeals of protest. That was when I saw that it had a collar on.

Luckily, nobody seemed to care about the demolished dessert. Instead, they were all gathered around the pig, touching its rough hair and letting it nuzzle its soft snout in their hands.

"Whose pig is he?" Lyla asked. I turned to look at Adele who was staring at the floor.

I pulled her aside and demanded she explain. "I told you the author of *Pig Tales* got sick. Maybe I didn't mention that she'd brought along Hamlet, the pig in the book. You can't take a pig to the hospital," Adele said. "I thought it would just be a little while, so I put him in the storage room." Something in Adele's voice said there was information she was leaving out.

"I just got a call from the hospital. Kate, the author, is going to recuperate at a relative's condo. No pigs allowed."

When I glanced back at the party, Thursday had found some rope to attach to the pig's collar like a leash.

"Pink, there's no place for the pig to go. It's a poor abandoned famous literary pig. I'd take it home with me, but I live in a condo that doesn't even allow cats."

For the rest of the party, everyone took turns taking care of the pig, which amounted to making sure it didn't live up to its name and eat too much.

I took away the ruined cupcake platter, apologizing profusely, but I'd barely gotten it off the table when Bob rushed in with his giant birthday cookie bar and set the tray on the table with a pleased look. I mouthed a thank-you, looking at the swirl of buttercream icing. He'd even written "Happy Bday" in chocolate chips and provided candles. We all joined in singing Happy Birthday and Lyla blew out the candles. Bob did the honors, cutting and serving the small treats. Bob was all smiles as I tasted one of the chocolate cake bars.

"You'll see, cookie bars are the next big trend," Bob said.

I had to admit that Bob's creation was a big hit. Everyone found them easier to eat and less messy than the cupcakes. The big surprise was how quickly the partygoers pushed aside their plates and went back to crocheting.

The only problem was the party went much longer than scheduled, and no one seemed to want to leave. Including Isa Susberg. I was worried Hamlet's appearance might have caused her to change her mind, but quite the contrary. She liked the added excitement. She gave me a deposit for the shower, but I had to tell her I couldn't promise that another pig would show up.

When the guests finally went home, all that was left was a pig and a mess. But as they left, I heard everyone saying what a great party it had been. Hamlet's entrance seemed to have been the icing on the cake.

Rhoda and CeeCee left with the crowd. Dinah wanted to help clean up, but the party had gone so long, she was meeting her boyfriend, Commander Blaine, who'd just gotten back in town. Adele collapsed in a chair, saying she was spent from her trying day.

"Looks like it's you and me," Thursday said. Hamlet seemed to have attached himself to Thursday and followed at her heels as she helped me clear the table. He was also grateful for any falling food.

I gathered up the wrapping paper from the presents and was going to put it all in the trash, but a card fell out. I picked it up, planning to set it aside and get it to Lyla. When I did, I noticed that the paper felt different than a usual store-bought card. Then I really looked at it.

It was a collage of Kewpie dolls and trolls with some colorful paper as a backdrop. I looked at it for a long time. At first, I admired the artistic quality of it, but then I noticed something more. It reminded me of another card I'd seen, but I couldn't place it. I thought if I stared at it hard enough, it would come back to me. Thursday came by with a handful of yarn ends. She stopped next to me and looked at the card, too. I mentioned the style of it reminded me of something.

"I know what you mean," Thursday said, touching the

paper. "The style was like this, but it was different. And the inside . . ." her voice trailed off and she looked at me with wide eyes. "The wedding card. The one with the skeleton bride and groom and the creepy greeting."

Now it came back to me. Thursday had shown the card to Barry. What was it he had said? That it might have been a calling card from the killer.

I remembered the message written in cutout magazine letters, which had seemed very retro. I went to open the card expecting to see those colorful letters again, but instead it just said, "To my darling daughter, Lyla, love Mother."

"The woman who did the flowers?" Thursday said. "Why would she be leaving a card like that at the wedding?"

I didn't want to say it, but I thought I knew the answer.

Adele, in her version of being helpful, showed me the carrier Hamlet traveled in. Thursday and I worked together to load him into it, and then Thursday took him to my house. Where else did every stray person or pet end up? I gave her instructions to keep Hamlet in her room until I got home. Who knew how he'd be with the cats and dogs, and who knew how they would be with him?

I myself went directly to Emerson's. She was surprised to see me when she opened the door and invited me in, saying that her husband and Lyla had gone out together. I looked directly at the almost-empty mantelpiece and realized what was missing. The first time I'd come there, the mantel had held photos and mementos, but when I'd come back, there was just a pair of candlesticks and some mail. Now I knew why. Emerson had realized they could connect her to the murder.

"You forgot this," I said, holding out the card. She must have known by looking at me that something was up because her expression grew wary. "It's such a lovely card. You made it, right?" I said and she nodded. "It's very similar to a card Thursday said someone handed her at the reception." I let the words sit for a moment. "You made that one, too. Didn't you?"

Emerson's demeanor changed, and her pleasant features sagged as she sighed heavily. "Why did I ever leave that card?"

"Nobody ordered fresh boutonnieres for the reception. That was your excuse to get close to Jonah Kingsley. I know your father was Felix Rooten and he worked for Kingsley Enterprises. And he was convicted of—"

"You just think you know," Emerson said. "My father was framed. Framed by Jackson Kingsley. He was in charge of products, and against Jackson Kingsley's orders, he had a shipment of the diet herbs that came in from China tested. When it turned out to contain a substance that had been banned because of health issues it had caused, my father said they should dump the shipment. Kingsley said it would just make the product more effective and wouldn't do anybody any harm, and they'd lose too many orders if they waited for another shipment.

"When my father objected, the next thing he knew, he was being charged with embezzlement. All the proof had been conveniently found in his office. He was convicted and his life was ruined. When he got out of jail, he could never get another job. The only one who believed him was me, but I could never prove anything.

"And Kingsley was wrong," she said growing more angry. "The banned substance was a heart stimulant. Only after there were some deaths that seemed connected with the product was Kingsley forced to get it tested. Then he claimed ignorance about the ingredient and blamed it on his supplier in China. The product was recalled, but it was a joke. Most of it had already been consumed."

"So you wanted revenge for your father," I said.

"Yes," Emerson said, nodding for emphasis. "I had it all planned. I knew from before that Jackson Kingsley liked ice in his wine. I'd brought ice cubes laced with cyanide in the flower cooler. I waited to replace his boutonniere until he had a glass of red wine. I knew he'd ask the closest server for ice and, even though I was bringing him a flower, since I was dressed like the servers, I knew he'd ask me. I brought him a glass with the poisoned ice cubes and he poured them into his wine." She stopped, looking distraught.

"But then I thought about it. I couldn't do it. No matter what he'd done, I couldn't kill someone. So I knocked over his glass of wine on myself and left."

"Wait a second. So you're saying you didn't kill Jonah Kingsley?"

Emerson seemed surprised. "I never had any intention of killing Jonah. My beef was with Jackson Kingsley, his father. I'd already given Thursday the card, so I just left. Well, I did some venting in the service tent first. I went in there and ranted a bit about what a horrible person Kingsley was, not caring if people died from his product as long as he got his money. Then I left. You have to believe me. I wasn't there when Jonah was stabbed."

Emerson then confessed she had put away the photographs of her father and his things after hearing about my amateur sleuthing.

"I'm glad to finally tell someone. You have no idea how this has been weighing on me. I didn't kill Jonah, but I'm afraid that what I said set off somebody else."

I could see her point. She goes and gives a speech about what a terrible person Jackson Kingsley is, and a few minutes later, his son Jonah is stabbed.

"I've thought and thought about who was in the tent and tried to remember if anyone seemed to particularly listen to what I said."

"Well," I said, "what did you come up with?"

"Nothing. With the severe dress code, everyone looked the same, and I don't know who even heard me."

"What about Ben Sherman? Was he in the tent?"

Emerson put up her hands. "I don't know. I just don't know."

CHAPTER 32

THURSDAY WAS WAITING FOR ME WHEN I GOT home. "What happened?" she said. I told her the whole story and she seemed let down. "I was hoping it would get Ben off the hook." Thursday looked dejected as she went back to her small room with Hamlet for company.

I was in one of those places where I didn't know what to do with myself. The party was over and had been a success despite the surprise guest pig. That meant there would be others to follow. But the buildup to confronting Emerson had gone kaput. I had a bad case of the loose ends.

When I felt that way, the best thing to do was to clean house. The movement, the mindlessness of it all, seemed to soothe me.

The animals had figured out there was someone new in the house and were searching around, sniffing and looking for it. Cleaning wasn't as relaxing as I thought it would be, because I kept having to dodge wandering cats and dogs.

At least I could clean out my car. As I looked in the backseat, I was embarrassed to see my things from the wedding reception were still there. Not that I was likely to miss a pair of sling-back heels.

As I grabbed the shoes, something fell out of one of them and rolled on the car floor. I thought back and remembered how my foot had suddenly begun to hurt as I was escorting Thursday out the back way. Now I realized the pain must have come from something getting into my shoe. I bent down and searched the floor, curious what it was. When I picked it up and examined it, I was stunned as I realized what it meant.

It was out of left field, but I saw that I'd been missing what was in front of me all along. What had I heard repeatedly—that the servers and help were all people in the area who had other jobs. And that was the case here.

This time I was going to tell Barry, but only after I'd made sure about the proof. It would be so simple, just locate it and take a picture with my smartphone. I left without telling Thursday and didn't even bother putting a jacket on over my vest.

It was getting close to closing at Caitlyn's Cupcakes when I went in. Caitlyn and Kirsty were both waiting on a customer when I asked for the restroom key.

With a weary sigh, Kirsty handed it to me and went back to listening to the woman complain that they were out of everything. I tried not to look at Kirsty too long, but my brain was spinning. Of course! Why hadn't I realized that when Kirsty told me Emerson had worked at the wedding, the only way Kirsty could have known was if she had been there, too. Hadn't Kirsty said something about working a bunch of jobs? Kirsty was a premed student and would certainly know just where to stab someone to dispatch them before they had a chance to react. She would have gotten away with it, except for what had fallen out of my shoe. The dangle earring with the clay bead was unmistakable.

The area near the restrooms had cubbies for the employees to leave their things. Kirsty had said the single earring was there if Adele wanted to see it. I saw Kirsty's books and backpack and realized which cubbie was hers. I reached around inside quickly, and bingo, my hand touched a small box and then an earring with a bead. I pulled it to the front and took out my BlackBerry, turning it to camera mode. It was shadowy dark back there, and if I used the flash, Kirsty might notice. I was about to move the earring into a light spot when I heard a rustle.

"What are you doing?" Kirsty said, staring at my Black-Berry. It took a moment before she saw that the things in her cubbie had been moved around.

I tried to make an excuse, but Kirsty knew something was up. "I know all about your amateur sleuth stuff. Why are you investigating my cubbie?"

I tried to make more excuses, but Kirsty finally saw the box with the earring. Obviously she knew where she had lost its mate. "You might think you know something, but you don't, and what can you prove by a single earring, anyway?"

If only I had shut up. But no, I had to tell her what I had figured out.

"You couldn't wear jewelry when you worked at the reception. So you must have taken off your earrings and put them in your pocket. But when you went to ditch the shirt, you took them out, maybe to put them in your pants pocket. But only one of them made it. The other one ended up in my shoe." Kirsty's expression changed when I got to the part about the beads. I'd called Adele on the drive there, and she'd explained she had made the beads for the earrings out of one piece of polymer clay she'd formed into a random pattern out of a bunch of scraps. She had cut the piece into two square beads that were mirror images of each other.

"Do you think I'm really going to believe that? Let me see if the other bead really is a twin." Did she think I was born yesterday and would fall for that? I just told her the other earring was someplace safe.

She shifted her weight a few times and glanced around. I heard Caitlyn call out good-night, and then the front door whoosh shut.

"Nice story," Kirsty said in a dismissive tone. But then her face began to cloud up, and the hard exterior she put on gave way. "I suppose you want to know why. My sister was one of the people who took that diet supplement, believing the label." Kirsty's voice rose in anger. "She wouldn't listen to me. I told her she was fine, but she was a fanatic about her weight. She had to wear a size zero. Who needs to wear a size zero? She went into arrhythmia and died. She was seventeen years old. I heard that there was a mistake with the supplement, and it was recalled. I was angry, but it seemed to just be circumstances. I didn't even put it together with the people at the wedding until Emerson came into the service tent and did her rant. When I heard that Kingsley had refused to hold back the shipment and knew that it was tainted, I lost it." She had started to cry, and her mascara was making black speckles on her cheek. "I loved my little sister. Things weren't so hot at my house, and it was always the two of us against the world. When she died, I felt like my right arm had been ripped off. I wanted Jackson Kingsley to lose someone the way I did. I was acting all on impulse. I stabbed Jonah before I knew what I'd done. It was automatic to dump the bloody shirt and pull out the spare I'd brought. I hid the bloody gloves in my shoes. It was all so surreal," she said.

"I'm sure if you get a good lawyer and explain about your sister, you'll be able to work something out," I said, feeling some sympathy for her. It sounded like she'd gone temporarily insane. I started to put away my BlackBerry. "If you want, I'll go with you when you turn yourself in. It's probably a good idea to talk to a lawyer first. I even know someone who might help."

I was starting to collect myself to go, but Kirsty didn't move. "How do you want to do this? Do you want to do it now, or maybe wait until tomorrow?" I said.

"How about never," Kirsty answered. Her tears had stopped, leaving tracks of thick mascara down her cheeks.

Her answer surprised me, and I was going to say something.

"Where did you say the other earring is?" Kirsty asked.

"In a safe place only I know," I said and Kirsty nodded.

"Good work. Then without you, nobody will find it." When I looked up, I saw that Kirsty had picked up a cleaver.

"You can take off a hand in one blow with something like this if you know just where to cut," she said, looking at my hand resting on the counter.

While I was contemplating what she said, she pulled out a long plastic tie. "When Caitlyn opened, she got a Welcome to Tarzana package with a bunch of these in case she had shoplifters." Kirsty made me place my hands on the counter in front of me and wrapped the plastic around my wrists, holding the cleaver in one hand as a threat. Once she'd gotten the tie tight, she put down the cleaver and used both hands to finish the job. As soon as she was done, she grabbed the cleaver again and said something about being able to take off both hands at once if I gave her any trouble.

"Did I mention that my father was a butcher?" she said, seeming to want to make sure I believed she could carry out the threat.

She pushed me into the back room where all the baking equipment was. The mixers looked just like mine, only built for a giant. There was a stove top and a glassed-in enclosure that worked as a vertical oven.

"That's it," she said, more to herself than me. "A little Hansel and Gretel action." She pushed me back toward the glass enclosure and pulled open a door as tall as I was.

"This oven is Caitlyn's pride and joy. She can put in a rack with trays of cupcakes and bake them perfectly all at once. But without the rack, there's enough room for a person to stand." She pushed me into the vertical oven and I stepped onto something round and could feel it move back and forth. "You've noticed the metal disc," she said with a malevolent smile. "It's the secret to baking everything evenly. It revolves when the oven is turned on."

I got the message. She was planning to bake me. She didn't share what plans she had for me after, and I really didn't want to hear. Talk about being caught between a rock and a hard place—either I got roasted or had my hands lopped off.

Having my hands in front gave me a little wiggle room. And Kirsty didn't object when I asked to scratch an itch, even though it delayed her shutting the glass door.

Then with a shove, she pushed it shut. I could see her looking at the controls. There was the hum of a motor, the disc began to turn, and a moment later, I felt the heating elements beginning to raise the temperature.

Kirsty stood watching me spin slowly in the hot air for a few turns, and then she walked out shutting off the light, sure my goose was cooked.

CHAPTER 33

I WISH I HAD BEEN THE ONE TO TACKLE KIRSTY. Any sympathy I had over her sister's death ended when she pushed the On button at the oven controls. Of all the ways to kill someone, this one really rated high on the scale of cruel and unusual.

But while she was being tackled, I was too busy trying to save myself.

After this, whenever my older son mentioned how old and creaky the greenmobile was, I was going to remind him of this night. It might be old, but the car was a blue-green color that was like a signature. Barry recognized it right away and figured that since it was the only car in the closed cupcake-store parking lot, something wasn't right.

By the time I came flying out the back door, Barry was handcuffing Kirsty to the stair railing.

"Babe, your hair is singed," he said with shock in his voice, rushing to catch me as I almost missed the top step in my haste to get into the cool air. He helped me sit on the top step of the short stairway down to the parking lot. As he looked me over, he was already on his phone calling out the troops.

He threw Kirsty a menacing look when I told him what she'd done. "I saw the cupcake store was closed, and only one person came out, and it wasn't you," Barry said as he sat next to me and instinctively hugged my shoulders. "As soon as I asked the cupcake counter girl about you, she made a run for it. My motto is that when somebody runs from a cop, there has to be a reason." In the background, Kirsty was pulling at her restraints and telling Barry that he had it wrong. That I was the one who should be handcuffed.

I could already hear the sirens in the distance. The sound kept getting louder, and after a few moments, three cruisers with their lights flashing roared into the parking lot followed by the red fire department rescue ambulance.

I tried to tell Barry that other than a few burned hairs and a melted headband, I was okay, but he insisted the paramedics check me over anyway.

Naturally, the lights and sounds drew a crowd from nearby restaurants and Whole Foods, and there was an audience as Barry put Kirsty in one of the cruisers. No one could accuse her of going quietly.

"Sunshine, where are you?" a worried-sounding Mason called out, pushing through the crowd. Thursday was trying to keep up with him. Judging by their expressions when they saw me, I must have looked worse than I thought. I quickly told Thursday about Kirsty's confession, and despite her concern for me, she let out a huge sigh of relief. Mason had no idea why, not that he even noticed. He was touching my hair and making worried noises while asking what had happened. Barry came by and stopped outside our little group. I was going to say something to him, but Mrs. Shedd and Adele came rushing through the crowd. And when I looked again, he was gone.

"We were afraid all the sirens and flashing lights had something to do with you, Molly," Mrs. Shedd said. Adele's eyes bugged out when she saw me, and she started to say something, but before she could stick her foot in her mouth, I stood up and hugged her.

"If it weren't for you, I'd be toast." Adele seemed stunned, then accepted the praise without question. It was Mrs. Shedd who asked for an explanation.

I held up the metal J hook and the off-white cotton yarn that now looked the worse for wear. "Adele was using this instead of the diet powder." I explained how Adele used it to distract herself when she wanted to eat a sundae. I had picked it up the other day and shoved it in the pocket of my vest. I demonstrated how when my hands had been re-strained, I'd used the excuse to scratch as a way to take it out. "It was the only weapon I had," I said. "A crochet hook against a cleaver wouldn't do much, but there was some-thing the cotton yarn could do. As Kirsty hustled me into the vertical oven, I had managed to slip the yarn into the lock so that when she shut it, it didn't quite engage. As soon as she and her cleaver left, I was able to use the hook to jimmy it open and escape."

"It's just like Dr. Wheel says," Adele said. "Crochet can save your life."

AND CROCHET HAD BECOME PART OF LYLA'S LIFE. As Emerson predicted, Lyla immediately campaigned for us

to start a junior crochet group. I chose to call it junior because it sounded better than kids. They weren't teens yet,
and well, Little Hookers just didn't sound right. Lyla was
talking about the group in an excited voice as I gave her
a lift home from their first meeting. "Come in," Emerson
said as Lyla ran into the town house and up the stairs. I
looked around the familiar room and saw that Emerson
had placed the photographs and mementos back on the
mantel.

"I can't help but feel sad for Kirsty and that it's all my
fault," Emerson said. "If I hadn't spouted off, Kirsty wouldn't
have killed Jonah Kingsley and tried to cover it up by pushing you in that oven." She cringed when she said it and then
went on. "She went from being a med student with a future
to being charged with second-degree murder for Jonah and
attempted murder for you."

"If she gets a good lawyer, she may be able to make some
kind of plea deal," I said. Emerson and I traded glances.

"But any way you look at it, the life she knew is over,"
Emerson said.

"If you want to blame anyone, it should be Jackson Kingsley," I said. Emerson glanced at the photo of her father
with a sad expression. Even after all that had happened,
Jackson Kingsley still insisted he'd known nothing about
the banned ingredient in the diet product until after the
problems had shown up and the product was analyzed.

"I don't care what he says. My father was framed because
he told Kingsley what was in the shipment. I just wish Kingsley would tell the truth."

Lyla came back in the room to show off the beanie she
had started. "I just love the group," she said to me. She told
her mother excitedly how CeeCee had come to their meeting

and invited her to go with when they took the pet mats to the animal shelter. "One of them is the one we made at the party."

Lyla went off with her hook and yarn, anxious to crochet a little more before she had to begin her homework.

I noticed the pen was back with the other things on the mantel. I picked it up and turned it around in my hand.

"It's kind of big for a pen and on the heavy side," I said.

Emerson shrugged. "My father took it everywhere with him."

As I ran my finger along the barrel, I felt something click and was surprised to hear a beep.

"Is this some kind of recording device?" I asked, and Emerson shrugged in answer. She took it from me and began to look it over with new interest. As she fiddled with it, suddenly voices started coming out of it. She found that turning the barrel controlled the volume.

"It's my father," she said as a conversation could be heard coming out of the pen. I saw Emerson begin to tear up as she listened. She was caught up in her father's voice, but I was more interested in what was being said. The quality was poor, but if I listened closely, I could hear their words.

"I think there is someone who should hear this," I said.

"I don't know if it will do any good, but maybe it will give me some closure," Emerson said.

Thursday agreed to go along, both for moral support and because she had the best chance of getting us past the receptionist.

It worked perfectly. Now that Jackson Kingsley realized neither Thursday nor her mother had anything to do with Jonah's death, he was much nicer to her. So when the receptionist passed along the message that Thursday said she needed to talk to him about something regarding Jonah, Kingsley told the receptionist to show her back.

He wasn't as happy to see Emerson and me.

"What's this all about?" Jackson said in his melodious deep voice. "I thought it was about Jonah."

"It is," Thursday said and then gave Emerson the floor. As she played the recording on the pen, Emerson said, "You can deny it all you want, but that is your voice asking my father for all the results on the tests of the weight-loss product. You can hear my father telling you about the banned substance in the batch you'd gotten in. He even says the reason it was banned was that there had been reported heart problems."

Thursday was hearing it for the first time, and she was shocked. Kingsley was stoic and denied it was him, saying her father had tried to play that card before.

"You can deny it all you want," Emerson said, standing over him. "But you know that it's your voice on the tape. And you are going to have to live for the rest of your life knowing that what you did ended up causing your son's death." She turned to the rest of us, and we headed out the door.

But at the doorway I paused and looked back. Jackson Kingsley's face had crumbled into agony. No matter what he said to us, he did know the truth. And now he had to live with it. The worst kind of prison is the one you create yourself.

"OKAY, NANCY PINK, MAYBE NOW YOU CAN FOCUS your sleuthing on figuring out the real identity of the yarn bomber," Adele said in a low voice, glancing nervously at the worktable in the yarn department where her boyfriend's mother sat knitting. "She's leaving soon, and I don't want her to go home thinking I'm a yarn criminal."

I hadn't really focused on the yarn bomber situation before, but now I gave it my full attention. "Maybe if I can find a pattern, I can figure out where the next yarn incident is going to be," I said to Dinah and Adele later as the Hooker meeting broke up.

The first thing I did was to gather up the monkey's jacket and lay it out beside the newspaper and cell phone pictures of the assorted yarn attacks. I put all the items in chronological order and examined them. I stared at the photos for a long time, and then, even though I didn't have pictures of everything, something jumped out at me. I laughed at how obvious it had been all along. Still, the only real way to prove my hunch was to catch the culprit in the midst of a bombing.

I thought Dinah and I could do it alone, but Adele insisted on coming along, claiming she was the one who had to clear her name.

"I don't know how you can be so sure you know where it's going to be," Adele said as we trudged up the street from Dinah's. It was late and everything was closed. It was the perfect time for a yarn attack.

"Pink, what if the cops drive by and see the three of us? Your plan could backfire."

I pointed out that I didn't think the cops would notice us, even if they drove by. We'd all dressed in black, down to Dinah's long scarf, and were invisible like a bunch of ninjas.

We slipped around the corner and took up a position near the entrance to the bookstore, hiding behind the topiary lion in a long flower box that had recently been added.

And then we waited. I was sure this was the spot, but there was no way of knowing the exact time.

After an hour, all of us were getting antsy, and I was about to call off our mission when I heard the clang of a ladder and the three of us ducked.

The ladder made a rhythmic sound as it got closer, and then I heard the sound of it being set up. I held the two of them back until I heard the soft sound of footsteps climbing up the ladder quickly.

I counted to three in a whisper, and we all stood up as I took out the flashlight I'd brought and pointed it upward.

"Elise!" Adele yelled. The small woman froze just as she hung a long colorful strip of crochet on the last *e* in Shedd & Royal Books and More.

"Remove that piece of crochet," Adele ordered. Elise pulled off the strip and slunk down the ladder. She stopped at the bottom and put her hands up.

Adele wanted to detain her and call Eric, so she could confess to him. But we talked Adele out of it. Eric didn't so much need to know who the yarn bomber was, just that the attacks were finished. We let Elise hang the strip back with one change. She had to add a note.

The next day when I got to work, Dinah was waiting for me and, as expected, there was a small crowd around the front of the bookstore, and Eric was in the center. He'd become the department point man in the yarn bombing incidents. Mr. Royal had finally returned from his travels. He came out with a ladder, which Eric used to climb up and remove the piece. He saw the note on it and after reading it over said, "It's about time."

He waved the note to the gathered group and read it out loud when he got to the bottom of the ladder. "'To All, I'm retiring and promise this is my final act. Thank you and good-bye.'"

Dinah and I followed him as he walked right into the bookstore and hugged Adele, even though he was in his uniform. "Cutchykins, thank you," he said. Then he lowered his voice, but we could hear him anyway as he said that he had to admit he liked that dangerous side to her.

"Why couldn't he have said that before?" I said to Dinah as we watched them call each other pet names.

"You never told us how you figured out it was Elise," Dinah said.

"It was easy when I looked at the pictures. The monkey's jacket had a long white line of surface crochet. I realized it was supposed to be the letter *I*. And in the picture of the second incident, the gazebo at the cultural center had hearts hanging from it. Everybody uses that to mean love." I continued on, showing how the next letter was a *V*, then the two figures wearing the ponchos were right under the *A* and *M*. "Eric had sent Adele a photo of the yarn bombing on the handles of the motorcycle. When I saw it again and was looking for letters, I noticed the *P*. Even with a missing letter, I figured it out. And when I looked at the monkey's jacket again, realized the answer was staring me in the face." I reached in my pocket and pulled it out, showing it to my friend.

"Now I get it." She laughed. "It's done in half double crochet. The stitch Elise does everything in because she thinks they look like fangs. With the *e* from the Shedd & Royal sign, she was trying to spell out 'I love vampire,'" Dinah said. "Shouldn't it say 'vampires'?"

I shook my head and pointed to the window display right below the bookstore sign. There was a whole assembly of the

Anthony books for Halloween with a large cutout of the crocheting vampire in the middle. It was an artist's rendering from the book, but it did look a lot like Hugh Jackman. "Elise only likes Anthony. So she only loves vampire."

AT LAST EVERYTHING WAS PEACEFUL AGAIN. Leonora went home and Adele went back to her wild outfits. It turned out that all her playacting at being prim had backfired. Leonora told her son that Adele was too bland for her taste and recommended he break up with her and find someone with more personality. When Adele heard, she immediately started making plans for them all to spend Thanksgiving together as a do-over. I could only imagine what that would be like.

My house was peaceful, too. Thursday moved out and into a sweet little guesthouse with a yard. She'd become attached to Hamlet the pig and took him with her. I wished I could have been a fly on the wall when her mother and the film crew came over to see Thursday's place for the first time. Did I mention Jaimee didn't know anything about the mini pig her daughter was fostering until his owner could take care of him again?

I didn't have the whole story, but it seemed Thursday and Ben were trying to work things out. Another surprise for her mother.

And remember how Dinah and I told Ben he should do the right thing and all that, and we thought maybe he was going to confess? There might have been a bit of miscommunication there. His idea of facing up to things was to turn in the Pinocchio nose and costume and become Mr.

Darcy from *Pride and Prejudice*. Now anyone from his writers' group who came into the Storybook Cabaret would know it was him. Though it looked like his days of working there were numbered. After the first of the year, he was going to be a writer on a Web-only continuing series about a bunch of people working at a bowling alley.

Even though Paxton Cline was off the hook, he didn't like the fact that nobody bought his alibi, so he managed to get a copy of a sports news broadcast that showed someone catching a foul ball. And Paxton was clearly in the seat next to him.

I was glad that everything was smoothed over because I loved his company's yarn, and he offered to be my contact.

THE SANTA ANAS HAD KICKED UP AGAIN AND died down, and for now, my yard was the picture of peace. I made myself a fragrant cup of rose tea and took it outside. Evening was coming faster now, and all that was left of the afternoon was a blush of apricot toward the west.

I heard the clank of my back gate followed by footsteps, and then Barry came into view. I couldn't see his expression in the semidarkness and was about to offer him a cup of tea, but he spoke before I could.

"I have to talk to you." He blew out his breath, a sure sign he was having a hard time with whatever he was about to say.

I asked him to sit, but he wanted to stand, which made me even more uneasy. A mourning dove landed in the grass and began to look over the ground for dinner.

"I've been thinking. It isn't right to keep vying with

Mason for your attention. We all know this just-friends thing is a sham." I could see Barry's expression now, and he didn't look happy.

"Mason is good for you. He's dependable and he doesn't have issues. Even his daughter said how good you were for each other. I've been trying so hard to act like I work nine to five. But my job is more than a job. It's a calling. I'm the one who speaks for the dead and gets them justice. I follow up on leads no matter what time it is. But that means part of me is always thinking about my job and ready to be called away at a moment's notice. You deserve more than that." He blew out his breath again.

"So, I'm stepping away." He didn't wait for me to say anything. A moment later, I heard the clank of the gate and then the sound of the Tahoe's engine. He was gone.

What was that story about King Solomon and the two women fighting over the baby? The one who loved it the most was the one who was willing to give up her claim.

Now what?

I sat there thinking for a long time. The sky had turned midnight blue, and the fragrant tea had grown cold. All along I'd said I wanted to be on my own, seeing what it was like to fly solo. I picked up the teacup and prepared to go in. Is that what I still wanted? Maybe it was time to make a change.

Party Scarf

Easy to Make

Supplies: K-10 ½ (6.5mm) hook
1 skein Ruby Red Lion Brand Vanna Glamour, 202 yards (185 meters) fine weight, 96% acrylic, 4% polyester metallic
1 skein Red Lion Brand Fun Fur (in the same color), 64 yards (58 meters)
Tapestry needle

Stitches: Chain stitch, single crochet

Finished Size: Approximately 68 inches long

Gauge is not important for this project.

Chain 180 with the Ruby Red Vanna Glamour

Row 1: Make a single crochet in the second chain from

hook. Make a single crochet in each of the chains. Chain 1 and turn work.

Row 2: Make 2 single crochets in each of the stitches in the previous row. Chain 1 and turn work. The stitches will begin to ruffle in this row.

Row 3: Make 2 single crochets in each of the stitches in the previous row. Attach the Red Fun Fur to the last stitch. Chain 1 using both yarns and turn work.

Row 4: Using both yarns together make a single crochet in each stitch across. Fasten off and weave in ends using the tapestry needle.

Dr. Wheel's Meditation Washcloth

Easy to Make

Supplies:	G-6 (4.00 mm) hook
	1 skein of Lion Brand Nature's Choice Organic Cotton yarn, 100% organically grown cotton, 103 yards (94 meters)
	Tapestry needle
Stitches:	Chain stitch, half double crochet, single crochet, slip stitch
Finished Size:	Approximately 7 inches x 7 ½ inches

Gauge is not important to this project.

Chain 21

Row 1: Make a half double crochet in the third chain from hook and in each of the chains across. Chain 2 (does not count as first stitch in the next row) and turn work. 19 stitches made.

Row 2: Make a half double crochet in first stitch and across. Chain 2 (does not count as first stitch in next row) and turn work. 19 stitches made.

Row 3–13: Repeat row 2. On last row do not chain 2 and turn. Do not fasten off.

Edging:

Round 1: Chain 1 and make 3 single crochets all in the same stitch (it's a corner). Then loosely make single crochets around, making 3 single crochets in each of the corner stitches. Join to the first stitch with a slip stitch.

Round 2: Chain 1 (do not turn work) and make 3 single crochets in the back loop of the same stitch (it's a corner). Make a single crochet in the back loop of each stitch, making three single crochets in each corner. Join to first stitch with a slip stitch. Finish off and weave in ends using the tapestry needle.

CeeCee's Pet Mat

Pet mats are quick to make and a good way to use up remnants of washable yarn. CeeCee made hers for a small dog or cat, but by starting with more chain stitches and making more rows, one can be made for larger dogs.

Supplies: Q-19 (15.75 mm) hook
3 lengths of washable yarn approximately 170 yards each
Tapestry needle
Stitches: Chain stitch, single crochet

Finished Size: Approximately 18 inches x 20 inches

Gauge is not important to this project.
   Chain 31 with all 3 strands of yarn together.

Row 1: Make a single crochet in the second chain from the hook and across. Chain 1 and turn work.

Row 2: Make a single crochet in each stitch across. Chain 1 and turn work.

Repeat Row 2 28 times, fasten off and weave in ends with tapestry needle.

Tea Sandwiches

Take a square loaf of egg bread, sliced thin, or good-quality sandwich bread of your choice. Cut off the crusts. Spread fillings on one slice, cover with another slice of bread. Cut across diagonally and then diagonally the other way, so that you have four triangles. Arrange on a platter in a pinwheel fashion. Garnish with parsley.

POSSIBLE FILLINGS:

Finely chopped egg salad
Cream cheese with finely sliced hothouse cucumbers
Butter with watercress
Cream cheese with julienned, seasoned sun-dried tomatoes
Cream cheese mixed with chopped walnuts and raisins
Peanut butter with thinly sliced bananas
Hummus with chopped olives

Bob's Birthday Chocolate Cake Cookie Bars

Preheat oven to 350 degrees. Grease and flour a 10 inch x 15 inch pan.

> ¾ cup butter melted and cooled
> 2 eggs
> 1½ cups sugar
> 2 teaspoons vanilla extract
> 2 cups all purpose flour
> 2 teaspoons baking powder
> ½ cup unsweetened cocoa powder
> 1½ cups milk

Melt the butter and let it cool. With an electric mixer, beat the eggs, sugar and vanilla until yellow and thick. In a separate bowl, mix the flour and baking powder. Sift the cocoa powder over the dry mixture and stir to blend. Add the dry ingredients, alternating with the milk and melted butter to the egg and sugar mixture. Pour the batter into the prepared pan. Bake for approximately 20 minutes until a toothpick comes out clean. Cool before frosting. Makes about 30 bars, depending on how they're cut.

VANILLA BUTTERCREAM FROSTING

6 tablespoons butter
1½ cups powdered sugar
1–2 tablespoons milk
2 teaspoons vanilla extract
Chocolate chips for decoration

Cream the butter and powdered sugar. Beat in the milk and vanilla. Spread on cooled cake. Decorate with chocolate chips.